Kismat
CONNECTION

Kismat
CONNECTION

ANANYA DEVARAJAN

inkyard PRESS

ISBN-13: 978-1-335-45368-6

Kismat Connection

Inkyard Press
22 Adelaide St. West, 41st Floor
Toronto, Ontario M5H 4E3, Canada
www.InkyardPress.com

Printed in U.S.A.

Recycling programs
for this product may
not exist in your area.

to Appa, Amma, and Anushka

my words would not exist without you

CHAPTER ONE

arjun

"The stars are absolutely in your favor."

A smile twisted Arjun Mehta's lips, his cosmic black eyes twinkling at the middle-aged woman sitting with her legs crossed in front of him. A fresh set of scratches blossomed on his skin, thanks to the mangled mat they sat on. Every year he'd have his astrological chart read, which meant pulling out the neon orange rug beforehand. He called it his good-luck charm.

"You're sure, Auntie Iyer?" Arjun asked, leaning forward with interest.

Auntie Iyer wasn't actually his aunt, but rather a next-door neighbor turned family friend. Like most Indian children, Arjun was raised to refer to the elders in his community by either Auntie or Uncle. The title was often used as a sign of respect, but Arjun saw it differently. Auntie Iyer was as much a part of his life as his own mother, and referring to her as an Aunt made their connection feel more concrete, even though it didn't stem from a pure blood tie.

"Have I ever been wrong?" When Arjun clicked his tongue in defeat, Auntie Iyer laughed. "Your senior year is characterized by one word: balance. Your hard work will be rewarded in the fields of education, athletics, and love, though there will be multiple obstacles in your path."

Arjun's heart slammed exactly twice through his rib cage. Once in fear. Once in hope.

"Love?" he sputtered. "We both know I'm not the most eligible bachelor in town."

That was a lie.

A total of fifteen thousand people lived in their town. His graduating class consisted of 122 seniors and Arjun knew from experience that a majority of his classmates did not find him attractive. That was, until his junior year of high school, when his culture became a trend.

In elementary school, Auntie Iyer would pack him lemon rice for lunch whenever his parents forgot, and his classmates would bully him half to death about its neon yellow color. Now they asked if he could make them "Golden Milk," a newly trademarked Starbucks drink born from the same yellow turmeric that stained his rice. The girls that once scorned his bronzed skin, calling it a tan that had somehow lost its way, now attached themselves to his arm. They marveled at his curly black hair as if his features had transformed from uncomfortably alien to fetishizably exotic. His town had ex-

panded its palate to include him last year, but that didn't mean
he wanted to appease their picky taste buds.

"You know better than anyone that the stars never lie,"
Auntie Iyer said as if she could read his mind. When he didn't
respond, she placed a hand on his cheek. "Are you okay, beta?"

Arjun was suddenly overwhelmed with heartburn so severe
it scorched his intestines to a crisp. He wondered if his body
was trying to distract him from what the stars could mean
for his relationship with a certain someone...

Who just so happened to be Auntie Iyer's beloved daughter.

He knew better than anyone that Madhuri Iyer couldn't
give two shits about astrology, or about anything Indian, for
that matter. Himself included. Even if his prophecy indicated
romance and even if that involved her, Madhuri wouldn't let
it happen. As much as he hoped otherwise, Arjun knew that
if it was Madhuri versus destiny, she'd win. Hands down.

"I'm alright," he responded after a beat of hesitation. "Do
you know any more information? Anything concrete I can
keep an eye out for?"

Auntie Iyer scanned his charts from the past seventeen
years, breathing life into the stacks of paper littering the floor.
He was overwhelmed by the memories flying out of the pages,
their edges frayed and made brittle by time. He saw the first
time he scored a goal as the varsity lacrosse team captain, his
school cheering his name louder than any sound he'd ever
heard before. The first time his teammates lifted him on their
shoulders when they won the state championships. The first
time Madhuri lunged at him to celebrate, clinging from his
shoulders like she was meant to be wrapped in his arms. He

recalled the way her smile sparkled like an undiscovered galaxy, as if she were seeing him in a way she never had before.

Wishful thinking.

"You're going to be given an opportunity by a woman who shields you from reason, and sometimes even basic common sense." Auntie Iyer's lips widened into a toothy grin. "She will have rejected you on multiple occasions and will continue to do so until she faces the truth of her feelings for you. And when that happens, it is up to you to decide if she is too late or right on time."

"Great," Arjun muttered. "The stars are sticking me with a girl who doesn't even *want* to love me. You're sure you're not interpreting this wrong?"

Auntie Iyer lifted a neatly threaded eyebrow, peering at him through her rounded spectacles. Her expression twisted into a deadly combination of hurt and annoyance. It was only a matter of time before she threw her chappal at him.

"I haven't read a chart wrong in my forty-four years of life. You should know better than to ask that," she chastised. "Have you suddenly turned into Madhuri? Do you need me to beg you to have faith in something other than cold logic?"

"That's not what I'm saying. You should know better than to think that of me." He cut his eyes at her, throwing his hands up in defense in case a slipper went flying at his head. Arjun was being disrespectful, but he couldn't help it. He didn't want a prophecy to be the reason he fell in love, especially not when it had Madhuri's name written all over it.

To say he and Madhuri had been best friends for years would be an understatement. When Arjun thought of his life as he knew it, he saw Madhuri. She was a constant, a single thread of gold bridging his past and his future, and he had long concluded that a world without her would be thoroughly mundane.

The truth was Arjun had fallen hopelessly in love with Madhuri by the ripe age of thirteen. And now, four years later, he was still trailing after her with hearts in his eyes, too afraid to speak up out of fear that he might lose the best friend he'd ever known. He'd nearly lost her once before—in their freshman year of high school after a particularly upsetting fight. In the aftermath, he'd resolved to never risk their stability again, not even for his own feelings.

Arjun was forced out of his thoughts when Auntie's chappal connected with his face. "Ow!" he yelled, scrunching his nose in anguish. "What was that for?"

"Disrespect." Auntie Iyer huffed. "I'll ask you one more time. Are you okay?"

He wanted to answer her, he really did. Madhuri, however, had other plans.

"Amma!" A shriek echoed through the living room. Madhuri's nimble fingers ran through her waist-length hair as she glared at the two of them, unquenchable flames blazing away in her pupils. "Are you seriously reading his chart? No one in the twenty-first century even believes in astrology other than you!"

Auntie Iyer rolled her eyes. "Spare us the theatrics. You have your chart read every year, but you're too embarrassed by your own culture to own it. Arjun, at the very least, is proud to be here with me. You could learn a thing or two from him."

"Mom!" Madhuri hissed, this time in English. Arjun couldn't help but chuckle at how dramatic she was. As soon as the sound left his lips, Madhuri spun on her heel to face him. "And what exactly are you laughing at?"

"Nothing," Arjun said. "Maybe you should sit down with us. You've never missed our annual reading before, so why start now?"

Before Madhuri could explode into another temper tantrum, Arjun reached for her hand. Their palms connected and she fell to the floor soon after, leaning her head onto his shoulder. "Fine. Let's get this over with."

Arjun smiled to himself. He knew her way too well. Her outbursts never lasted for longer than a few minutes, and they ended even quicker when he was there beside her. They were better as a pair, even if it would only ever be platonic.

Auntie Iyer flipped through her papers again and pulled out a bulky leather-bound book with a bow and arrow embossed on the cover in gold. Sagittarius in every way, Madhuri was her family's miracle child—astrologically speaking, that was. Every single planet of hers had fallen into the embrace of the Archer.

"Do you want the honest truth?" Auntie Iyer sighed.

"Obviously," Madhuri snapped.

Her mother averted her eyes back to the pages. "Your stars are conflicted. You, simply put, are going to crash and burn in your senior year. That's how the teens say it now, correct?"

Arjun raised an eyebrow at the information. Madhuri never failed. She was the kind of person who'd win every game, ace every test, beat every bully—whether she tried or not. He'd always envied that about her, not that he'd ever admit it.

"Crash and burn? Is that really all you have to say about my chart?"

"Fine, I'll move on to more tangible developments." Auntie

Iyer held up two air quotes when she said the word *tangible*. "You're arrogant. You're used to success and that comfort will result in your downfall. You'll face a future where you can't quite reach first place the way you used to."

Madhuri scoffed and squeezed Arjun's hand twice. A cry for help. They'd come up with the signal in fourth grade when Arjun was being bullied for spending all his free time with a girl.

This was the first time Madhuri had ever used it.

"You're so full of it, Amma. I'm not going to fail. I never do."

"That's the exact arrogance I'm talking about."

Madhuri ignored the snark. "What do you even mean by *downfall*? That's awfully vague. Am I going to crash and burn in academics? In social activities? In romance?"

Arjun choked on air when he heard the last part. Neither of the women noticed him.

"You're not going to fail, but you won't succeed as easily as you're used to." Auntie Iyer removed a sheet of paper from the book and pointed to the different angles between each planet, their orbits drawn by hand. "All of your alignments are disastrously weak, which means your internal compass leading you toward growth is damaged. Expect mediocre grades, misunderstood emotions, and failed relationships."

"I don't believe you. This unevidenced magic of yours doesn't fool anyone but Arjun, and he's hopeless."

"It's Vedic astrology, not unevidenced magic. If you're going to insult the craft, you might as well use the proper terminology." Auntie Iyer didn't even bother to comment on her daughter's tone, sporting a poker face instead. "Besides, you and I both know that these readings are not meant to be a foolproof prophecy, but rather an opportunity to reflect on the elements highlighted in your chart. At the end of the day, your destiny is entirely in your control."

Arjun cut in, his gaze lasered solely on Madhuri. "You think I'm hopeless? Believing in something larger than yourself is not hopeless. Bonding yourself to your culture is not hopeless, but it's not like you would understand. You're too busy whitewashing yourself to please the awful people in our town."

Madhuri gasped, yanking her hand out of Arjun's. "Take that back."

"No. Someone needed to put you in your place."

"You think you're so high and mighty because you act more Indian than me," Madhuri whispered, her once-playful voice now gaining an edge. "I watch the same Bollywood movies as you. I have my chart read annually. I eat Indian food three times a day, every day. I just don't parade through the streets, waving my ethnicity around like a flag, like you do."

Before Arjun could bite back with an equally heated retort, Auntie Iyer scrambled to her feet and clapped her hands. "My ears are bleeding. Will you two, for the love of Krishna, shut up?"

"But you started this!" Arjun exclaimed. "What about our horoscopes? Our senior year?"

"My world doesn't revolve around you two, sadly." Auntie Iyer was smiling, so he had a feeling she wasn't that sad about it at all. She snapped the book shut, a burst of dust leaving the pages on impact. "You will figure it out. You always do."

And then, much to Arjun's dismay, Auntie Iyer winked at him.

CHAPTER TWO

madhuri

Later that night at the dinner table, Madhuri curled her legs up to her chest as she flipped through a stack of graded schoolwork collected over the last semester. Her eyes landed on every A+ scrawled across the top of her exams and essays, often followed by a glowing message from her teachers. And yet, thanks to the unlucky prophecy looming over her head, academic validation no longer brought her any peace.

Madhuri sighed and tossed the assignments to the side, her once-steaming dosa forgotten on the plate in front of her. She watched as a gust of wind streamed through the open kitchen window, scattering her dirty crumbs across the table. Even the sound of her mother's laugh as her father cracked another corny joke didn't comfort her the way it normally would.

She was much too preoccupied with her history of success, boldly stamped on her transcript despite her mother's prediction otherwise. Madhuri couldn't imagine a future where she lost her ability to succeed simply because of an unfounded, overdramatic, scientifically impossible prophecy. The thought alone was enough to send a spark of pain through her already twisted stomach.

"Why is she sulking now?" Josie Gregorec, Madhuri's best friend of three years, asked aloud with a teasing lilt to her voice. Her mouth was stuffed with crispy dosa, the deep red of the crushed peppers staining her lips like an organic lipstick. "Did you put a curse or something in her chart this year, Auntie Iyer?"

Madhuri felt her shoulders tense at the mention of a curse, and she resisted the urge to lecture Josie for her curiosity. "I'm right here, you know. You can ask me to my face." Madhuri sent her mother a glare from across the dinner table. "Speaking of my mother, I hope she knows I'm not going to Arjun's game tonight."

It was Madhuri's father who chimed in. "What's with the change of heart? We always support him at his games as a family." When Josie flashed him a wounded look, he offered her a smile. "You're a part of the family, too, Josie, just like Arjun is."

"Arjun will survive without me. He's a big boy." Madhuri gritted her teeth, bleeding sarcasm from the enamel of her incisors. When her dad sighed, obviously disappointed by her reaction, she urged herself to soften. "I'm sorry. That was mean of me to say, but my overall point still stands. I'm just not in the mood to watch a game tonight."

"Oh, you can come up with a better excuse than that." Her father lifted an eyebrow at her. "There's something you're not telling us."

Before she could respond, Madhuri's mother cleared her throat from her seat at the head of the table. Madhuri turned to her in anticipation of a snarky response, but she focused on the empty spot beside her mother instead. It typically belonged to Madhuri's little sister, Raina, who'd ditched Arjun's game for Bharatanatyam class. Madhuri hadn't gone to a dance lesson since her freshman year, not since the harsh spotlight and quiet audiences scared her away. She envied Raina's courage to continue even as her older sister jumped ship.

"Oh, you're so in for it now," Josie mumbled under her breath as she expertly tore into her third dosa with one hand, using the other to squeeze Madhuri's shoulder in silent support.

"Didn't you know, Dev? Madhuri's convinced that her astrological reading is wrong, and she's throwing a pity party with the sheer purpose of spiting us. Like always, she's taking her emotions out on not only us, but Arjun, too." Her mother was speaking directly to her father, but that didn't stop her from shooting Madhuri a passive-aggressive smile. She was obviously irritated, but she wouldn't fight Madhuri over it. In their family, banter was how they practiced conflict resolution. "What are you so scared of? Failure? Disappointment?"

"All of the above. I don't like being told that I'm going to fail at everything and that there's nothing I can do to stop it because it's written in the stars, whatever that even means. I believe in my free will, but apparently that has no place in my future," she retorted.

"That's not true. You always have the ability to shift your fate, but running away from it does nothing." Her mother's eyes slowly softened. "And I hope you realize that, no matter what happens, you will always have us. Your family will never leave your side."

"You're not hearing me, Amma." Madhuri caught Josie's sympathetic gaze. Their friendship was already so comfortable that Josie was listening in on their most vulnerable discussions. Madhuri had never been more grateful for her presence. "I hate the idea that some unprovoked cosmic force can ruin all of my hard work. I don't want to fail, and I don't think I deserve to, either, not after everything I've done to succeed. I have an SAT score in the ninety-seventh percentile, a 4.0 GPA in the IB program, and attractive extracurriculars to boot. You can't expect me to believe that the Universe is suddenly going to destroy all of that for no reason."

"The Universe won't destroy it. You will, whether you realize it in the moment or not." Her mother swallowed a large bite of dosa before speaking again. "Are you sure this isn't about what the reading predicted about the relationships in your life?"

Her father choked on his chai, the steam from the tea fogging up his reading glasses. "Relationships? You're only seventeen. You don't need a relationship with anyone beyond your family, Arjun, and Josie."

Madhuri ignored her well-meaning father. "I'm not going to lie, that's part of the issue. It doesn't make sense that my prophecy thinks I'm going to be the victim of misunderstood emotions and failed relationships—not only is that claim incredibly vague, but it's also too easy to refute. For example, let's say I were to facilitate a positive experience with love despite the odds stacked against me. If that new relationship were to succeed, wouldn't that inherently prove my prophecy wrong?"

"First of all, it's not a prophecy. That implies perfect accuracy," her mother corrected. When her father snorted, her mother elbowed him in the gut.

"You know what I mean, Amma."

"You can't create a perfect relationship whenever you feel like it," her mother continued. "If that was possible, I wouldn't have fallen in love with your father when I was still establishing my clinic in India."

Her father shook his head. "You chose to follow me to the United States, Kamala. It's not like I asked you to leave the clinic behind when we fell in love."

Madhuri tried to imagine how it would feel to be touched by a love that wasn't platonic. She wasn't anything like her mother, who had the courage to leave her thriving medical clinic in India to start a family with her father in the United States, thousands of miles away from her own. Madhuri didn't inherit the selfless gene, nor did she have faith in any power beyond her own immediate control.

"All I'm trying to say is that this prophecy is way too unbelievable. My life isn't going to fall apart simply because the planets have decided it will, and nothing you say will make me believe otherwise," Madhuri bit out, her eyes firmly trained on her floppy dosa.

Her mother sighed. "You're thinking about the family curse, aren't you?"

"What does *that* have to do with this conversation?"

"Madhuri, my love, you're throwing a tantrum about how desperately you want to control your own destiny. You may be using the reading as the scapegoat in your argument this time, but I'm your mother, and I know that you always end up circling back to our curse somehow."

Madhuri noticed Josie lean forward, suddenly intrigued. Her stormy blue eyes, much like the waves of the ocean during a high tide, widened as she glanced between Madhuri and her parents. "Your family has curses? You seriously never tell me anything, Madhuri."

As Josie's complaint registered in her ears, Madhuri felt a combination of guilt and anxiety creep into her throat. Was her prophecy stumbling into effect already?

Josie cocked her head to the side when Madhuri didn't respond with an equally petty retort. "You know I'm kidding, right?" Madhuri shook herself out of her spiraling thoughts to offer Josie an affirmative, yet tired, smile. Her best friend nodded as if she'd understood her perfectly and turned back to Madhuri's parents. "Tell me more about this curse."

"It's not a curse, per se," her father said, lifting the mug back to his lips. "It's more of a coincidence that every single woman in your mother's bloodline has married their first romantic partner. We don't have any divorces, either, so you could call us one-hit wonders."

Josie's mouth opened, and thankfully, there wasn't more food there. "No way."

Madhuri groaned, burying her face into her arms before turning back to Josie. "We're not joking. And it's very much a curse, for your information. I want to be able to date whomever I want without worrying that I'll fall in love with them forever. It's way too much pressure."

Her mother scrunched up her nose, making it clear where

Madhuri got it from. "I can't believe you *want* to experience all the heartbreak and tears associated with traditional dating."

"Yeah, I would kill to never have to worry about dating!" Josie said. "If this is a genetic inheritance thing, then I'm screwed. My mom and dad had to suffer through quite a few shitty first dates before they found each other and lived happily ever after." Her face turned red when she registered the swear she'd used, but when Madhuri's parents laughed good-naturedly, she settled back down.

Madhuri opened her mouth to argue, but the incensed words she'd prepared suddenly disintegrated on her tongue. An uneasy emotion washed over her, the one that always accompanied the thought of her family curse and the happily-ever-after it promised. She felt as if she were being held hostage by the Universe, doomed to compromise her future and herself for the sake of love. Her latest prophecy only worsened that feeling.

Thankfully, the conversation at the dinner table drifted from curses and prophecies to Josie's passion project, which was finally coming to fruition in their senior year—a student-run talent show highlighting all the art and culture Southern California had to offer. Madhuri, who'd already spent most of her summer vacation fundraising for the show with her best friend, utilized the temporary shift in topic as an opportunity to plan her next steps.

Madhuri's family history haunted her, stories of true love passing from mother to daughter for centuries. She couldn't help but think about her mother's clinic in India, a dream that was once alive deep within her heart. A dream that was now nothing more than a distant memory, slowly replaced by the kind smile of her father.

Madhuri was overwhelmed with a burning desire to prove her family, particularly her mother, wrong about everything. Madhuri would never let herself be bound to a prophecy with no scientific backing, nor would she become the target of a curse like all the women who came before her. She had to find a way to kill both of those pesky birds with one stone, but it didn't seem like her family would be willing to listen to her with an open mind. She'd have to *show* them exactly how mistaken they were, exactly how much power she held in her own life.

All she needed to do was target a specific area of her prophecy for refutation—her academics, her personal growth, or her relationships. Compared to the former two, manipulating a successful relationship in the face of her prophecy's negative predictions shouldn't be that difficult. She'd pick some willing sucker to date her until June, when she'd inevitably break up with him before college. She'd take part in an experimental relationship that would only end when *she* wanted it to, and with one perfect shot, her family curse and her prophecy would cease to exist.

The only thing she needed was a boy who would help her destroy her own destiny. A boy she was guaranteed to never fall in love with.

She knew just the one.

CHAPTER THREE

arjun

A distinct shiver raced through Arjun's fingertips when he wielded his lacrosse stick. The feeling careened through his veins like an oxygenated blood vessel. He cradled the ball in its net, breaking into a sprint toward the goal on the opposite end of the field. The shiver transformed into a burst of wind, encouraging the adrenaline pumping in his eardrums to push for more. More endurance, more agility, more power.

From the corner of his eye, he saw Madhuri's family and Josie standing in the front row of the packed school bleachers. Josie screamed at the top of her lungs, jumping up and down like a cheerleader, and Auntie and Uncle Iyer held each other close, their gaze narrowed on the aggressive players he was blazing through. They were worried, as always, for his health. One concussion had already sent them into a spiral of anxiety. They couldn't handle another scare.

Madhuri, on the other hand, was nowhere to be found.

Arjun tried to shake off the disappointment that had suddenly replaced his energy. He couldn't expect her to attend his games like some sort of Trophy Girlfriend, even if it was the very first match of their senior year. She'd never be that girl, and he'd never ask that of her.

When Arjun tore his eyes away from the bleachers, ready to deliver a perfectly aimed shot, the opposing team's captain checked him. Hard. The lights hanging over the lacrosse field transformed into white spots, exploding in Arjun's vision with increasing intensity. He felt his heartbeat thudding in a shy corner of his brain until the pain ricocheted off his skull and into the rest of his body.

He crashed into the grass headfirst. His fingers raced to his forehead, checking for signs of another concussion. A thin stream of blood leaked from his hairline, and he groaned out loud, looking up toward the bleachers again. Auntie Iyer was clinging to the rails, screaming his name. He was sure that from their vantage point, it looked like he was knocked out. He'd have to tease her about her dramatics the next time he saw her.

The referee blew his whistle for a time-out as Coach Hegde grabbed him by the arms, hoisting him onto the brightly decorated bench beside them. One of the posters taped to the bench had his name painted in blue and gold ink, their school colors. He smiled when he caught sight of the famil-

iar signature at the bottom left corner. A curvy, barely rec-
ognizable *MI*.

Even when she wasn't there for him, she was.

His coach shone a bright light in his eyes, and when nothing out of the ordinary seemed to show, he let out an incredibly long sigh of relief. With a pat on the back, his coach ran
back to the field, leaving the school nurse to inform Arjun that
he was out for the rest of the game and that he could either sit
and watch or go home.

The smile was wiped clean off Arjun's face. He'd never
been kicked out of a game before. Did his coach see his moment of distraction, the weakness that gave their opponents
an advantage? If so, he was screwed. He'd be running laps
around the field until their next game.

"I'll watch," Arjun muttered, clenching his fists as the nurse
cleaned his wound with alcohol. When he turned to the
bleachers to send Auntie Iyer a comforting thumbs-up, the
nurse pulled his head back with a click of her tongue. His grin
turned into a grimace that he was sure Auntie Iyer's hawk eyes
caught. Great. He was truly in for it when they got home.

"How are you doing there, Arjun?" A familiar voice sang
from behind him. He whirled around to find the source, only
to have the nurse screech in dismay. With a huff, she pressed
an ice pack to his temple and left the bench. Madhuri occupied the seat next to him, a soft smile twisting her lips. "You
don't look too good."

"I appreciate the kind words." Arjun withheld the urge to
roll his eyes at her.

"Fine, I deserve that." Madhuri placed her palm against
his cheek, eyeing the bandage on the side of his head. She

leaned in so close that Arjun could smell the Orbit gum on her breath, the brand she used to cover up the remains of her garlic-infused meals. "I hope you know that I was watching your game the whole time. I just wasn't in the bleachers with the rest of the family."

She could read his mind, just like her mother.

"You should've been. I couldn't find you in the stands and I got distracted," he said, pointing to his injury like the outcome was obvious. Arjun couldn't see it at the moment, but from the way the cut stung, he knew that the blood caked into his skin would soon be replaced by a frighteningly large purple scab. "And then, this happened."

She sighed, her fingernail gently grazing the edge of his jaw. "I'm so sorry."

Another shiver danced through his spine, waltzing with the layers of cartilage and marrow etched into his bones. "You don't have to be sorry. It's not your fault. But where were you if you weren't in the bleachers?"

"Right here." Madhuri patted the bench they were sitting on. "I wanted to hold up your poster when you scored and scream at the top of my lungs, so you knew I'd be here for you even when we fight. Even if it's over something as ridiculous as astrology."

A small chuckle left his lips, and he bumped his shoulder with Madhuri's. "I was wondering why you were kissing my ass all of a sudden."

"I was not! I'm being a good friend."

"That's rare." He stuck his tongue out at her like he would when they were kids.

"I'll let that insult slide, for now. I have more pressing matters to discuss with you."

"Sounds ominous. Tell me more."

Madhuri didn't roll her eyes at his comment the way he'd expected her to. Instead, she toyed with the gold pendant on her necklace, a nervous tic Arjun had picked up on years ago.

"Right." She nodded, turning to face him clearly. "I want to date you, Arjun Mehta."

She couldn't possibly be serious. There was no way she wanted to date him, not in a million years, and not even if they were the last two people on the planet after an apocalypse.

Her words, not his.

Before Arjun could respond, the bleachers behind him erupted into cheers and the school band played their fanfare louder than before. He turned back to the field, and he saw that, despite his slipup, his team had managed to win the match by one point, which would have been fantastic if the sudden excitement hadn't distracted him from what really mattered. Madhuri, the girl who'd owned his heart ever since she stole a jalebi from him when they were six years old, wanted to date him.

Arjun didn't know what to say, so he blurted out the first thought that came to mind.

"Are you fucking with me right now?"

"How romantic," Madhuri deadpanned. "No, Arjun, I'm not—" she motioned two air quotes with her fingertips "—fucking with you."

Arjun nearly sank into the bench when he saw her face, serious and downright unamused. She obviously meant business, whereas he'd suddenly become incapable of having a normal conversation with his childhood best friend.

"Let me start over," he began, and in the process of drawing out his words long enough to figure out what to say next, he'd left an opening for his teammates to sprint toward the bench, pulling Madhuri and Arjun into a group hug turned mosh pit. The nurse grabbed Arjun by the jersey before he was thrown in, dropping him back on the bench with another huff.

When Madhuri entered the circle, she threw her head back, laughing, and for a split second, Arjun forgot all the pent-up anticipation and anxiety that came with the thought of Madhuri dating him at last. The wind caught her hair, swinging the highlighted strands of black and blond in the faces of his teammates. No more than a minute passed before Madhuri turned around and found Arjun sitting on the bench by himself, and her smile instantly faded. She forced her way out of the circle and sat back down beside him, squeezing his hand in hers.

He looked back to the bleachers that were now empty of people and littered with confetti. Auntie and Uncle Iyer were nowhere to be found and neither was Josie. He tugged on Madhuri's hand, which was still encased in his own, to get her attention. "Your family is going to come here soon, so I'll get straight to the point. Why do you want to date me? And why now?"

"Well, it's not really dating in the traditional sense. I mean, we'd have a set of hypotheses detailing the expectations of both parties involved, control variables that would scientifically guarantee our success, and we'd have an end date. June fourteenth, the day after our graduation," she said, both of her hands in Arjun's now. She leaned forward, so close that he was worried he'd smell the minty-fresh gum again, and he wasn't quite sure what he would do if that happened.

"This sounds more like an experiment than a relationship, Madhuri."

"An experiment is exactly what I have in mind."

Her words hit him like a bullet. Of course, there was always a catch.

That was also the exact moment his heart skipped multiple excited beats in a row because, oh, God, his reading was already coming true. He scanned the area around them for Auntie Iyer and saw her marching toward him, face set in a stern expression. Behind her was Uncle Iyer and Josie, smaller in size when compared to Auntie Iyer's booming presence.

He didn't have much more time to think, and Madhuri was giving him her trademark puppy-dog eyes. He felt himself melting away, tumbling into the hopes he'd hidden away in his soul for so long. Maybe that was why Arjun agreed to her terms. Maybe that was why he decided that, no matter what, Madhuri would always be perfectly on time when it came to their relationship—even if it was purely experimental.

"Yes. Let's do it."

CHAPTER FOUR

madhuri

In Madhuri's seventeen years of life, she had never been rejected by a potential boyfriend. She'd like to think it had something to do with her charm, her eloquence, that rendered boys at the mercy of her will. In reality, it was only true because she'd never asked someone out. That level of vulnerability scared her away.

When Arjun said yes to her request, her heart shone through her rib cage like a golden halo. It wasn't like she was actually attracted to him, but the validation after a nerve-racking leap of faith was the best feeling in the world. Even better than the chocolate chip cookies she baked after a stressful day, or the way her dad tucked her into bed every single night with a kiss on the cheek, despite the fact she was almost a legal adult.

There was something special about the way Arjun smiled at her, cautious and confident at the same time. The last thing Madhuri wanted was to take advantage of him, but she was certain he'd survive her dating scheme. There was no way Arjun had feelings for her, not when they'd only ever been best friends for the last eleven years. Madhuri was confident that the risk the experiment posed to his heart (as well as her own) was completely and utterly nonexistent.

Before she could give Arjun a rundown on the hypotheses she'd already developed for their scientific relationship, her mother came running to them. She pushed past Madhuri like she didn't even exist and knelt at Arjun's feet, fingers tapping away at the bandages on his head.

"You're so reckless, Arjun," she muttered under her breath. "I saw you looking at us instead of focusing on your game. Why would you lose your concentration over something so small?"

He sighed, leaning his cheek into her palm. "It's not a small thing to want the attention of the people I love. I couldn't have made the winning shot if I hadn't seen you all there, cheering me on."

"How reckless," her mother repeated, shaking her head. "And so cheesy, too."

Madhuri let out a dry chuckle and turned to face her father, who had his arms crossed over his chest. Did he happen to hear her asking Arjun out? Was that the cause of his pout, the worry lines creasing across his forehead?

"You okay, Appa?" Madhuri asked.

Josie threw an arm around her, and she smiled at the touch, unwittingly using her best friend as a human shield. They'd coordinated their outfits to match their school's colors, each sporting a blue tank top and white jeans.

Her father lifted a brow, watching her with an unrelenting stare. "Completely okay. I just thought you would have run it by your parents before you got yourself into your first relationship, but I guess that was a lot to expect of you."

From her periphery, she could see Arjun and her mother eavesdropping on their conversation. With a disgruntled sigh, she grabbed her father by the elbow and veered him off the field. She placed her hands on her hips, willing the courage to speak to him as a friend, the way she normally did. Something about that felt harder now.

"I was going to tell you when we got home, I promise." Madhuri tapped the pressure point on her hip with her finger, wondering if she could avoid confronting her father by forcing herself to pass out on the spot. Sure, that was dramatic, but if she could loop her best friend into an experimental relationship to prove an astrological prophecy wrong, nothing was off-limits. "I didn't want to make a scene in front of everyone."

A flash of hurt rebounded off her father's face. "I never would have made a scene." Her father looked down at the grass, toying with the button on his shirtsleeve. Madhuri wondered if he wasn't necessarily sad about the dating, but more about her needing him less and less. That would've been so much more adorable behind closed doors, rather than in front of her school's lacrosse team. "I thought we were close enough for you to talk to me about this, though. You've told me about all of your wacky ideas in the past. Why couldn't you tell me about Arjun? You know I would've approved without question."

How could she tell him that she was dating Arjun to prove a point, not to fall in love?

"I was going to, like I said earlier," she whispered. "I'm sorry I didn't tell you before I did it, though. I will next time."

"Next time?" her father repeated. When he saw Madhuri hiding her laughter behind her freshly manicured hand, he broke into a small smile. "You wish you had a next time. I know you're determined to only ever date for fun, not for love, but I have a good feeling about this one. You couldn't have chosen a better boy to spend your time with."

Madhuri grinned, trying to ignore the erratic beating of her heart. She didn't know how to tell her father that she'd never fall for Arjun, not even in her wildest dreams. Their relationship would only ever be an experiment with an expiration date that would end their family curse and reestablish her free will in the face of her prophecy. A plan, a strategy, a game.

It wasn't love, and it never would be.

"Give me some credit. When I choose, I choose the best," Madhuri lied through her teeth. There was no doubt that Arjun was objectively the best, but she wasn't choosing him. Her father, however, needed to believe that she was. Otherwise, she'd be on the receiving end of an ethics lecture presented by her hopelessly-in-love parents.

"That's how I know you're my daughter." Her father pulled her into a hug, and she relaxed into his arms like she had when she was a child. He smelled like the detergent her mother used on their clothes, the special kind she bought in bulk from India when they traveled there during the summer.

Someone tapped Madhuri on the shoulder, but her eyes were squeezed shut and she didn't have the motivation to leave the safety of her father's hug. Her mother cleared her throat. "Are you serious, Dev? You're going to start a family hug without me?"

"It's technically not a family hug yet," he teased, offering his second arm for his wife, and soon enough, the three of them were in a tight embrace.

It felt like Madhuri's world was coming together all at once. Her parents were the Sun, and she was the Earth, constantly revolving around their attention. She couldn't imagine fighting her battles without her mother's witty banter or her father's bouts of wisdom grounding her. She couldn't imagine not seeing Arjun there beside them, laughing at her dramatics like he were watching an entertaining play.

Her eyes flew open when she thought of him.

Madhuri squeezed herself out of the hug and scanned the field for Arjun. They hadn't discussed the plan yet and Arjun didn't always process surprising information in the healthiest way. For all she knew, he could be pacing down the length of the boys' locker room, plotting a last-minute escape before he was caught in her web of lies forever.

Right when Madhuri was seriously considering bursting into the locker room herself, Arjun walked up to them, his helmet swinging from his fingers. She heaved a relieved breath and made her way over, only to have him brush past her. Josie sent her a look, silently questioning Madhuri about the events transpiring on the field. It didn't quite make sense to her, either, so she shrugged in response.

Arjun stopped in front of her parents, who watched him with confused stares. His helmet fell from his hand with a thud, and he bent over, touching their feet. Her mother gasped, her eyes wide with shock, and made a feeble attempt to stop him out of fear for his head injury. Arjun followed through with the offering regardless. In Indian culture, it was a sign of respect to touch the feet of elders, especially when they were related to a romantic partner.

He was taking this much more seriously than she'd expected him to. Madhuri wanted to grab him by the shoulders and shake until he snapped into his senses, until he realized that their relationship wasn't that important and never would be.

However, and she would never admit this out loud, Arjun's knowledge of their shared culture made her feel understood. She tried to ignore the way his actions sent a warm flutter through her chest like she was being seen for the first time.

Her mother's lips slowly grew into a megawatt smile as she overcame her surprise. She placed a gentle hand over his head. "You have our blessing, as always. No matter what happens between you and Madhuri, we'll be in your corner."

Her father wrapped his arm around her mother, his eyes piercing Arjun's like a knife. "But you being a part of our family doesn't mean you can hurt Madhuri. There'll be consequences for your actions."

"To be quite frank, I think Madhuri is more likely to break my heart than the other way around." Arjun looked over his shoulder, sending her a wink that seemed to say that their secret was completely safe with him. It was like he *knew* he was at her mercy, and he still didn't care.

Josie watched their exchange with a raised eyebrow and Madhuri soon felt the burning gaze of her best friend drilling into the side of her head. There was no doubt that Josie would have a lot of questions, especially after Madhuri had squashed the idea of her and Arjun's romantic prospects from her brain years ago, but she'd give her the explanation she deserved soon.

Madhuri turned her vision to Arjun laughing with her parents, their teeth sparkling like the brightest stars, and all of a sudden, Madhuri worried if Arjun was right. It pained her to think she was taking advantage of Arjun's kindness, using his loyalty as a sacrificial pawn in her war against fate and family.

She wasn't sure what she'd do if she broke his heart and lost her best friend all at once.

CHAPTER FIVE

arjun

Arjun never celebrated his lacrosse games.

Even when he'd won State Championships and was named MVP of the season, Arjun had chosen to end the night alone. It wasn't like he didn't get invited places. There was always the option of sharing celebratory gulab jamun with Madhuri and her family, or hitting up a party with Liam, his best friend, and the rest of his teammates. Still, Arjun had spent most of his life feeling like a burden, and it didn't come naturally to him to accept those invites, as genuine as they might be. He'd much rather choose himself, the only human being he knew he could *always* depend on.

And so, the cheering crowds of the student section were replaced by the hum of an empty refrigerator. The lacrosse field that had quickly become his second home gave way to his living room, which had just about frozen over since he left for school that morning. He'd forgotten to turn off the air conditioner again.

Arjun unlocked the front door to his house with a years-old rusting key.

"I'm home," he whispered under his breath to no one, and shrugged his coat onto the staircase. His mother would've chastised him for his laziness when the coatrack was standing *right there*. But weeks had passed since they'd last spoken in person—another business trip to another foreign country, as usual.

He decided that what she didn't know wouldn't hurt her.

Arjun settled onto the leather couch in front of the television, pulled a blanket over himself that smelled ever so slightly like dust, and rested his head on his mother's favorite pillow, hand-quilted and gifted by his great-grandmother. He made sure not to lean on his injured side, making a mental note to change his bandages before he dozed off. If he didn't do it himself, he'd have no choice but to ask Auntie Iyer for help, and that was the last thing he wanted now that he was Madhuri's boyfriend.

Overall, there was only one difference to his bedtime routine. Rather than replaying memories from his game as he coaxed himself to sleep, Arjun thought about the warmth of Madhuri's smile when she'd asked him to partake in her experiment. He wished that it would be enough to keep him company on yet another lonely night—which was uncharacteristically interrupted by the ring of his doorbell. Not once, not twice, but over and over again like the most torturous alarm clock known to man.

Arjun didn't need to guess who was responsible for the disturbance. Ever since they were kids, Madhuri found a way to announce her presence without uttering a single word, and it seemed that the doorbell was her choice tonight.

Her forthrightness would be the death of him, but honestly, he didn't think there was any better way to die.

"Coming!" Arjun shouted as he folded his blanket back into a neat square and hung it over the couch as if it had come straight out of a catalog. On his way to the front door, he turned on the lights in the kitchen and the hallway, hoping that it gave his house a bare-minimum semblance of liveliness.

"Could you possibly take any longer? It's freezing out here."

Arjun could envision the scowl on Madhuri's face when she spoke, and it took all of his self-restraint not to laugh at the image his brain had concocted of her—hands on her hips, lips downturned, and eyes blazing.

"Well, now I'm going to take even longer." He turned the front doorknob at a snail's pace, and it creaked so loudly that he was positive she could hear it from the other side. "Try not to catch hypothermia in the meantime."

"If you don't open this door right now, I'll—"

"You'll what?"

A beat of silence passed between them before Madhuri muttered, "I don't think you want to know what I'm capable of."

"Try me." He swung open the door with a flourish and flashed her a boyish grin. As soon as he saw Madhuri, though, with her hair laid flat against her back from the sudden downpour of rain, whatever charisma Arjun thought he had vanished into thin air.

She wore a bright yellow churidar, which made sense because it was a Friday night and that was when Madhuri and her family went to the Malibu Temple, a tradition that was never broken, even if it meant they could only attend after his game ended. A glimmering necklace adorned her collarbone, matching in color to the bindi—also known as a pottu, if Arjun was remembering the bit of Tamil Madhuri had taught him correctly—placed between her threaded eyebrows. Looking at her now, radiant even in the darkest of skies, Arjun somehow forgot to breathe.

Madhuri sent him a glare and shoved a small cardboard box into his hands, walking into his house without an ounce of hesitation. She found the blanket he'd been using earlier and wrapped it around her shoulders. "Cat got your tongue? Or are you feeling guilty for leaving me out in the rain for the sake of your own amusement?"

Arjun let out a strained cough as he tried to find his regular breathing pattern again. "Me? Guilty? Never." He leaned against the door with his ankles crossed, trying to appear as effortlessly cool and collected as Madhuri. "What's with the box?"

She settled into his typical spot on the couch and pulled his great-grandmother's pillow into her lap with the utmost care. "Why don't you open it and find out?"

Arjun turned his attention to the Insomnia Cookies label and the fresh scent of double chocolate chip. He smiled at the gesture, simple proof of how well she knew him.

"Thank you." He couldn't remain at a distance from her, so he also moved to the couch, their knees just barely grazing as he sat down. She didn't pull herself away when they touched, likely because she was so used to him that these little moments didn't matter anymore. Still, he wondered if she felt the same electric spark that he did. "What's the occasion?"

Madhuri opened the box and split a cookie in half, placing the larger of the two in his open hand. "I wanted to congratulate you on a good game. Plus, I thought you'd like some company tonight."

"The game where I made a fool of myself and got knocked out on the field? That's worthy of cookies to you?" He popped a piece into his mouth, and the taste of sweet chocolate flooded his senses. "I do appreciate you wanting to keep me company, though."

"Why can't you let me be nice to you in peace, Arjun?"

"Because I know an ulterior motive when I see one, especially when it comes to you. Spit it out, Madhuri. Why are you really here?"

"Fine, fine, you caught me, but I'll have you know that you were only correct in the cookies having an ulterior motive. Me coming to see you was purely because you're my best friend and I love you."

I love you. The three words echoed through his ears, though he should've known better than to be so affected by them. She said she loved him because it was safe to do so, because he was irrevocably defined as her best friend. He needed to remember that.

Arjun sent her a pointed look. "You're avoiding the subject."

"Alright, I'll get to the point. I was hoping to set a date and a time to go over the ground rules for our little dating scheme, and I brought your favorite cookies to make sure you didn't get cold feet."

"First of all, even if I did get cold feet, a box of cookies would not be enough to change my mind. I'm not that easy." Madhuri chuckled, and Arjun felt his heart glow the way it always did when she so much as looked in his direction, let alone laughed at one of his jokes. "Secondly, you didn't have to come all the way here just to set a date and a time. Our phones exist for this reason, you know."

"Maybe I needed an excuse to see you, and the experiment was the easiest way to do it."

"Don't start making me feel special," Arjun teased. "What's gotten into you?"

Madhuri looked up at him through her lashes, fluttering like the butterflies careening through his stomach in that very moment. "I guess I felt bad about how I treated you at our reading and at the game. I wanted to apologize to you properly, when we were alone and not preoccupied by my family or the prophecy or the experiment."

"You don't need to apologize for arguing with me. We've been that way for ages, and I know it's not personal." Arjun locked his eyes on to hers. "I also know how you are when it comes to your destiny. If you need to take your frustration at the Universe out on me, I'm completely okay with that."

"Well, you shouldn't have to be, and I'm sorry for making you feel like you need to be my punching bag in order to be my friend." Madhuri shook her head at him as if what he was saying was somehow amusing and sad all at once. "Now, finish your cookie. I've had enough sentimentality for the evening, and I'd say it's finally time we get into the fun stuff."

Madhuri flashed him a smile before continuing on with business as usual, her apology slowly fading into the depths of Arjun's memory. "Why don't we develop our hypotheses tomorrow? I think we need to get the details of our experiment locked down before people start to ask questions, and trust me, they will. You're a pretty hot commodity, and I'm positive it'll cause a riot once the girls at school notice you've been taken off the market."

"Correct me if I'm wrong, but what you're saying is that we should be prepared for crowds of girls to throw themselves at me in protest. I don't think I'd complain if that were to happen." Arjun let out a quiet chuckle. "Unless that makes you jealous?"

"Jealous, yeah, sure." Madhuri rolled her eyes. "I just don't want to be caught in a lie if we were to be interrogated about our relationship. Besides, I think it's more likely that those girls will throw themselves at me, and not in the fun and flirty sort of way."

"More the off-with-her-head sort of way?"

"Exactly."

Arjun knew that if two average teenagers agreed to date, they didn't do it through scientific hypotheses. There was nothing typical about Madhuri's proposal, but he should've seen that coming. Most teenagers weren't ruled by the planets, nor did they have something to prove the way that she did. And Arjun wasn't going to pass up the opportunity to show Madhuri exactly what she'd been missing her whole life—a happily-ever-after with him.

"Well, I'll be free tomorrow to work on those hypotheses. You can count me in."

Madhuri's smile widened into a brilliant grin, and she pulled him into a hug. They didn't do that often, the whole physical displays of affection thing, but he didn't have the heart to stop her. "Thank you, Arjun. I seriously don't know what I'd do without you."

Arjun couldn't bring himself to let her go, not when Madhuri leaving meant facing his deserted house all over again, so he didn't. Much to his surprise, the two of them stayed that way for quite some time before he finally found the right words to respond.

"I promise you'll never have to find out."

CHAPTER SIX

madhuri

Madhuri loved the smell of books. Old or new. Torn or polished. That was why she wanted to create their experiment in her mother's study, a room dedicated to the art of Vedic astrology. It was only right for Madhuri and Arjun to sign their agreement beneath the watchful eyes of fate, hidden within the intricate planetary charts on her mother's bookshelf. There was something peaceful about the whimsical language scrawled across each page, and Madhuri needed all the peace she could get before her plan went into action and effectively turned her life into a Bollywood film.

Arjun fell into the swivel chair in front of her, dropping his gym bag to the floor without a care in the world. Beads of sweat dangled from his hair, specifically the stray strand that curled toward his forehead. For someone who'd probably spent the morning working out, he didn't smell too bad. In fact, Madhuri couldn't smell anything but the floral perfume that belonged to the lingering presence of her mother.

Arjun shot her a smile. "Ready to start?"

Madhuri nodded, picking up her sparkly pink pen. She wrote *The Kismat Experiment* across the top of the page with a clean flourish. When directly translated from Hindi, *kismat* meant *destiny*, the very force Madhuri set out to fight. Beneath the title, she wrote a clarifying note.

Disclaimer: This is not a fake relationship. This is a scientific investigation with all control variables held steady in order to create a data set that will aid Madhuri Iyer and Arjun Mehta in their future dating endeavors.

Madhuri knew a STEM lab like the back of her hand, considering she wanted to be a scientist conducting immunology research at Stanford University in the future. Her passion was the sole reason she had the necessary knowledge to create such an experiment.

She turned the paper to Arjun. "What do you want to add?"

His eyes widened as he read over what she had written. "You're taking this really seriously."

"Considering you outright asked my parents for their blessing after the game, I'd say that you're more into this than me," she retorted. "Speaking of, why are you so into this?"

Madhuri needed to make sure that Arjun wouldn't screw with her control variables. She didn't know what she'd do if she'd misunderstood their friendship and he'd developed some sort of feelings for her.

She shook her head. That was impossible.

"Why are you?" he asked.

"I need to prove my reading wrong." Madhuri shrugged. That wasn't her only motive, but she couldn't tell him more without revealing her own insecurities. Their relationship was much more than an act of defiance against her prophecy. It was a pawn in Madhuri's battle against her Indian culture, as well as the family curse that came with it. Every tradition strangled the breath from her lips, much like the jewelry she wore on her neck for a dance recital. "Your turn."

Arjun chewed on the back of her sparkly pen, deep in thought. She didn't have the heart to stop him. "I don't really have a reason other than the fact that you're desperate for my help and I wouldn't be a good friend if I wasn't there for you when you needed me."

A shiver ran through her toes, and she curled them on instinct, wishing she'd worn sneakers instead of her open-toed, heeled sandals. "Fair enough." She pulled out a new pen, bright purple this time. "Are you going to write anything down?"

He clicked the pen open with his teeth. "Well, I actually have a question."

"Shoot."

"If this is a real relationship, albeit with very weird motives behind it, does that mean we have to do more than go on dates together? Do you expect me to pay for your dinner? Bring you gifts?" He swallowed, averting his eyes to the chewed-up pen in his hand. "Should I kiss you?"

Madhuri raised a brow. She hadn't thought about that. She

leaned over the table, and a whisk of cologne danced through her nostrils. For a scent mixed with a tinge of sweat, it was really nice. "Depends. How do you feel about kissing? Is it something you want to save until you're ready?"

"I've already had my first kiss and that was with you, back in sixth grade." Arjun paused. "I don't think it would be a big deal if the second and third were with you, too."

Madhuri couldn't forget that moment even if she tried.

The autumn breeze was fresh, sending golden leaves soaring through the air like free birds. A lone pumpkin sat on their front lawn, a mediocre grin carved into the skin by her and her father the night before. Cobwebs were stuck to every corner of the rooftop, fuzzy spiders bouncing from the center in pursuit of their next victim. Her father was so proud of her for helping with the decorations despite her fear of everything Halloween. He even convinced her mother that she was old enough to stay home alone for the first time while they were at work.

Madhuri pulled on the front door handle over and over again, hoping it would magically open on its own. The final tug was too forceful for her petite frame, and she stumbled backward, falling onto their patio with a groan. The thought of her silver house key, lying forgotten on the kitchen counter, sent irritated tears to her eyes. Her parents would never trust her to be independent after this.

Twelve-year-old Arjun, who had walked her home from the bus stop, noticed her distress the way he always did. When it came to her, he was always so observant. He sat down beside her and bumped her shoulder with his, flashing her a timid smile like he was afraid she'd explode at him otherwise. And once she'd relaxed into his arms, he kissed her on the forehead.

Looking back on that memory at the age of seventeen meant finding the humor in its innocence. Even the youngest of children knew that a typical first kiss was a gesture saved for the lips and the lips only, but Madhuri disagreed. Somehow, Arjun's kiss felt just as real and meaningful.

Madhuri's eyes moved to her fingers subconsciously resting atop Arjun's hand. Her heart leaped and she withdrew from him as if she were burnt. *Madhuri, get your shit together.* She picked up the first pen she found, the disgusting pink one that Arjun's teeth had destroyed in seconds, and decisively scribbled down the rule.

To ensure optimal trial accuracy, kissing is allowed. Other control variables include splitting dinner checks, posting photos on social media with Madhuri's explicit consent, and buying gifts only when necessary (birthdays, Christmas, and Valentine's Day).

She dropped the pen back down, rubbing her hand against her jeans to get Arjun's saliva off. "Anything else you want to add?"

He scratched his chin, thinking to himself. "At the moment, no."

Madhuri nodded and wrote another line down with a purple pen this time.

The Kismat Experiment aims to prove Madhuri's hypothesis: if Madhuri's destiny predicts failure, then a positive relationship would refute it.

"Wait!" Arjun exclaimed, pulling the purple pen from her hands. God, he was going to slobber all over that one, too. "I have to add something, too."

The Kismat Experiment also aims to prove Arjun's hypothesis: if Arjun's destiny predicts success, then a positive relationship would support it.

"Our hypotheses are conflicted." Madhuri's eyebrows furrowed together as she reread the experiment. "If we're going to break up by the end of our experiment, wouldn't that be a failure for you? Wouldn't that mean your destiny was wrong?"

"Does it really matter? Both outcomes prove your point." When Madhuri cocked her head to the side, trying to mask her confusion for the sake of preserving her own ego, Arjun laughed out loud. "The only difference is why. If your hypothesis fails, it would be because our experimental relationship didn't succeed, and your prophecy was right all along—you are, in fact, a colossal failure."

"Shut up, Arjun."

He ignored her, a playful smile tugging at his lips. "If my hypothesis fails, it would also be because our experimental relationship didn't succeed, but that means my prophecy wasn't accurate. I wasn't meant to be a winner this year."

"And in both conditions, our destiny would no longer be what we expected." Madhuri grimaced as she finished his train of thought for him.

She'd once found solace in the certainty of science, that an intellectual, pragmatically crafted hypothesis had a predictable yield based on some law of physics or chemistry or biology. Yet with one sentence, Arjun broke her safe space into smithereens. The stakes of their relationship caught up to her with the realization that she may not have as much control as she'd once thought. All Madhuri could do was hope that her negative prophecy would outweigh his cosmic luck.

She needed to change the topic before her anxiety got the best of her.

"Any other suggestions?"

Arjun went silent as if he were replaying their conversation in his head the same way she was. When he came to his senses, he twirled the purple pen between his fingers and let it fly across the paper as if of its own accord.

Primary Control Variable: Madhuri and Arjun must remain best friends throughout the experiment, and even when it ends.

"I'm surprised I didn't think of that first," Madhuri said. As much as she teased Arjun for clinging on to her, she found solace in his unwavering loyalty, his constant presence in her life. In her mind, there wasn't a single reality where they weren't best friends.

"I'm not. You've been trying to get rid of me for ages."

Madhuri pulled her shoe off on instinct, waving it around in the air the way her mother would do when she'd been disrespected. A witchlike cackle left his lips, and she wondered how he was so comfortable with himself to laugh so outrageously.

Arjun inhaled a deep breath and wiped his eyes like he had been crying. "I can't believe you're threatening your boyfriend with a chappal before we've even been on our first date."

"Calm down, Drama Queen. I haven't thrown it at you yet." Madhuri tried to digest the authoritative title of *boyfriend*, but she couldn't quite manage it. There was something concrete about it, realer than anything she'd ever known before. Their status was definitely going to take some getting used to. "I'm adding one last touch, and then we can sign this into existence."

The relationship will begin on September 29 and will end on June 14 of the next year.

"Don't get too attached," she warned. "This one is non-negotiable. I don't want to bring you with me to Stanford."

"You're not accepted yet, you know."

The thought of Madhuri not getting into her dream school was enough to make her throat close in on itself. Ever since she'd visited the campus with her parents four years ago, she'd wanted nothing more than to study Biochemistry at Stanford University. If that didn't happen, she didn't know what she'd do with herself.

"Hey, there's no harm in manifesting it out loud."

Arjun didn't respond. He nodded when he read the final line, his face completely expressionless. Without a beat of hesitation, he signed his name underneath and she signed right next to his.

Madhuri Iyer was no longer a single woman.

CHAPTER SEVEN

arjun

Arjun wasn't sure if it was a result of his head injury or the haze-like state of an early morning before school, but he seriously believed he was dreaming when he saw his mother sitting on the black leather couch in front of him. According to the itinerary stuck to their otherwise bare refrigerator, she'd returned from her business trip five days earlier than expected. As much as he'd grown accustomed to her constant travel, Arjun couldn't help but feel his chest brim with childlike excitement at the sight of her.

His mother looked incredibly real, so much so that if he reached out to her, he'd feel her breath on his palm. She had the remote in her hand and was clicking through channels, her feet propped up on the center coffee table. She had a content smile on her face, and for the first time, she looked like she was completely relaxed. Like she wanted to be with him, in their home, as a family.

If Arjun played his cards right, he could rekindle his relationship with his mother after years of emotional distance. His prophecy did say it'd be a lucky year for him, after all.

"What are you doing back?" Arjun asked in what he hoped was the most nonchalant manner possible. He didn't want to burden her with the sheer force of his emotions—the excitement, the anxiety, the cautious optimism. He fell into the La-Z-Boy beside her and popped the recliner out, releasing a sigh from his lips. "Your trip wasn't scheduled to end for another few days."

"Actually," his mother started, flashing him a smile, "the trip is still going on, but I realized that I needed to set my priorities straight. I didn't want to miss your senior year the way I missed all the others."

His mother often forgot the big events, but Arjun could've forgiven that if she were there for the smaller moments. He wanted nothing more than to share takeout from their favorite Indian restaurant, to spend sunny days at the beach and waste time with trips to the grocery store. He didn't think that was a lot to ask of his mother, especially with his father out of the picture.

His parents were lucky to have fallen in love with each other, but unlucky to be trapped in a community that looked down upon any sort of separation once their love died. Arjun would never forget the day his mother filed for divorce and his father packed his bags, the day his grandparents took sides in the war of his broken family while the Aunties and

Uncles in their neighborhood whispered judgments behind their backs.

His father had the privilege of running away. Within a few years, he built a new life with a new family, and no one ever disrespected him for it. Arjun's mother, on the other hand, would always be known in their community as the woman who ruined her own family, the woman whose career came in the way of her marriage, the woman who asked for too much and was rightfully punished for it.

His mother had a lot on her mind, and Arjun had come to terms with the fact that he was an unfortunate hitch in her life. He was the boy she created with forever in mind, only to have that forever ripped out from beneath her feet. It didn't surprise him that his mother didn't want to be around him then, not when he smiled like his father and laughed like her former in-laws.

His mother sniffled as she continued on, snapping Arjun out of his thoughts. "What I'm trying to say is that I'm sorry. I'm sorry for choosing myself over you, for neglecting you and your needs. And I'm sorry for trying to reconcile that now when it might already be too late." His mother tilted her head to the side, peering at him curiously. "Is it?"

Could he ever forgive her for the birthdays and the championship tournaments she'd missed, the countless times she'd forgotten to leave food in the fridge before one of her trips? He still remembered the first time he'd knocked on Auntie Iyer's door, his hair dripping wet because he didn't know how to drive and had no choice but to walk through the rain in search of a decent meal. It was that or eating RITZ Crackers for dinner, so the decision was relatively easy.

Despite his mother's absence, he'd found another family

that loved him unconditionally. Did he really need the conflict that came with having two?

At the same time, he wouldn't have to burden the Iyers anymore. He couldn't keep eating their food and sleeping in their home, not when he was stealing their eldest daughter, too. The Iyer family gave him everything when he had nothing, but their kindness couldn't be sustainable for long. The least he could do was get out of their hair until his mother inevitably scurried back to the office.

"It is not too late," he whispered, enunciating each syllable so the words felt more real. His chest filled with an incredible warmth, the kind of heat that only came from unadulterated hope—and a lucky prophecy that predicted this reconciliation days in advance. His mother's words, which were nearly identical to Auntie Iyer's reading, propelled him to accept her apology immediately.

Maybe Arjun and his mother were meant to be.

His mother screamed with joy and jumped off the couch, tackling Arjun with a bear hug. The force shook the recliner like an earthquake. Arjun almost tumbled off as a result, but his mother caught him by the arm before he hit the marble floor.

He could get used to this.

"I missed you."

Arjun didn't know who said it or if they both were thinking it and couldn't quite put it into words, but the sentiment resonated through his body. Waves of happiness washed over him, enveloping him like his mother's embrace.

For one beautiful moment, they were complete and not a single part of him questioned when they'd fall apart. For one beautiful moment, Arjun had all the faith in the world that they could last, that they could be like Madhuri and her parents one day. A real family.

When they finally pulled away, his mother's eyes landed on the bandage on Arjun's head. "What happened to you? You didn't get into a fight, did you?"

Arjun chuckled. "I don't fight, Mom. I was checked by an opponent during the game the other day and hit my head. Auntie Iyer changed my bandages and cleaned my wound before I came home, so don't worry about me. I've been in very good hands while you were gone."

His mother's eyes glazed over, and she fell back onto the couch, nibbling at the stray strip of skin on the side of her thumbnail. "Auntie Iyer, ready to save the day as always," she murmured under her breath, her voice edging on scornful.

"What is that supposed to mean?"

"Don't get me wrong—I'm very happy that Kamala and Dev are there to take care of you when you need them, but that's not their job." His mother turned to face him. "Sometimes, I find myself wishing I could be that person for you."

Sometimes. Arjun hadn't thought a word could feel so needlessly cruel.

He couldn't help the scornful thoughts that entered his mind, that she didn't have to *wish* to be that person for him—she simply *could be*. If only she were actually here long enough.

But he didn't think there was much use in voicing his emotions to his mother. He'd much rather continue to make excuses for her than risk her running away again because she couldn't handle how he truly felt. Besides, maybe he was overreacting. He could be quite prone to sensitivity, as his father used to put it.

Arjun squared his shoulders. "You can be that person for me now. If you want."

"I would love that." With the topic of Auntie Iyer aside, his mother relaxed into her chair and asked another question from her mental list.

It seemed like she was trying her hardest to reconnect with him and that was all he'd ever asked for, a bare-minimum semblance of effort and affection. And yet Madhuri never came up. Maybe it was natural for their conversation to take other avenues, or maybe it was because Arjun didn't know if he trusted his mother with the idea of her as more than a friend. If his mother found out about their relationship, she'd want to meet Madhuri again, and they hadn't interacted since his freshman year of high school.

After years of feeding Arjun's starving stomach, Madhuri and her parents knew that he wasn't raised by the most thoughtful family, but that wasn't the same as seeing the way he and his mother interacted. He couldn't bear their pity when they noticed that Arjun didn't tell his mother everything that was on his mind, the way Madhuri chatted with her parents like they were longtime best friends. When they noticed that Arjun's mother never said *I love you*.

His mother's eyes clicked to the digital clock on their kitchen counter, and she gasped. "Don't you have to go to school? I wouldn't want to make you late."

Arjun had definitely missed first period by now. Normally, he wouldn't have any issues with skipping school if it meant spending quality time with his mother, but this morning was different. Madhuri planned to publicly debut their relationship at school today, and she'd make him pay if he ditched her.

"Thank you for reminding me." Arjun picked up his keys and twirled them around his index finger, one foot already out the front door. "I'll see you this afternoon?"

His mother smiled at him. "I'm here to stay, beta."

"Arjun, we'll never turn in our lab on time if you don't finish writing down our procedure," Madhuri reminded him with a frantic edge to her voice. She didn't look up from her notes, her nose buried in the hearts dotting her *i*'s. She'd formed the habit last year in an act of reclaiming her identity as a woman in STEM. "What's going on with you?"

Arjun had a lot on his mind. His mother was back, and she was here to stay.

Maybe that was what his horoscope was talking about. Maybe the love that the Universe had in store for him was the familial kind—the one that Madhuri had with her parents, that he'd spent his entire life pining for.

What did Auntie Iyer say exactly? Something about how he'd be given an opportunity by a woman who typically destroyed any ounce of common sense he had, and how it was up to him to decide if she was too late or right on time. His mother checked off those boxes. She gave him the opportunity to reconnect with her and even asked if she was too late, exactly like Auntie Iyer predicted.

Although the faint disappointment that Madhuri was not his endgame rumbled through him, Arjun's heart still brimmed with joy. He'd spent years wishing for his mother to come home, and finally, she had. He made a mental note to ask Auntie Iyer to confirm his theory about his prophecy, perhaps when he and his mother went to visit the Iyer family later that evening. That should give him the courage to fully accept his mother back into his life.

"Arjun? You in there?" Madhuri waved her hand in front of his face. When he didn't answer, she yanked the paper from his hand and scribbled a numbered list of procedures down the middle with a disgruntled huff. "You can't just sit there while I do all the work, you know."

He could tell she was still upset about that morning.

As they walked down the hall hand in hand, they were approached by Olivia and Brynn, Madhuri's two ex-best friends from middle school. Their eyes ran up and down Madhuri's frame as if searching for an aspect of her identity to dissect.

"Good morning, Madhuri," Olivia said, drawing out her name with horrific pronunciation. A white flash of rage passed through Arjun's vision when he heard it—Mad-Oo-Ree, instead of Mah-Dhoo-Ree. Back in middle school, Olivia would pronounce it correctly, but now she weaponized Madhuri's own name against her. "You and Arjun are just so adorable together. How'd you manage to pull him?"

Brynn giggled. Arjun could see the crowd of students around them watching the interaction. "Her parents must've set it up. Arranged-marriage style, you know?"

Madhuri averted her gaze to the ground, choosing to remain silent instead of offering her bullies any more ammunition. Arjun, however, couldn't let Olivia and Brynn continue to hurt his best friend. He'd stand up for Madhuri, even if it meant paying the price for it later.

"Nice microaggression, Brynn. How long did it take you to come up with that one?" Arjun turned to Olivia. "And by the way, I pulled Madhuri, not the other way around. She's a catch, and you're too ignorant to see it."

"Not worth it, Arjun." Madhuri tugged on his shirtsleeve, and Arjun could feel her staring daggers into the side of his skull. "Come on, let's go to class. It's getting late."

Olivia ignored them and exchanged a knowing look with Brynn. "I completely forgot about that weird Indian shit, but you're so right. I can't imagine Arjun dating her by choice, not when he has so many better options." She tossed her blond hair over her shoulder. "Oh, and, Arjun, you were so amazing at your last game. I didn't know if you saw, but Brynn and I made a poster for you. We were holding it up in the student section of the bleachers, cheering you on."

"I didn't notice." Arjun set his jaw into a straight line.

"So sad." Olivia clicked her tongue and checked her watch. "Well, as much as I loved chatting with you both, I think Little Miss Spelling Bee Champion is right. It's time for class."

That was the breaking point for Madhuri. She shook her head, pulled her textbooks to her chest, and ran away toward the chemistry lab, tears sparkling in her eyes. Olivia and Brynn chuckled to themselves before walking in the other direction, and just like that, their other classmates scattered to their respective classrooms. Within a minute, the hallways were empty, and Arjun was standing alone, silently cursing himself for not doing enough to protect Madhuri when it truly mattered.

And now Madhuri was taking her emotions out on him, the way she always did.

"Do you plan on ever starting the data analysis section, or do you want me to do that for you, too, Arjun?"

"I was getting to it. Patience is a virtue, darling." He rolled his eyes at her, unbothered by her subtle dig. Madhuri's inability to cope with her own feelings was something he'd grown used to—not in a sad-wounded-puppy sort of way, but in a she-doesn't-really-mean-it sort of way.

Liam, his closest friend outside of Madhuri's inner circle, brushed past him with a bump of the shoulder. "This lab's the worst, man. You're lucky you have that one on your team." An easy smirk played on Liam's lips as he nodded to Madhuri, who awkwardly squirmed in her seat. "Before I forget, Coach wants me to ask if you're still coming to practice after class. He said something about your mom coming home early, but that has to be a joke, right?"

"Actually, it's true." When Liam raised a brow at him, the surprise clearly evident in his expression, Arjun continued, "I'm caught off guard by it, too, but it doesn't change anything. We have State Championships to win, so I'm not slacking off."

"I'm happy for you, Arjun." Liam flashed a smile, his eyes crinkling at the corners. Arjun could never get enough of it—the genuine happiness his friends experienced on his behalf whenever his mother came back home. Even Madhuri, despite everything she'd been through that morning, had offered him a tight hug when she'd heard the news. He could still feel the ghost of her touch now, a gentle current that ran up and down his arms with no end in sight. "I'm guessing this means you can't make it to Spiked Milkshake Night, though."

Before Arjun could respond with a definitive no, Liam made eye contact with their instructor and scurried up to the front of the laboratory with a sheepish grin, leaving Arjun to face Madhuri's taut grimace alone.

"I don't like it when you call me your darling," she snapped once she was sure Liam was out of earshot. She pushed her goggles up the slant of her slightly crooked nose and narrowed her eyes on the pink titration in front of her. "Not in a school setting, and especially not when I'm taking charge of an experiment we're supposed to work on together."

Her voice gradually decreased in volume as she spoke, probably because she was conscious of their classmates listening in. He caught her scanning the laboratory, her chest rising and falling at a heightened pace. He hated when Madhuri did that—when she screamed her thoughts and regretted them right after for no reason besides a deeply held insecurity.

Their instructor walked past them at that exact moment, ignoring Arjun in favor of offering Madhuri a thumbs-up. "Keep up the good work, Miss Iyer. As for you, Mr. Mehta, I would recommend putting in your fair share of the work on this lab report. Otherwise, I'll have no choice but to make you repeat the lab—*independently*."

Obviously, Madhuri wasn't speaking quietly enough.

Arjun couldn't mask his annoyance anymore. That was the first time a teacher hadn't stopped by his side of the table, striking up a conversation about last night's game or his particularly stellar performance on an exam. Even when the people around him doubted his abilities, be it due to his circumstances at home or the external-jock stereotype he often embodied, he always ended up as the all-around favorite. He'd never had a teacher scold him before.

Madhuri, on the other hand, was a quiet sort of brilliant. She was the type of student advanced-placement teachers noticed, the stereotypical valedictorian in training. Her charisma was reserved for the few who dared to know her, namely her family, Josie, and himself. The rest of the world thought she was invisible—until they wanted to hurt her, that was—and she seemed to prefer it that way.

As if she could read his mind, Madhuri sighed. "I'm sorry for lashing out. It's been an awful day. Are you sure you're alright?"

"I always am," he responded with a stiff smile, and snapped his goggles back onto his face. "You don't need to worry about me."

Arjun bent over the table, scribbling answers into the open spaces that Madhuri had left for him. He was determined to write the best lab report in the history of his high school, and he'd turn it in at the end of the period, unlike any of the other students. He'd do anything to make every aspect of his prophecy, academics included, a reality.

After all, this year was destined for his success. It was literally written in the stars.

CHAPTER EIGHT

madhuri

Karma ruled Madhuri's life with an iron fist. It was a boomerang that'd come back to smack her in the face if she made any sort of questionable decision. But unlike the other devout Hindus that had a love-hate relationship with Karma, she was unlucky enough to have another moral equalizer: her parents.

The Iyer family was a pillar of generosity and kindness. Her father volunteered his work-mandated vacation days to India, where he visited estranged family members and gave back to the community that had given him everything. Her mother was similarly selfless, devoting herself to her family while simultaneously working full-time as a psychiatrist. Madhuri could never get away with anything under their watchful eyes and was forced to stifle her more selfish tendencies, some-

thing her parents never truly understood. They were unde-
niably good, while Madhuri was firmly gray.

When Madhuri woke up from her afternoon nap with a
roaring fever and a painful cough, she knew with absolute
certainty that her sickness was Karmically induced. She'd
dared to keep a secret as extreme as her motivations for dating Arjun from her oh-so-perfect parents, and now she was
being punished for it.

"Amma!" Madhuri shouted, wrapping her weighted blanket tighter around herself. "Can you come upstairs? I need to
talk to you and Appa."

No response. Even the ever-present sound of her mother
cooking onions with red peppers and flaming hot oil was suspiciously absent. They were definitely ignoring her, so she'd
have to resort to drastic measures.

"Raina!" she screamed, clenching her sheets in her fists
until her knuckles turned white.

Right on cue, her little sister bounced into the bedroom.
Her hair was forced into a high ponytail and Madhuri's eyes
lasered on to the very-cute, very-much-hers scrunchie that
held up the style. She'd have to steal it back when she had
the energy to leave her bed. Raina wore a pair of ripped blue
jeans and a baggy white crop top. Even at sixteen, she never
cared much for superficial appearances. Comfort was most
important to her.

"What do you want?" Raina asked with a fake deadpan.
She offered Madhuri a cheery smile, trying to make it obvious that she wasn't actually being mean.

"I'm sick." A spark of pain seared through her brain. "I need
Mom and Dad, and for some weird reason, they're pretend-

ing not to hear me!" she yelled, only to spiral into a coughing fit that ripped her throat apart like it was being stabbed by a series of freshly sharpened knives.

Raina jumped back, covering her face out of precaution. She peeked through the space between her fingers. "They said they'd take me to a dance workshop in LA if I told you they weren't home." Raina lowered her voice to a whisper. "If you beat their offer, I'll snitch."

"How do I know you won't go back to wherever they're hiding and throw me under the bus for an even better offer?" Madhuri pulled her blanket up so it covered her neck. A flurry of warmth bloomed in her chest, subduing the fever chills and waves of nausea overcoming her.

"I swear on our sister bond that I won't." Raina grinned. "Have an offer?"

"I'll take you to the workshop and I'll buy you the costume sari you've had your eye on since last Christmas." Madhuri winced at the thought of her obliterated wallet and the soft memory of her own costumes, collecting dust in the back of her closet. "How's that?"

"The costume isn't complete without a jewelry set. Don't try to rip me off, Madhu."

"You can't be serious."

Her sister made a move for the door. "I can always go ask Amma for the same deal."

"Fine, I'll get you the jewelry set, too." Madhuri groaned. "Will you tell me why Mom and Dad are ignoring me now?"

Raina threw herself onto Madhuri's bed without a care for the infectious diseases she might be carrying. "They're downstairs, brewing tea before the Mehta family comes over.

They told me they didn't want you to disturb them." She wiggled her eyebrows suggestively. "Maybe they're arranging your marriage."

She chucked a pillow at her sister, who had dissolved into a fit of giggles. Arranged marriages were such a messy Indian stereotype, which was why Raina loved to make a joke of it—after all, their own parents were the product of an arranged marriage, and they were more in love than the majority of the couples in their community who weren't. Still, Madhuri wasn't a huge fan of relationships born from partnership rather than true, unyielding love. It also didn't help that arranged marriages were also used against her by people like Olivia and Brynn—a way of mocking her culture without being explicitly racist.

The whole concept was so complicated, and it pissed her off to no end.

"I could've figured that out myself! You little hustler!"

"You swore on our bond. There's no escaping now unless you don't care for me at all." Raina's trademark puppy-dog eyes cut into her soul. "You're not that bad of a sister, right?"

Madhuri threw the covers off the bed and rose to her feet. The throbbing in her head intensified, and for one unbearable second, she thought she was about to pass out. Unfortunately, she was still conscious and in excruciating pain.

"You're in for it when I get back, Raina," Madhuri warned under her breath, tying her hair into a relaxed bun.

Raina shrugged. "Yeah, right." With that, her sister walked back to her own room across the hall with a cocky skip in her step. Raina had survived this battle, but Madhuri made a mental note to get her back in the future. Little sisters never won the war, especially if a stolen scrunchie was involved.

Grumbling to herself, Madhuri made her way down the stairs at a snail's pace. Her parents' voices rang through the corridor, bouncing off her eardrums like a toddler at Sky Zone. Her lips twisted into a scowl when she saw her father sitting on the living room sofa, drinking his chai in peace.

"I'm sick, and none of you care," Madhuri announced from the top of the staircase, her softest blanket wrapped around her like a tightly wound cape.

He didn't even look up from his newspaper. "Of course we care, Madhu."

She mustered up the energy to storm over to him, kneeling beside the adjacent coffee table. "Oh, yeah? Then why are you ignoring me and bribing Raina to lie about your whereabouts?"

"What are you, my mother?" He snorted.

Madhuri crossed her arms. "Don't avoid the subject. What are you hiding?"

Her father put his newspaper down and turned his head so he could see into the kitchen, where her mother was making another cup of tea. As she waited for the chai to boil, Madhuri's mother tossed two pills into her mouth, blanching at the dusty taste of her Crohn's disease medication.

"Kamala," her father complained, drawing out the last letter of her mother's name like a child. "Your daughter thinks I'm hiding things from her."

Her mother laughed out loud once she'd swallowed the large tablets. "*My* daughter? She gets her quirks from you." She strolled out of the kitchen and handed Madhuri a cup of her own. "And, Madhuri, we're not hiding anything from you, but we'd really appreciate if you left us alone before Mrs. Mehta comes over."

Madhuri lifted an eyebrow at the mention of Arjun's estranged mother. "Nope. Whatever you have to say in front of Auntie Mehta, you can say in front of me."

Her parents exchanged a look before her mother responded. "If you insist."

They waited for no more than a few seconds before the doorbell rang. Her mother offered Arjun and Auntie Mehta each a steaming cup of tea as they stepped through the door, even though Arjun was a total coffee person. That didn't matter, though. Chai during crucial discussions was an Indian Auntie tradition and her mother knew he would never disrespect that.

"Madhuri, you look like total shit," Arjun said, all in one breath.

Madhuri made eye contact with Auntie Mehta, and she tried to hide the way her lips curled into a scowl when she heard his comment. She wanted to make a good impression on Arjun's mother, and she was somehow failing already.

But Auntie Mehta smacked her son upside the head, ignoring his pained yelp. "How dare you speak to your girlfriend like that? Let alone in front of your elders!"

"My girlfriend? How did you—"

"Find out? First of all, you can't hide anything from me, and secondly, you forget that I'm still in contact with Mrs. Iyer." Arjun's mother sent him a smug look before she turned back to the Iyer family. "It's so lovely to see you all again. It's been much too long."

Madhuri's mother patted two empty chairs near her own spot on the couch, stifling her laughter as well as she could. Her smile didn't quite reach her eyes, though. Every moment Auntie Iyer spent with Auntie Mehta seemed forced. "Please, come sit."

As Arjun and Auntie Mehta sat down, Madhuri's father cleared his throat. "To what do we owe this visit? It's been quite some time since we've heard from you."

"I just wanted to say how glad I was that Arjun picked Madhuri for his first girlfriend." Auntie Mehta beamed at her. If Madhuri wasn't worried that she'd dissolve into another coughing fit with any sudden movement, she would have smiled back. "But considering that they're both teenagers, I wanted to have some say in the foundation of their relationship. I know you would like that, too."

By the way Auntie Mehta was speaking, it was looking like they'd have to include a few parental addendums to their experiment. Madhuri looked to Arjun, hoping he would notice the desperate plea in her eyes. Someone had to stop them and it sure as hell wouldn't be her.

He pretended not to see her. Arjun would never damage his reputation as the Golden Boy in front of her parents, but honestly, nothing could hurt his relationship with them. Her parents loved him so much that Arjun teasingly insulting her and swearing under his breath only made them laugh.

"That's a great idea," her mother said. "What do you have in mind?"

"Why don't we decide on their first date?"

Madhuri's mother nodded before speaking. Her words sounded alive, but her voice was distant. "If that date doesn't work, they'll have their answer loud and clear. And if it results in a proper match, then they can continue without our input."

While the thought of a chaperoned first date sent a rush of bitter bile to Madhuri's taste buds, she knew her disapproval was no match for their parents' stubborn plans. Besides, it couldn't be that difficult to make it through one family-approved date. If she pulled it off, she could move on to the experimental relationship she'd originally planned, no questions asked.

"You read my mind! In fact, my niece, Arjun's cousin, is getting married next weekend at The Beverly Hills Hotel in Los Angeles. We were hoping that your family would join us for the occasion."

"You're inviting Madhuri's family?" Arjun asked, his lips twisting into a frown. Madhuri noticed how his once-still leg was bouncing up and down like a caffeine-ridden toddler. His vision was firmly trained on his mother, who squeezed his shoulder with a stern hand. Arjun's leg went motionless at the touch.

Auntie Mehta shook her head. "Of course I'm inviting them. What's the point in planning the first date if the parents don't get to keep an eye on the couple?"

"After all, we don't want there to be any funny business," Madhuri's father added, challenging Arjun with a stone-cold stare. Madhuri elbowed him in the gut, and he grimaced, lowering his eyes back to the center table.

Maybe their experimental relationship would be harder to pull off than she had originally thought.

Auntie Mehta jumped to her feet. "It's settled, then. We will see you at the wedding." The adults chatted away, saying goodbye over and over while promptly forgetting to leave once another conversation point came to their attention.

Madhuri took advantage of their distraction and grabbed Arjun's arm, steering him toward the kitchen. "Why didn't you tell them to get out of our business?" Madhuri growled, pulling him close by his shirt collar. "They're being so Indian about this."

"Well, they are Indian. What else did you expect?" His arm snaked around her waist. "Besides, don't you love weddings? What's the harm in that being our first date?"

Madhuri was caught off guard by the sensations tingling away under the skin of her hip, the way her throat clenched in anticipation, though she didn't quite know for what. Something about the way Arjun spoke felt electric, mature in a way that was so unlike his boy-next-door self. She'd never been attracted to him in any sense before, and she brushed the feeling off as nothing more than experimental-relationship jitters. The whole thing was so fresh that it was probably messing with her brain chemistry. Surely, it'd fade with time.

Madhuri hoped he couldn't read her mind, and she continued on with their conversation. "They're going to be supervising the whole thing. Doesn't that bother you?"

"Not at all. If I can get away with holding you like this with our parents in the other room, what's to say I can't pull this off at the wedding, too?" He flashed her a smirk that was a little too cocky for her to recognize. Madhuri wondered if he was overcompensating after his mother stole the conversation from beneath him a moment ago. "By the way, your breath reeks."

"Well, I'm sick. What else did you expect?" She blew a stream of air at his nose.

He didn't flinch and instead infiltrated her space with confidence. Arjun had lost all sense of restraint, his eyes locked on to hers with urgency, his fingers digging into the crook of her waist. Even when he spoke, his voice resembling a light tease, Madhuri didn't detect a hint of caution. "That's disgusting, Madhuri. You're lucky I like you as much as I do."

"You know, my mother always told me that when you choose to like someone that much, it becomes a little too easy for them to hurt you." She released his collar, pulling back like he'd burned her. A pinkish tinge of color made its way back to her skin, and she sneaked out of his grasp before he could lean in any closer. "That's the last thing I'd want to do to you."

"So don't," Arjun called out as she rushed back to her parents, who were still in the process of sending Auntie Mehta home. Before Madhuri could disappear through the doors to the living room, he sent her a knowing look. "Don't hurt me, and I can like you as much as I want."

Madhuri offered him a smile, silently hoping the same. Arjun's feelings were the one variable she had to control the most, and she didn't think her experiment would be able to survive if he suddenly experienced a change of heart.

"I won't."

CHAPTER NINE

arjun

Arjun sat on top of the granite island at the center of his kitchen, dangling his legs in the air. He watched his mother make breakfast as she hummed a classic Bollywood song to herself, flipping her omelet from the pan to her toast. She pulled out a Maggi hot sauce bottle from their refrigerator and spooned a dollop onto her eggs. With a contented sigh, she smashed the omelet and hot sauce between two pieces of almost-burnt toast and took a large bite out of it.

Arjun shook his head when she dug in. "Ew, Mom."

His mother smiled, covering her mouth so she could respond while chewing. "You have Americanized taste buds. You wouldn't understand this cultural delicacy."

"The only cultural part of that meal is the hot sauce, and I already have that with my grilled cheese." Arjun kicked himself off the countertop, depositing his coffee mug into the sink.

"Now, *that* is an ew-worthy combination." His mother stuck her tongue out and he ignored the flaky bread crumbs scattered across it. He missed this the most—his family's utter disregard for hiding their nasty habits from each other.

"My taste buds are much more evolved than yours," he responded in what he hoped was a posh British accent. It must have felt real, because his mother's nostrils flared when she heard him.

"Since when did you become one of those colonizers?" His mother shook her head, dusting her hands of bread crumbs. "Don't make me lecture you on their crimes against India again."

Arjun chuckled, kissing his mother on the cheek. "You don't need to. I remember."

His mother clicked her tongue as if she didn't quite believe him, but she smiled at him anyway. Her phone, forgotten on the dining room table, buzzed with a new email. Although it caught her attention momentarily, she focused back on him. "When will you be back?"

Wow. He hadn't heard a question like that in ages.

"I'm visiting Madhuri at work since I didn't have a chance to catch up with her at school yesterday, but I can come home in a few hours if you need me to."

His mother left the kitchen and handed Arjun a yellow banana. It reminded him of Madhuri's outfit when she'd come to visit him at the house. "I'd really appreciate that. I thought we could have lunch together and plan out the details of the wedding coming up. As you know, members of your father's family will be in attendance, and I want to talk through the logistics of that with you beforehand."

Arjun cocked his head to the side. His father's family had no reason to show up at his maternal cousin's wedding, but the thought of facing them again after so many years was enough to flood his heart with waves of discomfort. And if that was how *he* felt, he couldn't imagine what his mother was going through. He'd need to be there for her.

"I'll be back for lunch, then," he said, drawing out each syllable as he swiped his keys off the kitchen counter. "I promise I won't let you down."

His mother beamed. "I love you, Arjun."

No way. That couldn't be real.

His mother obviously loved him, but in a subtle way. She preferred to show her love by cutting him fruits during an intense study session, which she hadn't done since his freshman year, or by catching him before he fell off a leather recliner.

She never said it out loud, though. Not once.

He looked over his shoulder and caught his mother's hopeful gaze. The thumping of his heart rang in his ears, screaming the words back to her. His mouth didn't get the memo, though.

"I…uhhh…" When his mother furrowed her eyebrows, the way she did when she was confused and trying to figure him out, he cursed under his breath. He needed to say something before he hurt her feelings.

"Thank you so much for that, Mom!" he exclaimed, and slammed the door behind him.

A fluorescent beam of light fixated on Arjun's forehead from the ceiling, accenting his sharply lined features in the fitting room mirror across the aisle. He saw a gleaming Tillys logo in his reflection, framed by hanging floral skirts and distressed band T-shirts. The clothing outlet had a foot in every Californian subculture, from Hollister surfer to Hot Topic grunge, and it was giving him a roaring migraine. He had no idea how Madhuri worked here every day, serving customers who didn't know what they wanted before or after entering the storefront.

With a sigh, he turned to the left of the menacing wall of short-short shorts and found Madhuri at the cash register, a smile plastered to her face as she made small talk with a pack of girls from their AP English Literature class. He recognized them as friends of Olivia and Brynn, and he wondered how Madhuri scanned and bagged their items as if they didn't affect her at all. It was so different from who she was at school, where the mere sight of her ex-best friends was enough to ruin her mood for the rest of the day.

Arjun picked up the cheapest item he could find: a fifteen-dollar lanyard with different Star Wars characters lining the cloth. Nerdy and extraordinarily expensive, but it was unapologetically him. He approached the register after the girls left, although they continued to loiter behind him. Madhuri counted their change with incredible concentration, her frizzy hair covering her face like a shield. When she noticed someone at her register, she jumped and hurriedly forced the same smile she had on before.

"All set?" she asked cheerfully before she noticed Arjun swinging his pathetic lanyard from his fingertips. In hindsight, he really shouldn't have picked that item. She'd make so much fun of him when she was off the clock. Madhuri's eyes landed on the girls Arjun was desperately trying to ignore, their whispers drilling a hole through his eardrums. She leaned over the counter with a grimace. "What are you doing here?"

"Buying a lanyard, obviously." He dropped it onto the counter and shoved his hands into his pockets. All he had to do was be confident in himself, even if it meant confirming his love for Star Wars merchandise. Wasn't that the real key to winning a girl's heart?

As if to escape the inquisitive stares and flashing phones of their classmates, Madhuri let herself out from the confines of the register and pulled Arjun toward the front of the store by the sleeve of his shirt. "How did you know I even worked here?"

"I have my ways." He shrugged. In reality, Raina had a big mouth and Arjun knew exactly how to crack her. All it took was a pack of French fries from the McDonald's down the street from their house. "Why are you keeping it a secret? It's not like this is an embarrassing job or anything."

Madhuri groaned, tugging on her crop top like she felt the need to cover her exposed midriff. She turned on her walkie and mumbled something about taking her ten. Another voice screeched through the headset, affirming her request. Madhuri slipped her hand into his, which he prayed wasn't sweaty, and led him to the break room.

He focused intensely on the employees-only sign pinned to the front, no more than a few feet away from the girls who'd suddenly gone silent at the sight of their interlaced fingers. He had no doubt that word, or rather a Snapchat, of their subtle PDA had made it to Olivia and Brynn by now. "Are you sure I'm allowed to be here?"

"It's not a big deal. I'm my manager's favorite, so I can get away with whatever I want around here," Madhuri said once they entered, leaning against a tower of storage boxes. He gingerly sat down on the spinning chair in front of her. He didn't want to break anything and have Madhuri pay the price for it. "To answer your question, I didn't want my parents to know about this job. I don't think they'd react favorably."

Arjun raised his eyebrows, unable to contain his surprise. "I thought you told your parents everything."

"I do, but certain things are exceptions."

"Like what?"

Madhuri took a moment to think, and Arjun knew she was analyzing all the possible ways their conversation could go. He wondered if her technique originated from a coping mechanism, a way to reel in her trust issues when confessing secrets to anyone outside of her family.

"My family doesn't believe in their children working when they're supposed to be focusing on their academics. They think that me having a job would only distract from my education, but I know the real reason." She took her voice down an octave and Arjun found himself leaning in to hear her clearly. "They've been saving for college since I was born, but they still can't cover more than a four-year degree at a public university. When I told them that I wanted to go to Stanford to kick-start my career in research, they were so supportive, but I know that they don't have the funds for it."

Madhuri's eyes landed on absolutely anything but him. "If they knew I was working, it would hurt them. To them, having a daughter means also having the responsibility of supporting me emotionally, mentally, and financially. I don't want them to feel like they're failing to do that because I'm working."

Arjun nodded. He knew that tradition well. His mother wouldn't let him get a job, either, but his family was more financially privileged than Madhuri's. With no work-life balance, their money piled up quickly. Still, he would've rather been in Madhuri's position than his own.

"Anyway, I want to help my parents pay for school, and if that means working a part-time job without them knowing, so be it. It's not hard to get away with it, either—all I need to do is tell them I'm with you." Madhuri's lips contorted into a sad smile. She pushed herself off the sturdy storage boxes, making her way to Arjun. "They gave me an American dream before they got their own. I have to repay them somehow. It's the least I can do."

He had never been more in awe of Madhuri than in that moment.

He'd spent most of their childhood reconciling the two versions of Madhuri he saw every day. There was the American Madhuri, who loved to cause a scene as long as it didn't catch the attention of the kids at school. And then there was the unbreakable Indian Madhuri, who was so incredibly proud of herself and where she came from.

In that dusty storage room, he saw a third.

Madhuri embodied India through her unconditional love for her family and America through her burning desire to accomplish even the most difficult of dreams. She alleviated her diaspora and blessed him with the opportunity to see it firsthand.

That was the real reason why he'd agreed to *The Kismat Experiment*. He would've done anything if it meant being there for moments like this, where he got the chance to understand the girl he'd spent his entire life with.

"I'm sorry to be such a downer. I know it's a pretty heavy topic." Madhuri pulled him into a hug, resting her head on his chest. Arjun hoped she couldn't hear his heart beating faster and faster as if he was on the brink of disaster. "I guess I needed to talk to someone who'd understand the position I was in. I've tried telling Josie about it, but it's hard for her to see the cultural reasoning behind my parents' rule."

Arjun didn't know what compelled him to do it, but he kissed her on the top of her head. A whiff of rose shampoo danced up his nose. Within seconds, the beautiful scent faded away and he wished he could've held on to it for a while longer. "Don't apologize to me. I'm always here for you, no matter what happens."

"Thank you," she whispered, although her spine stiffened slightly. Arjun pulled back as soon as he felt her body language shift. The last thing he wanted to do was make her uncomfortable. "That means everything to me."

What would it have been like if she'd said that he, specifically, meant everything to her? Maybe he'd muster the courage to confess the full extent of his feelings, the confusion and the anxiety and the unrelenting hope that she may somehow feel the same.

But no amount of hope would change what she actually said—his *presence* was what meant everything to her, not him as a person. As much as she needed him for moments like these, Arjun knew that Madhuri would never let herself fall for him. She had a prophecy to prove wrong, and he had no choice but to come to terms with their experimental relationship, silently praying that his own heart wouldn't break in the process.

CHAPTER TEN

madhuri

"Josie, I know you told Arjun about my job."

Madhuri cornered her best friend after their last period, the final bell ringing in her ears. She placed her hands on her hips and tried to appear irritated, even though she was happier than ever. Telling Arjun about her position at Tillys lifted a burdensome weight off her shoulders. She'd never thought to mention it to him before, even though he would've been the only person to understand the complexity of her situation. Maybe that was because she'd only seen Arjun as the little boy she grew up with, laughing to himself about some comic book or coercing her into a game of competitive freeze tag.

"Actually, Raina did." Josie must have noticed the slight uptick in Madhuri's temper and promptly linked their arms together in the form of an infinity symbol. "It doesn't matter who said what, though. Isn't Tillys something he should know about?"

"Why should he?"

Josie offered her a blank stare. "For starters, he is your boyfriend now."

"Oh, yes, exactly. That makes sense." Hoping to distract from her momentary slipup, Madhuri steered Josie toward the student parking lot among a crowd of their classmates, unable to wipe the smile off her face. "You're right—he should know that side of me. Plus, it gave him a chance to prove himself. He was so thoughtful and kind when I brought it up."

Josie leaned her head on Madhuri's shoulder with a sigh. "See? He's perfect for you. I'm surprised it took you so long to notice."

Madhuri hopped onto the hood of Josie's black Toyota, swinging her legs through the air with a contented sigh. Josie joined her, staring at her with a knowing glimmer in her eye.

"Dreaming of Arjun?" she asked, leaning close to Madhuri's face.

Madhuri hated keeping *The Kismat Experiment* a secret from her best friend. She knew that it was for the best, that confounding variables like nosy friends and family members could destroy her hypothesis before it even began.

Still, Madhuri couldn't help but feel excited. In a few hours, she was going on her first ever date, where they'd be attending a big fat Indian wedding.

After spending her childhood watching Bollywood films filled with colorful receptions and wondrous magic, she would finally get to experience a fairy tale of her own. Sure, she'd be breaking up with Arjun in the summer, but that didn't mean she couldn't enjoy the process of being swept up by the whirlwind, albeit short-term, romance. She wouldn't let herself fall for her boyfriend, but she could always fall in love with love itself.

"Something like that." Madhuri flashed her a grin. "I'm going to a wedding tonight. Well, it's actually a Sangeet. It's a party with dancing and free food and an open bar to kick off the celebration. The next morning, we have the actual ceremonial wedding and the reception after."

She tentatively showed Josie her palms, which were stained by dark maroon henna. Her mother had spent hours the night before weaving intricate designs for her and her sister to flaunt at the wedding.

"That's gorgeous." Josie leaned forward to marvel at the blooming flowers and snaking vines. "It smells so good, too!"

Madhuri rubbed her sleeve against her nose with a sniffle, a leftover symptom from when she spent her break between AP Calculus and AP Biology crying in the restroom. Olivia had mentioned that her mehndi looked like she'd drenched her hands in mud. "You think so?"

"The henna is beautiful, Madhuri. Everything about you and your culture is." Josie squeezed her hand. "Now, tell me more about this wedding and what it has to do with Arjun."

Grateful for the shift in topic, Madhuri smiled. "Well, it's my first date with Arjun."

"You're messing with me, aren't you?"

"Nope."

"I've always dreamed of a romantic first date, and instead, I was stuck eating a boring meal with a boring boy and his nervous, yet somehow still grabby, hands." Her best friend playfully shoved Madhuri and flashed her a grin. "Whereas you get to dress up like a princess and impress your boyfriend all at once. Not that you have to, considering y'all used to bathe in the same tub as kids."

Whenever Josie got excited, her Midwestern accent would force its way into her voice. It was absolutely adorable, seeing those little slips of the person she was before she moved to California. She wondered if Josie felt the same way when she saw Madhuri's Indian side, like the subtle roll of her tongue when she pronounced the *r* in her own name.

"Oh, shut up." Madhuri waved her last comment away with a laugh. "There's one downside, though. Our parents are going to be there the whole time. Apparently, they want to supervise to make sure there's no funny business."

Josie made a disgusted face, before it morphed into an expression Madhuri couldn't quite place. She tapped the side of her head like she was in the middle of a brilliant discovery. "I have an idea. What if you had a buffer at the wedding? Someone to distract your families if you and Arjun need some alone time."

That was an objectively great idea, and she knew the perfect woman for the job—Raina, her sneaky little sister, who needed to be reckoned with after she'd conned Madhuri out of two hundred dollars' worth of dance costumes.

Madhuri tackled Josie with a hug. "You're a genius."

"Don't I know it."

Madhuri shivered against the brisk autumn air that swept through the rooftop lounge at The Beverly Hills Hotel. Her eyes caught a glimpse of the various constellations sparkling from the night sky. They lit up the dance floor without the help of the flashing neon beams on either side of the DJ. The bride, adorned with gold jewelry and a bloodred lehenga, sat on a decorative plush couch in front of the dance floor. Beside her was her grinning groom, feeding her bite-size pieces of tandoori chicken pizza and white wine through a pink straw in a last-ditch attempt to keep his fiancée's lipstick intact. Their closest friends and family performed a choreographed dance routine until it was time to open up the floor to the rest of the guests.

Madhuri noticed the way the Aunties at the function pointed at Raina, who was publicly stuffing her face with every item on the menu while trying to coerce the bartender to serve her a whiskey on the rocks. As the Aunties passed judgments among themselves like a steaming pile of samosas, she silently urged her sister to escort herself out of the limelight. Instead, Raina made eye contact with Madhuri and the Aunties behind her before flashing her a dazzling, confident smile in their direction. Madhuri wished she could channel even an ounce of that energy into her own life.

Madhuri shifted her attention to her father, who pulled her mother to the center stage, spinning her around in the center of the crowd to the tune of "Sadi Gali," their favorite Bollywood song. Auntie Mehta followed, her carefree laughter filling Madhuri's heart with a pang of envy. There was a time when Madhuri used to be like them, screaming out the lyrics without a care in the world.

As a classically trained Bharatanatyam dancer, she remembered the way the audience would watch her when she danced, unable to look away from her grace. She'd never forget how it felt to close her eyes when she spun, committing every single moment to memory forever. The South Indian art form helped her to feel connected to her culture as a child.

But Madhuri quit after eighth grade, when her fear of nonconformity outweighed her passion for dance. Once the girls at school found out about her colorful costumes and dramatic makeup, the Hindu folklore and foreign instruments, they ripped her to shreds with their cruel words. Her Arangetram, a culminating solo for dancers who successfully completed their training in Bharatanatyam, was supposed to be an accomplishment, but instead it led to ridicule by her classmates.

Arjun posted a series of photos and videos from her Arangetram to congratulate her, and given his newfound popularity, the Instagram went viral with the kids in their community. Olivia and Brynn, both of whom had never explored art beyond their ballet classes and the Steve Miller Band discography, immediately ended their friendship with her. Before she even made it to her freshman year of high school, Madhuri had become her small town's local embarrassment.

She still felt pain aching through her heart as she watched her parents spin across the dance floor. She shook her head and turned her gaze to the antique clock on the wall of the lounge, watching as the time ticked away and Arjun remained absent. She'd only been at the Sangeet for thirty minutes, but even his mom was here. Was he standing her up? Maybe he got nervous, but that was still unforgivable. Because of him, she looked like a fool, standing alone and waiting for him.

Madhuri sneaked a sip of wine from her father's long-forgotten glass on the table, twirling her freshly curled hair around a finger as she waited for the bitter taste to wash her anxiety away.

"Come on, Madhu!" her father called after she'd pushed the wineglass away from her possession, extending an arm out to her with joy glittering in his smile.

Auntie Mehta whispered something to her parents and her father's arm fell back to his side. The confusion must have shown on her face, because her mother caught her gaze and sent her a comforting, all-knowing wink. With that, they left the dance floor. The sea of guests parted as the song came to an end, moving back to their tables all at once. Madhuri stood up from her chair, trying to better understand what exactly was happening. From the corner of her eye, she saw her father holding his beat-up camcorder, aiming it at her.

The dance floor was empty. The soft beginning of her favorite song, "Ajab Si," cascaded from the speakers. Her heart slammed out of her chest as a singular spotlight turned on in the center of the room and Arjun Mehta walked right into it.

He wore an extravagant black kurta with gold stitching, but his hair was unkempt as ever. She could hear his heavy breathing from a distance as if he'd run a marathon to prepare for his performance, and she noticed the frantic look he exchanged with his mother. When Auntie Mehta sent him a thumbs-up, he broke into the most charming smile Madhuri had ever seen him wear.

The singer's voice reverberated through her eardrums. Her mind translated the melody of the Hindi song within seconds— *in your eyes, there is a special kind of grace.* She was soothed by the slow instrumentals and somehow mustered up the courage to meet Arjun's gaze.

He offered his arm to her. She'd have done anything to keep that beautiful smile on his face, even if it meant dancing in front of a public audience after so long. She walked toward him, her emerald sari trailing behind her like a wedding gown. When their hands connected, a spark jolted through her fingertips. This time, she didn't pull away.

He spun her into his arms and a burst of warmth erupted in her chest. She closed her eyes, praying that she never forgot the feeling of dancing with someone like Arjun. Someone who made her feel safe from the judgment she'd spent her entire life running from.

"I thought you stood me up," she whispered.

He pulled her closer to him, if that were even possible. "I would never."

The song swelled, as did her heart when he moved with her.

She immersed herself in the moment, in the way Arjun gently traced a circle over her hip bone. The feeling of his fingertips brushing against her exposed skin was enough to set her aflame, and suddenly Madhuri had no recollection of their experiment or their prophecies. She was hopelessly lost in the boy dancing beside her, the boy she was once so certain was a friend and nothing more.

Arjun's breathing locked into a unison with hers, a rare and beautiful thing that she couldn't bring herself to leave behind in the spotlight, as the song's final chord faded into silence. A burst of loud cheering and applause overwhelmed her as she slowly opened her eyes. Her head rested on Arjun's chest, his arms around her waist. Without a single word, he stepped to the side. His touch lingered on Madhuri's skin, and she had a feeling it would never leave.

The DJ spun his disc and the next upbeat song faded in. The crowd rushed back to the floor, erupting into cheers, and suddenly their moment had become a thing of the past.

Arjun grabbed her hand, escorting her out of the mess of guests she was stuck between. She searched for her parents and found them cornered at the food table by Raina. Her father's camcorder flashed a red light—still recording, even as it faced the floor. A soft chuckle left her lips. She wasn't surprised that her engineer of a father would be the one person to misunderstand basic technology.

"Where are we going?" Madhuri asked as Arjun moved them across the room. She tried to commit every single element of her surroundings, from the twinkling stars to Arjun's pointed shoes, to memory.

He nodded toward a flight of stairs at the back of the rooftop lounge. A red carpet covered the cement and Madhuri prayed the sharp edge of her stiletto wouldn't catch on the intricate stitches. "It's a surprise."

Madhuri hated surprises, especially when it meant compromising her plans. If she had no logical way to predict the future or analyze the decisions that led up to it, she'd break down. But for the first time, not a single feeling of anxiety rumbled through her body. For the first time, she made a split-second decision to trust him, even if it meant facing the unknown.

All she wanted was to exist in the present, so she did.

CHAPTER ELEVEN

arjun

Madhuri's sari, combined with a particularly steep flight of stairs, left Arjun hopelessly breathless. He didn't quite have the courage to tell her outright that she was as gorgeous as an angel, which was ironic, considering he'd just serenaded her through a dance in front of six hundred guests. Maybe it was because he knew that she'd make fun of how cheesy he was being for a boy trapped in a lab experiment of a relationship.

She turned to him as they climbed the stairs. "You're really out of breath for a varsity athlete. It's only a single flight of stairs."

Arjun withheld the urge to roll his eyes. He wasn't going to be Best Friend Arjun, who bumped her shoulder and fought with her over silly things. Tonight, he wanted to be Boyfriend Arjun. He wasn't exactly sure what that entailed, but he'd made a promise to Madhuri. He had to do his part in making their first relationship feel as real as possible, even if they were bound by an expiration date that doomed them from the start.

"I'm out of breath from our dance, not the stairs." He smiled at her. "Unlike you, I'm not naturally talented at that. I practiced with my mom every day since she planned our first date."

Madhuri stopped dead in her tracks at the top of the staircase, peering at him from beneath her dark eyelashes. Even the evening sky, right within his periphery, couldn't distract him from her. "You practiced dancing? For me?" Her voice fell to a whisper like she was speaking to herself, trying to believe the words she was saying.

Score. Boyfriend Arjun was killing it already.

"Why wouldn't I?" He tucked a stray curl behind Madhuri's ear. He noticed the way her hair wasn't exactly soft, yet still comforting in its layered texture. "How else was I going to impress you with my two left feet?"

"You've always impressed me, ever since we were kids." She stood up on her tiptoes, her fingers grazing the stubble on his chin.

Why did she always pull that move on him? Didn't she realize how her touch, as subtle as it was, single-handedly gave him arrhythmia?

"I have to thank you, though. Thank you for going above and beyond just to make me smile. No one outside of my family has ever cared that much about me, and I don't know how I would've managed without your love."

Arjun's hands were frozen at his sides while his mind raced at the speed of light. The way she threw out the word *love*, as if it meant nothing to her, sent him into a spiral.

Her fingers were beginning to slip away, the hopeful glint in her eyes fading with every passing second. He had to do something before they lost their moment forever.

"Did I say something wrong?" she asked.

"Never," he responded, forcing himself to stay cool. If Madhuri even had an idea as to what he was thinking, she'd end the experiment immediately. His feelings were too real, too intense. "And by the way, you're welcome. For everything."

She broke into the most beautiful smile, one Arjun wished he could witness up close, closer than they already were. He was incredibly aware of the mere inches separating his lips from hers, and the stars shining down on them as if they were swinging chandeliers. If only they could take one more step forward, away from the elegant staircase beneath their feet and into the open air.

Her fingers were running over the sharp edges of his jaw again, her eyes examining his with a sense of urgency. He regained his composure and gingerly placed his hands on her hips, pulling her in as if he feared she'd be ripped away at any minute.

He should've known that she would be. Madhuri always had an exit plan, whether she knew of it at the moment or not.

The door to the staircase flew open, thanks to Raina. Her mouth was full of biryani, and she held a half-empty glass of alcohol in her hand.

"There you are!" Raina exclaimed, rushing up the stairs.

Arjun let Madhuri go on instinct, and she sent him a grateful look as she repositioned herself. She leaned against the concrete wall behind her with her arms crossed tightly across her chest. "Amma and Appa are looking everywhere for you, and they don't seem happy at all." She looked between the two of them, her eyebrows stitching together to form one thin line. "What did you do, Madhuri?"

Madhuri's eyes flashed, and she swatted at Raina with her purse. "I haven't done anything. At least, I don't think so." With that, she nodded her head toward the open door. "Come on, Arjun. If they're actually upset with me, I'm going to need you for moral support."

Madhuri had once told him how she wanted to learn more about the Universe around them, one galaxy at a time. If they had made it up the staircase, she would have found his state-of-the-art telescope and his astronomy almanac waiting for her. He dreamed of holding her hand as they stargazed from The Beverly Hills Hotel rooftop like two teenagers falling in love.

Instead, his dream disappeared before his eyes. He wanted to run after it like a wayward balloon, find it before Madhuri left him and their perfect moment in the dust, but it was too late. Their time was up.

"We both know you didn't do anything wrong. Can't your parents wait until later?"

"My parents think I did something, though," Madhuri responded. "I want to set them straight before they get the wrong idea in their heads."

Arjun averted his eyes to the grand mahogany door, turning his expression to stone. He couldn't bring himself to fight with her, to risk losing her the way he had in freshman year. "Shouldn't they trust you?"

"My parents trust me completely, but I don't want to risk it. You should know that better than anyone." Her voice shook like she was trying very hard not to cry from frustration.

"Then go," Arjun muttered. "I'll stay here."

Madhuri hesitated. For a naive moment, he wondered if she'd come back once she'd reassured her family of whatever had upset them, but he knew her better than anyone else. Madhuri never returned after an argument. She took days to process, to analyze the why and the how of their situation, and finally she'd pretend the whole confrontation never happened.

Without another word, Madhuri turned on her heel and stormed away.

CHAPTER TWELVE

madhuri

Madhuri couldn't quit thinking about the stairs separating her and Arjun. How, if she'd taken just one step forward, she'd have ended the distance rippling between them. She felt herself losing sight of her experiment as Arjun's smile encapsulated her vision.

But she couldn't go there with him even if she wanted to. She had something to prove, an agenda against her family and the stupid curse that got her into this situation in the first place, and she couldn't afford to lose her ambition—especially not for a boy.

Arjun probably thought she was being selfish, that she was running away instead of choosing to stay. He'd think she was overreacting over a minor conflict that wouldn't matter in the long run, but he didn't understand that while she did often argue with her parents, she never wanted to be the cause of their unhappiness. If she had a chance to avoid the drama, she'd take it.

Madhuri found her parents after Raina pulled her away from the staircase. They were still dancing together as if nothing had happened, and she turned to Raina, who was slowly digging her acrylic black nails into Madhuri's upper arm.

"Amma and Appa seem fine, Raina. Did you lie to me?"

Raina steered Madhuri to the dimly lit coat check-in station at the entrance to the Sangeet. The young boy employed at the booth winced when he saw Raina, and he held up a twenty-dollar bill—a bribe, no doubt—in his right hand as if it were a white flag of surrender. Raina nodded at him, and he scurried away to the dessert table a few feet over, keeping watch for them from afar. Once they were alone, Raina dropped her voice to a low whisper, and Madhuri suddenly remembered why she used to be scared of her little sister when they were growing up.

"I did, but only because you lied to me first."

Madhuri had no problem admitting that she lied to her parents about Tillys, but she never kept secrets from Raina. Her sister was the exception, her person through it all, and there was no way she'd risk that over something as frivolous as a lie. Raina had to be mistaken.

"I don't lie to you. You know that."

"Explain this, then." Raina fished around in the pockets of her lehenga and pulled out a neatly folded piece of lined paper.

Madhuri didn't have to open it to recognize what it was, taking a mental note of the tight creases framing their hypotheses. But still, her heart leaped out of her chest when she saw the title scrawled across the page in her handwriting.

The Kismat Experiment.

"How did you find that?" Madhuri whispered, unable to regain her composure.

"I wanted to borrow your gold jhumkis and I found this so-called experiment in your suitcase by accident. I'd make a better attempt at hiding it next time, if I was you." Her sister turned her body away from her and narrowed her eyes toward their parents, who were chatting up a storm with the other Aunties and Uncles invited to the wedding. "Amma and Appa would've been devastated if they were the ones to find out about this."

Madhuri couldn't believe her carelessness. She knew what a mistake it would be to involve her family, Raina included, in the experiment—they were an unpredictable confounding variable that needlessly complicated her thesis. Her parents would never understand her motives, and that was the exact reason why she'd never wanted to tell them about it in the first place. They'd try to reset her moral compass and, worst of all, they'd take Arjun's side.

Her parents would think that Madhuri was carelessly leading him on without an ounce of remorse for his feelings, not that the experiment was why she even had a fighting chance at securing the future she wanted.

But that didn't explain Raina's reaction.

"That's exactly why I didn't want to tell them!" Madhuri snatched the paper back from her sister and tucked it into the waistband of her skirt. "Why are you being so dramatic about this? Not everyone can have a perfect relationship like you and Aditya, you know. Some of us have no choice but to take matters into our own hands."

Aditya Kumar, her little sister's boyfriend of the last four years. He'd asked Raina out before they'd even hit puberty, and now they were the renowned cocaptains of their high school's premier Bollywood dance team. The Aunties in their community absolutely adored them—the golden couple with an effortless love story rooted well within their own culture. Sometimes, Madhuri wondered if the attention went straight to Raina's head, since she often felt compelled to give Madhuri relationship advice despite being younger than her.

"Have you ever considered the fact that maybe, just maybe, Aditya and I have a perfect relationship because I trusted our family curse?" A flash of anger sparked in Raina's eyes, a defense mechanism Madhuri noticed in her sister whenever her boyfriend was name-checked in an argument. "But this isn't about us. It's about you and Arjun, and how you've decided to use him as a pawn in your fight against destiny."

"Why do you even care? This isn't any of your business."

"I wouldn't have cared if you'd told me about it!" Raina raised her voice, and when the coat-check boy sent them a warning glare from his lookout spot, she settled back down. "I thought we didn't keep secrets from each other. I thought you were my best friend."

Madhuri couldn't muster the nerve to meet her sister's gaze. "I couldn't risk it. I need this experiment to succeed, Raina. The future I want depends on it."

Raina's demeanor visibly softened. "And what about Arjun? Don't you think he deserves to know your true intentions?"

"Arjun signed this experiment, too. He knew what he was getting into."

"For a girl as intelligent as you, you sure are oblivious. Can't you see the way he looks at you? That boy would do anything for you because of how he feels, and clearly, you're taking advantage of that."

"Arjun doesn't have feelings for me." Madhuri groaned out loud, wiping the kajal off the corner of her eye with her dupatta. Raina ducked beneath the coatrack and rifled through various hanging coats until she found a plaid handkerchief. She handed it to Madhuri with earnest, who cringed at the sight. "Ew! You don't know what Auntie blew from her nose into that."

Raina held back a chuckle. "It would be better than ruining your new lehenga, though."

"I highly disagree." Madhuri swatted at Raina's hand until she deposited the handkerchief back into the coat it belonged to. "But seriously, Arjun and I have been best friends for the last eleven years, and he's never once given me any indication that he likes me as anything more than that. I'm positive he doesn't see me that way."

"How can you be so sure? Maybe he's intimidated. Most boys tend to be when it comes to you." Before Madhuri could bite back with a snarky response, Raina sighed and moved her fingers to her temple, squeezing so hard Madhuri worried she'd break the bones underneath. "Let's not veer off topic. What are you even trying to accomplish through this relationship?"

"I want to prove Amma and Appa wrong." Madhuri nodded her head toward her parents, back on the dance floor again. "I want to take charge of my own future and make sure that I don't fail, even in my relationships. And if I have to do that by destroying my prophecy and our family curse with this experiment, then so be it."

"You're using Arjun to break the curse? To prove a point against our family?" Raina released an exasperated sigh from her lips. "And that means you walked into this relationship knowing full well you were going to dump him?"

"Yes, we have an end date. It's clearly written in the experiment—that we *both* signed."

"Yes, but your reasons behind the expiration of your relationship are so wrong." Her sister pulled her hair out of its high ponytail, snapping the hair tie onto her wrist aggressively. "You can't follow through with this, Madhuri. You can't use an innocent human being to disobey Amma and Appa or your destiny."

"Raina, if you want to rat me out to them, just do it. I don't need the lecture."

"Don't worry. I plan to keep your secret, but only on one condition. You never—" Raina sent her a pointed look "—and I mean *never*, lie to me ever again."

Madhuri's eyes brimmed with tears when she heard Raina's simple request, a sign that the trust between them had suffered a devastating blow because of her experiment, and she willed herself not to let them fall down her cheeks. Her prophecy and the complications it predicted in her relationships flashed through her mind, and suddenly the idea of Madhuri finally being in control of her own destiny didn't seem quite possible anymore.

"I promise I won't."

"Good." Raina used the edge of her fingertip to dab away the moisture at Madhuri's waterline. She pulled her into a hug, whispering a soft reassurance into the curls of her hair. "I'm on your side, okay? Forever and always."

Madhuri nodded, trying her best to ignore the waves of guilt crashing inside her heart, and she urged herself not to choke on her words when she finally found the courage to respond.

"Forever and always."

CHAPTER THIRTEEN

arjun

Arjun straightened his tie with his eyes set on the mirror in front of him. The reception started in an hour, and he knew that his mother wanted to get there early with the rest of their family. Arjun, however, needed his mother more than some last-minute wedding organization.

"Mom, I was hoping to talk to you about something," he said.

His mother screwed on the back of her earring, staring into a mirror of her own. "Can it wait until after the reception?"

"It really can't." Arjun bit his lip, facing his mother. "I need your advice."

She looked up, tilting her head to the side like a confused parrot. He couldn't help but hope that she would be willing to delay her presence at the reception by a few minutes, and to his delighted surprise, she did. "What's going on, beta?"

The soft maternal lilt to the word *beta*, comforting and curious at the same time, broke him into a needy little boy all over again. "Have you ever felt that, no matter what you do, people will always find a reason to leave you?"

"That's been my reality for as long as I can remember. Ever since the divorce, I've found myself weary of people who need me less than I need them." His mother sat down on the edge of the dressing table, tilting it forward with a weighted creak. Her face swirled with a multitude of emotions before it settled into her usual contemplative, yet woefully closed-off, expression. "Is this about your father's family? Did they say anything to you at the Sangeet?"

"They congratulated me on my dancing, and they tried to pry into my relationship with Madhuri, but they didn't say much else." Arjun had become numb to the pain of his father leaving him, but he knew his mother would never recover the way he had. He lifted an eyebrow at her, hoping that for once she might open up to him. "Did they say anything to you?"

"Of course they did, but I'm used to it now." His mother shook her head, and Arjun's heart broke for her. His father was once the primary breadwinner of their family, which left Arjun an entire childhood's worth of time to bond with his mother. Even now, he could sense her emotions—her highs and her lows—whether she verbalized them out loud or not. "If this issue of yours doesn't regard your father, then what is it actually about?"

"It's about Madhuri, but I can't be like you and distance myself from her solely to protect my heart. She means too

much to me." Arjun sighed and fell onto the carpet in front
of his mother, craning his neck upward to see her face.

"Wait a minute. Madhuri is the person who you're afraid
of losing?" When he nodded slowly, his mother burst into a
bout of laughter. "That girl wouldn't let you go even if you
wanted her to. Can't you see the way she looks at you?"

Arjun's eyebrows furrowed into a confused line. "I don't
think she looks at me the way you think she does."

His mother hopped off the dressing table and turned back
to the mirror, touching up her lipstick. "I see a lot of myself
in Madhuri, so trust me when I say that she's in it for the long
run. Whether she wants to admit that to herself or not is a
whole other question, but I have a feeling you're in good hands
with her." She kissed him on the forehead, leaving a soft red
hue behind. Before he could respond, she opened the door,
one foot already out. "Ready to go?"

Arjun needed to think, needed to process the hope his
mother instilled in him so easily. Was it as simple as Madhuri
sending a meaningful look in his direction? Was that all it
took for his mother to predict who would stay in his life and
who would leave?

"I'll meet up with you in a bit." He waved as she walked
out the door, her heels clicking down the hall to the hotel
elevators. Once her footsteps faded into silence, he exited the
room. Instead of making his way to the reception, he searched
his floor for a door with an Iyer name tag stapled to it.

If the conversation with his mother had taught him anything, it was that he needed to take his future with Madhuri
in his own hands. He couldn't wait around for a stolen glance
to prove the safety of their relationship, not after she'd to-

tally avoided him for the past twenty-four hours. He'd have to confront Madhuri immediately, before she self-destructed and took their entire relationship, fake or not, down with her.

As soon as Arjun left his hotel room, the sound of quiet voices floated through the air. He felt compelled to follow it, leading him toward the Iyers' room a few doors down. It wasn't long before he identified the source—Madhuri. He turned a corner and skidded to a clumsy halt against the freshly mopped tile floors. Madhuri was sitting with her back flat against the wall of the hallway, talking animatedly with her hands while Raina stood beside her.

Arjun froze in shock when Madhuri looked up at him, midconversation with her sister.

"What are you doing here?" Madhuri whispered.

Arjun slowly flashed her and Raina a sheepish smile. "I, uh, came to talk to you. You seem kind of busy, though, so I can leave, and we could, you know, put a pin in it." He scratched the back of his neck, cursing himself for being flustered. "So, yeah."

"I'm not busy. We're mourning the loss of my favorite jhumka, that's all." Madhuri rubbed her dupatta against her nose. "Raina, why don't you go meet our parents at the reception? I'll join you after I chat with Arjun."

"Please use a tissue," Raina responded, handing her a package of Kleenex before disappearing into the elevator.

Madhuri deposited the tissues into her pocket and turned back to Arjun. "What do you want to talk—"

"Do you need help searching for your jhumka?" Arjun immediately blushed when he realized he'd cut her off midsentence. In his defense, he'd do anything to fix the problems in Madhuri's life, even if it was nothing more than a missing gold earring. He couldn't help himself.

Her lips quirked up at the corner. "Eager to be of service, I see."

"Anything for you."

"You're such a knight in shining armor," Madhuri teased as she held out her hand, and Arjun pulled her to her feet. The touch sent sparks of electricity along his fingertips. "I believe I lost it somewhere on this floor, but Raina and I couldn't find it."

He nodded, urging himself not to stare at the way the skirt of her lehenga fell into a perfect circle of fabric at her ankles. "We can look for it together."

"And you can tell me why you're here to see me."

"Can't a boyfriend want to see his girlfriend for no reason?"

"Hilarious. Now, what's the real reason?"

Arjun walked along the hallway, focusing his eyes on the carpet in case something glinted at him. "I wanted to talk about the Sangeet. You ran away so suddenly, and I never got the chance to check in with you. Did you figure everything out with your parents?"

"Raina made that up." Madhuri waved her hand dismissively. "My parents were never upset."

"Then what's the problem? Why'd she need to pull you away so urgently last night?"

Madhuri folded her hanging dupatta into the waistband of her skirt, her fingers running over the pack of tissues in her pocket absentmindedly. Arjun tried really hard not to watch as the delicate Indian fabric fell against the curve of her waist.

"I think I messed up, Arjun."

"What'd you do?" he asked, his curiosity getting the better of him.

Madhuri dropped to a squat, narrowing her gaze toward the boundary between the ice-machine room and the carpeted hallway. With her eyes focused anywhere but on him, she said, "Raina found out about our experiment, and she thinks I'm hurting you with it."

That was the last thing Arjun had expected to hear.

"Doesn't she know that I agreed to it?" Arjun asked, trying to summon the courage he had the night before.

"She knows, but she doesn't like my motives for the experiment, and she thinks…" She hesitated, chewing on her bottom lip. "She thinks you have feelings for me and that those feelings distract you from the consequences of what we're getting into."

For the love of Krishna, was Arjun that obvious?

No, he couldn't be. Arjun knew, without a doubt, that if Madhuri thought he liked her as more than a friend, she would've broken it off with him immediately. That would've introduced a confounding variable into her experiment. She would've found another boy, one who could bend to her will and break her curse without any sort of external complications. But for some reason, Madhuri chose to stay with him.

The thought of Madhuri figuring out the full extent of his feelings didn't fill him with dread the way it used to. After all, Arjun had agreed to their experiment with the sole intention of showing Madhuri how perfect they were together, how they were destined to be so much more than best friends. He knew that by the end of their relationship, he *would* confess his love for her, and perhaps Raina had simply expedited his plans by planting the idea in Madhuri's stubborn mind on his behalf.

Arjun crouched down beside her and let his open palm find Madhuri's cheek. "As much as I adore your sister, she can't read my mind. Trust me, if there was something in my life worth telling you, you'd know right away."

She leaned into his touch. "Thank you."

He opened his mouth, trying to find a romantic way to continue their conversation, but a sparkle in the periphery of his vision distracted him. He let Madhuri go and shifted to his knees to scan the inside of the ice-machine room, and there it was—her jhumka, an Indian statement earring with intricate beads dangling from the base, tucked into the corner of the room as if it were patiently waiting for its rightful owner to find it.

"Come on, Madhuri. How'd you miss this the first time?" Arjun lifted an eyebrow at her and picked up the earring. He cleaned it with the edge of his kurta before handing it over. "I can see why you were mourning its loss. It must look amazing on you."

"You're seriously the best." Madhuri beamed at him, and instead of taking the earring, she tossed a lock of hair over her shoulder and exposed the side of her face to him. "Do you think you could put it on for me?"

Arjun was going to pass out, but he couldn't let her know that. "Of course."

In what he hoped was the smoothest manner possible, Arjun leaned into her space. He noticed the subtle hint of her rose perfume and forced himself to ignore it, tightening his grip around the jhumka.

"You can come closer," she said softly, looking up at him from beneath her lashes.

God, this girl was going to be the end of him.

He shifted toward her, and when his fingertips brushed the slope of her neck, he saw Madhuri shiver. Was it possible that she wasn't immune to his touch, either, no matter how much she refused to admit it?

Arjun slowly pressed the jhumka into her ear, and a charged silence passed between them. He couldn't stand the tension much longer, so he rekindled their conversation from earlier. "I am curious, though. What does your sister dislike about your motive behind our experiment? I didn't think it was that bad when you told me."

Madhuri hesitated again before she responded. "She thinks I'm using you to break my prophecy and my family curse."

The infamous Iyer curse that destined Madhuri to marry her first boyfriend in a grand happily-ever-after. He wished he were subject to a force as powerful, an otherworldly magic guiding his life to perfection.

"What if you are?" Arjun forced out a laugh and pulled his hand away from her. The jhumka was successfully in place, and he couldn't let himself fall into the strands of her hair again. Nor could he afford to hold her under the disguise of a best friend. Every second of restraint ripped Arjun apart, clawing against his aching heart. "I don't care."

It killed him that Madhuri would much rather seek one heartbreak after another, rather than be with him from the very beginning. She wanted to challenge her fate, to prove the existence of her free will, and she was using him to do so. But he was in no position to complain, not when he was at his happiest when he was with her.

She watched him carefully, her dark eyes gleaming with hope and all of the words they never said. "Are you sure?"

Arjun thought back to their fight in freshman year, when he let his emotions get in the way of their relationship. He wouldn't make that mistake ever again. All he needed was one more convincing smile, and Madhuri would continue on with their experiment. It didn't matter if each lie meant destroying his resolve, engulfing his desire in a burning flame. She was worth every promise, every misguided wish upon a star, and he couldn't deny her much longer.

"I'm positive."

CHAPTER FOURTEEN

madhuri

Madhuri could list the sheer number of qualities she didn't like about Raina off the top of her head, like how she was physically unable to talk about her emotions or how, even at sixteen, she had the maturity of a kid who'd just hit double digits. And yet she couldn't ignore how fantastic Raina was at cheering Madhuri up and how she'd go to extreme lengths to do so. Raina once parkoured off their garbage can, knocking it over and sending trash flying through their suburban streets, just to make her smile.

After the reception ended, Madhuri spent over an hour recounting her time with Arjun to Raina. Madhuri resolved to never give her sister another reason to doubt their bond, so she didn't leave a single detail out, from the jhumka hiding in the ice-machine room to the way he held her when she owned up to the experiment and her motivations behind it.

Raina blinked at her from her spot on the hotel bed. "How does your love life affect me in any way?" she asked, her focus drifting back on the AP Calculus homework she'd brought with her to the wedding.

"First of all, this isn't considered a love life. I don't love Arjun as anything more than a friend, and that's never going to change. We've been over this." Madhuri rolled her eyes. "Secondly, you're my little sister, and I thought you'd want to know, especially after what happened last night."

Raina lifted an eyebrow, and a moment of understanding passed between them. "I do want to know the important things, like the experiment and Tillys, but I don't really need to hear you gush about your fake boyfriend."

"And why is that?" Madhuri flopped onto their bed, letting her head dangle off the edge. The blood rushed to her cheeks on instinct. She knew getting back up would be an absolute hassle, thanks to her anemia. She'd see flashing white light in her vision for days.

"Well, I want the majority of my conversations to pass the Bechdel Test." Raina sat up a little straighter, a self-assured smile on her face. "I don't think fawning over Arjun would fit this goal of mine. Do you?"

"I think Bechdel Tests are another method of shaming women for no reason." Madhuri threw the pillow she was leaning on, a Beverly Hills Hotel logo stamped proudly across the front, at her sister. "It isn't such a bad thing for me to talk about Arjun with you. And you never mention this Bechdel

Test rule when you're gushing to me about Aditya. Is your boyfriend immune to your rules?"

"That's a good point, and I admit, I'm a bit hypocritical when it comes to him. How could I not be? He's perfect." Raina caught the pillow in her hand and pulled it closer to her chest, resting her chin on the fabric. She stared at Madhuri from beneath her long lashes, and Madhuri could practically see the hearts in her eyes. "And I never said you talking about Arjun wasn't something I liked. You two are adorable, but there are so many other things I want to know about you."

"Like what?"

Raina pulled her phone out of her pocket, and swiped through her photo library until she found a video of Madhuri and Arjun from the Sangeet. "Like this. Look at how happy you are when you're dancing with him."

"I thought we weren't talking about Arjun," Madhuri pointed out.

"We're not. We're talking about dance, and how you haven't smiled like this—" Raina paused the video and zoomed in on a frame where Arjun had led Madhuri into a seamless dip. She was grinning up at him, and for the first time, she didn't care what the audience or the Aunties or her bullies thought about her. "—since you quit Bharatanatyam three years ago. You were the best dancer at the studio. Better than me even, and you know that's a feat in and of itself."

Madhuri wondered if she should tell her sister about how much her experience with the girls at her school and their constant, cruel judgment affected her. Her family, Arjun, and Josie knew the details of what had happened in middle school, but she never told them how the bullying made her *feel*. Madhuri couldn't bring herself to be so vulnerable, not when it meant saying the truth out loud for the very first time—that she let the words of two white girls destroy her love for Bharatanatyam, for Indian culture, for herself.

She let them win.

Raina deserved an answer, though, and Madhuri wouldn't risk upsetting her again.

"Honestly, I quit dancing because I hated the attention. I couldn't handle the way random strangers would stare at my costumes or how the girls at school would mock my choreography behind my back." Madhuri's lips twisted into a grimace at the thought of her complicated past. "Bharatanatyam wasn't worth the emotional sacrifice anymore, so I dropped out."

Raina sighed as if she were a middle-aged woman with years of wisdom beneath her belt. "I wish you'd talked to me about how you felt earlier, preferably before the decision to quit even entered your stubborn head. I could've taught you how to ignore all weird looks and snide comments."

Madhuri didn't have the heart to tell Raina that she never would have been able to talk her out of quitting, so she offered her a small smile instead. "I wish I had, too."

Raina leaned across the hotel bed to squeeze Madhuri's hand, choosing not to respond when their silence spoke volumes. Even with Raina's faults, her endless snark, and roaring sarcasm, Madhuri couldn't help but feel warm when their palms connected.

Raina snapped out of her loving-sister role and loudly tapped her pencil against her textbook. "Now, could you annoy someone who doesn't have seven hours of calculus homework to finish in one night?"

"It's not my fault that you waited until the last minute." Madhuri chuckled at Raina's inability to maintain an emotional conversation for more than a few minutes. "You know, I finished my homework early because I knew we'd be at the wedding all weekend."

"Yeah, well, procrastination is my middle name and I'm in no mood to change it." Raina didn't even look up from her homework as she spoke. She scribbled in a few notes in the margins of her paper, squinting through her black-rimmed glasses. "Before I forget, there's a note for you on the coffee table. I read it already."

Madhuri lifted a brow, heading toward the coffee table. "Didn't I tell you not to stick your nose in my personal business?"

"I've already read your diary twice. There isn't much you can still hide from me."

Madhuri's heart dropped. She'd written her most intimate feelings in that beat-up diary, including quite a few paragraphs about Raina. When Madhuri was left alone to her thoughts, she'd envy Raina's ability to filter out the world around her. She'd written countless sentences wishing she could dance with Raina, cursing her sister for personality traits she couldn't change. As a wave of guilt washed over her, she caught Raina stifling a bout of laughter. Maybe she'd skipped over those sections. Maybe it hadn't hurt her the way Madhuri feared it would.

Raina flashed her a genuine smile and, just like that, Madhuri knew her theories were wrong. Her little sister had definitely read all of her thoughts, but she'd chosen to discard them for the best of their relationship. That was Raina's most redeeming quality—her unwillingness to let the actions of others affect her self-worth, even when it came to her loved ones.

"The note's kind of creepy, I'm not going to lie," Raina said. "If it wasn't in a romantic context, I'd probably put you in witness protection."

"You're so dramatic." Madhuri picked up the note, folded neatly on the table. Her name was scrawled across in pink ink, similar to the pen she'd given to Arjun after they signed their experiment. He must've kept that slobbery old thing for over a month now. She opened the paper, her eyes scanning the message inside.

If you want a second date, meet me under the stars you left me with.

Her heart fluttered like a newborn butterfly spreading its wings. As soon as she registered the rush of emotion, she frowned. What was going on with her? It wasn't like she was suddenly into Arjun or anything, but God, she had only ever dreamed about the kind of affection Arjun consistently showered her with. Just remembering the way his hands felt on her hips in the stairwell was enough to make her smile.

"You look like a fool, Madhuri." Raina slammed her textbook shut. "Stop wasting all of your time thinking and please just act. If you don't get that second date from Arjun, I'll have no choice but to smack the sense into you."

Madhuri smiled to herself, pocketing the note into her denim miniskirt. "What happened to your precious Bechdel Test when it comes to me and Arjun?"

"I'd consider this conversation to be about your flaws and

how you can fix them, not about a man." Raina pushed her glasses up the crook of her nose. "I might be a feminist kill-joy, but I'm not immune to a good old romance."

Madhuri couldn't help but tackle her little sister with a giant hug. "I can't even be mad at you for reading the note when you say things like that, Raina."

Raina pushed her off half-heartedly, grinning wildly despite her actions. "Yeah, yeah, I know. I can be sweet sometimes, but don't get used to it." Her eyes flicked to the clock ticking away on the wall beside them. "That note got here over thirty minutes ago. You should probably get going before Arjun thinks you stood him up."

Madhuri kissed Raina on the cheek before pulling on her windbreaker, in case the Southern Californian autumn grew teeth overnight. "Thanks, Raina!" she called out as the door slammed shut behind her.

A burst of adrenaline coursed through her, slamming against her eardrums with a distinct thump. The energy spiked like an electrical current, reminding her of the time she drank an entire venti black coffee after avoiding caffeine for a year.

Madhuri was overwhelmed by an unshakable urge to run to the roof before Arjun thought she wasn't going to come. She knew that she didn't like him romantically, so she couldn't quite understand why she was so excited to find him. Why did she want to race up the hotel stairs, instead of waiting for an elevator? Why couldn't she get his face out of her mind, no matter how hard she tried to remove it, and why did the image itself inspire her to move even faster?

It must be because they were best friends, because Arjun

meant everything to her, and she didn't want to ever risk being the one to hurt him. It was completely and utterly platonic.

Madhuri passed her parents and Auntie Mehta, who were chatting near the staircase. She mumbled a quick greeting, pushing the staircase door with her back. She must have looked more frazzled than what was normal for her type A self, because her parents simply stared at her, unable to respond. She'd have to explain herself later.

Madhuri climbed up the single flight of steps from their floor, her fingers shaking against the railing. Her excitement bled into anxiety, which she didn't understand, either. Arjun was her person, someone who knew everything about her in a comforting, forever kind of way. They'd grown up together, leaning on each other without realizing it and without labeling it. Why did this note suddenly change everything?

When Madhuri made it to the top of the staircase, she saw Arjun standing beneath the breathtaking starry night, the brisk wind defining the curls in his hair. His hand was wrapped protectively around the neck of his most prized possession—his state-of-the-art telescope, gifted to him by her parents for his sixteenth birthday. A plethora of books lay open on a blanket, and even from her spot dozens of feet away, Madhuri saw constellations outlined within the pages.

Arjun looked at his watch and a long sigh left his lips. He muttered curses under his breath as he slowly folded the legs of his telescope. He must have given up on waiting. Was his faith in her that rocky?

Madhuri made her way toward him, her stomach twisting when she realized that she was seeing his heart break in real time. The adrenaline slamming through her rib cage morphed into pure courage. She let her fingers run down Arjun's arm, turning him around to face her.

"I'm here," she whispered. "I'll always be here."

Madhuri wished she could read his mind, especially when his eyes widened into the size of a black hole, threatening to swallow her up. He broke into a smile that was completely un-restricted, unconditional in a way that felt too good to be true. Too soft and genuine and wholesome to be the victim of her experiment.

Suddenly, the warm feeling in her chest crumbled into dread.

Madhuri knew Arjun better than she knew herself, and in that moment, there was nothing more obvious than the fact that Arjun's feelings for her had changed. He didn't look at her like a best friend anymore—there was something roman-tic and sweet and definitely not platonic in the way he smiled, like all his wishes had been granted by her simply being there.

A pit of guilt opened up in her stomach.

Arjun must have noticed her expression dull, because his hand squeezed hers, attempting to bring her back to life. His smile was long gone, and she knew it was because of her.

She didn't deserve him.

CHAPTER FIFTEEN

arjun

Arjun wasn't sure what he did to deserve Madhuri finally finding him. He had never been more grateful for his good Karma than in that moment.

His left hand held on to his telescope tightly, careful not to drop his prized possession while reaching for Madhuri. He was quite skilled at multitasking.

But Madhuri's eyes glazed over, her smile disappearing like the words off her tongue. She was drifting away, and quickly at that. He always knew she was a flight risk, that one negative thought was enough to send her off in the opposite direction. The bitter voice in his mind didn't take long to call her out, reminding Arjun of how she'd run away a night ago, at the Sangeet. How she'd been running ever since they were kids. He'd built up his walls for a reason and she was breaking them down, one brick at a time.

Arjun bent down, placing his telescope on the soft picnic blanket, and by the time he looked up, Madhuri was backing away from him. She whispered the same phrase under her breath, something about not deserving him. Arjun knew that if she left, he wouldn't have the strength to follow. He needed to stop her before it was too late—before she broke his heart all over again.

His hand found hers and he interlaced their fingers, squeezing twice. Above all else, they were best friends. Madhuri wouldn't leave him if he was asking for her help, for her to stay. Her eyes softened and she squeezed his hand back, two times instead of a single affirmation.

She needed him, too.

"Why do you always run away?" he asked, edging toward her like she was a deer caught in the headlights of a roaring truck. "What are you so scared of?"

Madhuri shook her head, her feet rooted in place. "I'm not scared of anything."

"That's a lie." He closed the space between them, his eyes searching hers. He didn't see any tears in them, but her anxiety was evident in the stiffness of her spine and in the way she actively avoided his gaze. "I'm your best friend. You can trust me."

A wave of silence crashed over them, threatening to drown him if she never responded. If she took off and ripped apart their experiment. If she buried herself in her family's embrace, never showing her face to him ever again.

She'd done it once already, when they were fourteen years

old and falling apart at the seams. Arjun's mother had left him alone for three months, the longest she'd ever been physically absent from his life, and Arjun was constantly fluctuating between red-hot rage and crippling depression. With no one left to talk to, he made the mistake of taking his emotions out on Madhuri.

He remembered when she came to him in tears, complaining about how her parents wouldn't let her quit Bharatanatyam. Arjun knew she was in distress from the bullying she was constantly faced with at school, but that didn't stop him from cutting her off midsentence.

He stumbled to his feet, white spots flashing through his vision, and screamed at Madhuri for not appreciating what she had. He cursed her for being born into a family who loved her without fine print underscoring their connection, for having the nerve to be upset with The World's Best Parents while he was destined to beg for scraps from his own mother.

And just like that, he lost her.

Madhuri stopped taking the bus, choosing to wait an extra hour at the library for her father to pick her up because it meant she didn't have to see him on the way home. His phone stopped ringing, devoid of texts with silly emoji or random memes that reminded her of him. He tried to find his shine again through his love for astronomy, but even the brightest constellations lost their sparkle when Madhuri left him.

Arjun couldn't take another heartbreak like that.

"I trust you, but I'm also scared of you," Madhuri said in front of him. "You are the most forgiving boy I've ever known. I'm scared that I'll change you into someone worse, someone who can no longer afford second chances because

I used all of them up." She looked away, staring at the sky-line surrounding them. "I don't deserve your trust, Arjun."

Arjun let go of her hand. He sat down on the picnic blanket and his head fell into his open palms. His words came out muffled, but he was sure Madhuri heard them, because she was already sitting right beside him. "If you think you're going to break my heart, why did you pick me to sign your experiment? There are plenty of other boys in the world."

Madhuri inhaled a sharp breath, so sharp that he heard the air scratching her throat. "You knew what you were getting into, Arjun."

It didn't take a genius to see her changing the topic. He wouldn't let her.

"I still do," he muttered. "I'm tired of you finding a new way to let me go, a new excuse about how you're not good enough for me. If anything, I'm not good enough for you, either." He sat up straight, lasering his vision on Madhuri. "I want to move forward. I want to have a second and a third and an infinite number of dates with you. I don't want to let you go until our deadline. That is, unless you don't want me anymore."

Madhuri didn't even take a second to think before she responded. At any other time, Arjun would've analyzed that action as a positive sign—that she'd understood his importance in her life. Now his heart filled with dread when he noticed the way her hesitation conveniently dispersed into thin air. He knew the truth—that she didn't want their experiment to end when it wasn't on her terms.

"I don't want to let you go, either. Not again," she whispered.

Arjun forced a smile to his lips. "Then shut up about you not deserving me."

Madhuri inhaled again as if to signal an incoming shift in conversation. She was never the type to dwell on conflict, so Arjun followed her lead. It was what he did best.

"Hey, Arjun?"

"Yeah?"

"I need you to explain what's happening here." Madhuri made a wide gesture, encompassing the various astronomy textbooks and cosmic diagrams neatly stacked in front of them. He'd hung fairy lights around the perimeter of The Beverly Hills Hotel roof, bursts of gold masking the natural shine of the galaxies above them, and laid a soft cerulean blanket across the cement floor. His trusted telescope sat atop the blanket, positioned at an angle perfect for a night of stargazing.

As Arjun took in the visual result of his hard work, he felt his chest brim with pride. Although Madhuri was still tiptoeing around him, he knew she couldn't deny a brilliant date when she saw one. She was a hopeless romantic, too, even if she didn't like to admit it.

"Well, on the night of the Sangeet, I had a surprise for you. I had all of this set up so we could watch the stars. I remember you telling me that was on your bucket list." His smile grew a little larger, despite his efforts to control it. "Anyway, that obviously didn't happen, so I thought I'd try again before we have to get back to our normal lives."

"You did all of this for me?" she asked, pulling her Science Olympiad windbreaker tighter around her body. Arjun wrapped an arm around her, and she fell into the crook of his body. When she looked up at him, he noticed that her anxiety had faded away and was replaced by an emotion he couldn't quite place.

"I can't believe that still surprises you."

Madhuri's eyes gleamed for the first time since the Sangeet. "It always will. I'm not used to kindness."

"That's another lie. Your family showers you with affection constantly."

"That's not the same and you know it," she said. "They're stuck with me, so they have to make the best of their situation. You, on the other hand, are purposefully choosing to go above and beyond to make me happy."

Arjun shrugged. "It's not a big deal. I wanted to do this for you."

"And that's why I chose you." She leaned forward, the scent of her Orbit gum shocking him alive. Every hair on his arm stood on edge, waiting in anticipation for whatever came next. "You're too good to be true, Arjun."

"If that's the case, what's stopping you from continuing to choose me after our experiment ends?" he blurted out. When Madhuri's face dimmed, Arjun cursed himself for not thinking. He blamed his lack of emotional responsibility on the smell of that godforsaken gum.

She shook her head, leaning her shoulder into his. "I can't do that, Arjun. The only two Indian kids at school dating each other? God, it's such a cliché, and I really don't want to be ridiculed for falling into the stereotypes I've been trying to prove wrong my whole life."

"Aren't we already falling into that stereotype with this experiment?"

"Right, but our experiment isn't a real relationship," she said. "So, it doesn't matter."

A jolt of pain tore through his heart. "That's one hell of a technicality, Madhuri."

Her body tensed at his sharp tone, and he made a mental note to cool himself back down. Any more conflict and their relationship would snap right in half. He squeezed her shoulder when she didn't respond, hoping it would dim the tension simmering between them, but Arjun could tell that she was thinking hard. The gears in her brain were visceral, cranking and puffing smog into the air around them.

"This is our destiny, isn't it?" she whispered after a beat of silence.

Despite the beautiful connotation of her words, something about the way Madhuri said it, hesitant and cautious, made it very clear to Arjun that she resented the very forces that had brought them together in the first place.

Arjun dropped Madhuri off at her hotel room at exactly midnight, which earned him a firm nod and a kind smile from Uncle Iyer. Score.

After they'd said their goodbyes, Arjun circled around the hallway and took a moment to stop at the ice machine just because. The faint memory of Madhuri and her earring was enough to send him over the moon, and he kept that feeling close to his heart when he finally opened the door to his family's hotel room.

He didn't think his mother would still be awake, but she sat in the corner with her eyes glued to the melodramatic daytime serial playing on her phone. She clicked her tongue just as a slap sound effect reverberated from the living room television, and she looked up at him with a smile.

"How was your first date, beta?"

Arjun stuffed his phone into his back pocket and made his way over to her. His mother didn't notice when he almost tripped over the binders of work documents scattered across the floor. "It was perfect," he said. "I can't believe we're finally happening."

"Did you give her a good-night kiss?" his mother teased.

Arjun's cheeks heated, threatening to burn him alive. "Madhuri and I don't do that," he muttered, his eyes focusing on the Hindi soap opera and the gaudy sari the lead actress wore. The main character was arguing with her husband, and loudly at that, before she pushed him down a marble staircase. The music swelled, as did the visual effects.

His mother turned her phone off. She pulled her legs into a crisscross position, rocking back and forth on the pullout couch. Much like Auntie Iyer, his mother watched him like she knew exactly what was going through his mind. "You didn't kiss her after the first date?"

"I'm a gentleman." He lifted his nose into the air as he shook his jacket off onto the floor. The sleeves were puffy, a style Madhuri often teased him for wearing. Something about him looking like the Michelin tire guy. "Besides, it's way too soon in the relationship."

"You've been the one for Madhuri since you both were kids, whether she admits it or not. The romantic attraction between you two is so obvious that everyone around you, even complete strangers at the wedding, can see it. With chemistry like that, I'd like to think you'd be allowed to skip a few steps in the typical dating process." She fidgeted with the phone in her hand, tracing over the home button, and Arjun wished she'd just turn it back on. "What are you so afraid of?"

Despite his reluctance, Arjun really tried to understand the depth of what his mother was saying. He couldn't brush her off like a typical teenager, not when he worried that the slightest hint of trouble would make her disappear into her career all over again.

"I'm scared that if I make even one mistake with Madhuri, she'll let me go, and I can't risk losing her," he whispered. His eyes caught his mother's, and for a brief second, a sense of pain soared through him. "And I think I have this fear because of you."

His mother's eyebrows threaded into a concerned line. "You must be joking. What did I do to destroy your trust in her?"

"You left." Arjun inhaled a sharp breath of air, digging his toes into the intricately stitched rug beneath his feet. "You're my mother and you left me, so what's stopping her?"

His mother pulled a pillow into her lap and held it tight against her chest as if it would be enough to protect her from the consequences of her mistakes. He wasn't sure what she was defending herself from—if she was frightened of her own son or of the rippling distance wedged between them. "I gave you a choice when I first came back. I asked for your forgiveness, but at the end of the day, it was a question with a yes or no answer. You said yes. You took me back. You promised me that everything would be okay. That *you* were okay."

"I was supposed to say yes!" he exclaimed as a sudden chill ran through him, warning him against starting a fight with his mother after the perfect weekend together. He couldn't lose her hard-earned presence. "Auntie Iyer's charts told me that a woman that had hurt me in the past would give me an opportunity in the present and it was up to me to decide if it was too late for her. If I could truly forgive her after everything she did wrong."

"You forgave me because of Kamala's nonsense prophecy?" she cried, throwing the pillow to the side without a care for its satin exterior. It landed in front of a glass of Maaza mango juice, barely escaping a nasty stain. The inflection of his mother's voice told him more than her words—she didn't believe in Auntie Iyer's readings, nor did she approve of his reliance on them. "You didn't actually want me back?"

"Of course I wanted you back! Auntie Iyer's prophecy simply gave me the courage to act on how I felt, to take a chance on trusting you even when I had every reason not to."

His mother's expression fell back into its typical poker face. She left the couch, her body as still as ever, and took his face into her hands. Her touch was warm, as always, but something about it wasn't comforting anymore. If anything, it left him on edge. "Every reason not to, huh? Well, I'm sorry you feel that way."

When her hands slipped away, his face froze. His eyes glazed over, a trail of ice making its way down to his heart.

"That's not an apology," he whispered. He left the living room before his mother could chastise him for his tone or beg for his forgiveness all over again. He didn't think he could sit through another person he loved convincing him that he was a priority, only to make him their second choice without an ounce of remorse.

And for the first time in his life, Arjun wondered if he deserved better.

CHAPTER SIXTEEN

madhuri

There were certain moments in Madhuri's life that she could never forget, like the time she tried to teach herself how to drive in the middle of the night using her father's beat-up Honda Civic, Arjun scared stiff in the passenger seat. Or the time she went to her first red-Solo-cup party and drank well past her limit, throwing up over Arjun's brand-new sneakers.

Arjun showing up at her front door a week after they'd accidentally fallen asleep on the rooftop of The Beverly Hills Hotel was one of those moments. The kind that felt important, but she didn't have enough evidence yet to be certain.

And something about Arjun standing in front of her now, with his hands shoved into his jean pockets and his eyes glistening with tears, felt just like that.

Madhuri closed the door behind her with a decisive thud, coughing as the sharp December wind hit her body. White fog burst into the space between them, and the hairs on her arm stood on edge. Arjun must have noticed her shivering, for he threw his coat to her, leaving himself in a thin shirt and jeans. When she attempted to give it back, he flashed her a deadly look that said nothing short of *wear it before I make you*. She threw her hands up in surrender and slipped the coat on. It smelled like him, the unmistakable aroma of freshly squeezed lemon and chaat masala.

"Are you okay?" Madhuri asked, unable to find the courage to move toward him. For the first time in years, Arjun felt closed off to her.

"No," he muttered, sitting down on the stairs leading up to the front patio. He watched her wearily, like he didn't fully understand why he was with her. "I'm not okay. I feel like literal shit seconds before it flings itself into a fan. Does that make sense?"

It didn't, but Madhuri nodded anyway.

Arjun continued, "I should've listened to you from the very beginning. These prophecies are a total waste. I don't know why I'd believe in something that only hurt me in the end."

Madhuri couldn't help but find that funny. It was just their luck that when she was finally beginning to believe her horoscope, finally starting to trust Arjun's hypothesis to protect her as much as her own, that he would turn away from it.

"I thought you loved astrology. How did it suddenly hurt you? What went wrong in the little time since I last saw you?" She willed herself to slow down so she didn't overwhelm him.

"There's obviously something on your mind. Maybe we can work it out together."

Arjun picked up the tiny pumpkin sitting on her porch. It was barely orange, browning from the inside until its outer layer looked as demonic as the face she'd hastily drawn across the front in purple Sharpie. He turned it over in his hands, soft and gentle.

"You kept this?" He lifted the pumpkin to his nose and cringed. "These have an expiration date, Madhuri."

"Yeah, but you gave it to me. I didn't have the heart to throw it out after you spent a whole sixty-nine cents on me." When Arjun snorted at the crude joke rumbling silently through both of their brains, a little smile crawled across her face. "Now, do you want to tell me what's going on, or would you rather we chat about a poor decaying squash?"

"Why can't you be like every teenager ever and avoid conflict?"

"Because I thrive off conflict." He smirked at her, and for a second, Madhuri worried that her heart had stopped entirely. She tried to regain her composure by sending him what she hoped was an effortlessly cool wink. Instead, her contact folded in her eye and the wink quickly turned into a very unattractive twitch. "Spill it, Arjun."

Arjun used his shirtsleeve to wipe away a stray contact-induced tear from beneath her eye. He sighed, like one of those old men who had nothing better to do than plot their retirement, annoy their wives, and sigh over and over again.

"My mother and I got into another fight, just like every other day this week. The smallest things are starting to annoy me, like how she flaked on our plans because of some conference call or how she forgot about dinner and left me alone at the table while I waited for her. It's like I don't matter to her anymore." Arjun groaned, running his fingers through his tangled hair.

"I'm so sorry, Arjun," Madhuri said. "What suddenly changed with your mother?"

"Well, I told her that she was the reason I couldn't trust anyone anymore, and that unraveled into countless other bottled-up fights."

Arjun's face noticeably drained of all color when Madhuri gasped. She should've held her tongue, but if she spoke that way to her own mother, she'd have a chappal thrown at her head. "How did this argument even start? What sparked it?"

"You, Madhuri. It's always you."

Normally, his words would spark her temper. Arjun had a knack for blaming her whenever his life went down the drain, but she couldn't challenge Arjun this time. If she pushed him any further, especially when he was at his worst, his patience for her would thin out into nothingness.

"What does that mean?" Her fingers grazed his shoulder in an attempt to memorize every inch of his skin before he pulled himself away again. "I didn't do anything wrong at the wedding, did I?"

"I was telling her how hard it is to believe you. To believe that this relationship wasn't a mistake and that you might one day reciprocate the very obvious affection I have for you. Then again, my own mother couldn't do that for me, so maybe I'm expecting too much from you." He chewed on his bottom lip as if he was planning what to say next, concocting the perfect response to whatever question he'd expected her to ask. When silence enveloped them, he squared his shoulders back and watched her with an intense stare, waiting for her answer.

"You promised you'd tell me if your feelings changed," she whispered, her voice cracking on the word *promised*. "I didn't listen to Raina because of our conversation at the wedding, and now you're saying she was right all along? You want us to be more than friends?"

"I've always wanted that, Madhuri, but I couldn't tell you unless I thought there was at least a slight chance that you might feel the same way. I wouldn't risk our friendship over something as unimportant as my feelings if it wasn't absolutely worth it." Arjun tilted his head to the side. "Is it worth it?"

Madhuri's breath caught in her throat as the world around her fell into a hesitant silence. The dead leaves rustling on branches halted as the wind took a well-deserved break. Her heart slowed and burned simultaneously. She never wanted their frozen time to end.

If it did, she'd have to face the reality of her growing feelings for Arjun. How, in that moment, she couldn't think of anything but what it would be like to kiss him. How the warmth would creep into her chest, rendering his jacket useless. How she'd melt in his arms and her ice-queen heart would thaw at last. She wasn't sure when everything had changed between her and Arjun, when they'd transitioned from platonic friends to something much deeper, and she wasn't sure if she could continue to ignore her growing feelings any longer.

A leaf fell off the tree swaying in her front yard. Her time had ended.

"You knew what you were getting into when you signed the experiment," Madhuri whispered. Her fingers left him, reluctantly returning to their cold home at her side. "You can't blame me for your feelings. I can't control that."

Arjun leaned in, and God, Madhuri hated him for it. It was so hard to deny him when he pulled moves like that. His touch ignited sparks of faith throughout her body, inspiring her to believe in a force larger than herself. His eyes glimmered like a series of flashing lights, a reminder to embrace the love standing right in front of her, even if the timing wasn't quite what she had in mind—even if the boy who was offering her everything was the boy she never saw coming.

As much as Madhuri wanted to listen to the sensations running down her spine, she couldn't lose sight of her endgame. She had to prove her family and her destiny wrong, and Arjun was the way to do it. Finding a home in him meant accepting a lack of free will in her own life.

"Madhuri, I've liked you since we were kids. I've tried to convince myself that I moved on, since you clearly never felt the same, but something about us makes me believe we're meant to be." He pulled her shivering hands into his own and she could swear that she heard herself sigh at the touch. "I can't be the only one that feels our chemistry, right?"

"Chemistry isn't a happily-ever-after, Arjun."

"It could be, if you tried." When Madhuri watched him quietly, he squeezed her hands. "And by try, I mean really try. No experimental relationships or ulterior motives of proving your destiny wrong. Just you and me, the way it was supposed to be from the very beginning."

A shiver ran down her spine, and suddenly, she was tired of

the experimenting, tired of the endless planning, the painful yearning for even a semblance of control. Perhaps her reality would shift the way she wanted if she simply let go, hoping against all hope that Arjun would catch her before she crashed into the stubborn ground.

"Maybe you're right. Maybe this—no, *us*—really is worth it, and maybe I've been so distracted with my prophecy and my family curse that I didn't realize how badly I've wanted to kiss you all this time," Madhuri said slowly as she considered every possible consequence to this moment. "Do you think it's too late for me to make up for it?"

"Never." The softest smile blossomed across his lips. "What are you waiting for?"

Madhuri took the time to find an answer to his question, but she quickly realized that she didn't have an excuse for running away anymore. Her fingers found the satin collar of his shirt, pulling him closer. Within seconds, his arms were wrapped around her waist. Nothing about his touch felt foreign, but a delightful spark danced through her bloodstream anyway. The space between them grew thick with tension and it just about killed her.

"I'm not waiting anymore. I've wasted too much time."

Arjun closed the distance between them at last, his lips effortlessly molding against hers. Madhuri felt the tension dissipate around her, and for the first time since they'd signed their experiment, she felt like she could breathe.

She hadn't known what it would feel like to kiss Arjun until now, but she did know that she'd been searching for that feeling her entire life. Whether it was because of the kiss itself or the unadulterated, heart-stopping confidence it spurred within her, Madhuri felt herself wonder if she really could choose Arjun without losing herself. Maybe she could have both.

She broke into a smile that almost split her face in half. In a romance novel, that would've been cute, but in real life, smiling that widely during a kiss meant knocking her teeth against Arjun's. Hard.

His eyes shot open at the harsh impact, and he jumped back, sufficiently breathless. When he caught sight of her expression, a pained combination of utter embarrassment and mortification, Arjun burst into a fit of laughter. His uproarious tone soared through the air, singing off-tune melodies in her ear.

She'd never heard him laugh like that before. She found it cute, so cute that she wanted to kiss him all over again, especially if that would make him shut up.

"You've got some killer teeth there, Madhuri," Arjun managed to say between cackles. "Surprised you didn't bite my lip right off."

A sting of heat creeped into her cheeks. She was never gladder for her dark brown skin and its foolproof ability to shield a blush. "That's totally an exaggeration."

"Maybe, but that doesn't make it any less amusing." When she pouted at him, her arms crossed over her chest, Arjun groaned out loud. He pulled her hand into his again, but this time he interlaced their fingers. "I'm sorry for laughing."

"You've spent most of our lives teasing me about everything, Arjun. I can handle it." Madhuri cast a sly gaze toward their molded fingers. It felt natural to hold him like that, like puzzle pieces that were forgotten in the wrong boxes and found each other years later. Arjun was her connection to her childhood as an American teenager and her culture as an

Indian daughter. He was the bridge between her two worlds, a path she'd always thought she'd have to ignore for the sake of her reputation.

"So, what does this mean for us? For our experiment?"

Madhuri sighed. The questions brought her back down to reality, a world where open communication mattered if she wanted to have any stable relationships left. She couldn't quite answer him, though. To be honest, she hadn't really thought about what happened next. All she knew was that she couldn't imagine missing another opportunity to kiss him.

"I don't know." She combed her hands through her hair in an attempt to regain the warmth they'd lost when Arjun's lips left hers. "Do we need to know what our feelings mean right now? Do you think we could see where this takes us over time, day by day?"

"I'm tired of second-guessing what we are, Madhuri. I've been doing it my whole life."

Madhuri didn't know how to respond to that, but thankfully she didn't have to.

A tall shadow fell over them. Arjun's mother stood behind him with black mascara smudged under her eyes. A wool blanket was draped over her shoulders, covering the slipping strap of her tank top.

"Is something wrong?" Arjun tracked her line of vision, dropping her hand onto the dewy grass beside them before he turned around. When he caught sight of his mother, he scrambled to his feet. "What are you doing here, Mom?"

His mother avoided eye contact when she spoke, and Madhuri was not only positive that Arjun's life was seconds away from falling apart, but that his mother would be the sole culprit of their downfall.

"I'm here to take you home. We need to talk."

Arjun turned back to Madhuri, who was rooted in her spot on the patio. He didn't seem concerned by his mother's appearance on their doorstep, but Madhuri could clearly see the guilt lining her lashes, the tears frozen against her cheeks. Still, maybe that was all in her head. Maybe she'd listened to her own mother rant about Auntie Mehta's awful parenting for too long to be able to give her the benefit of the doubt. Or maybe Madhuri had become a little too protective of the boy who'd stolen her heart and had no intention of ever giving it back.

Madhuri waved him off with a small smile, hoping it would mask the questions rumbling through her brain, the relief of a successfully avoided confrontation burning away at the lining of her stomach. "You should go."

Arjun didn't need to be told twice. He linked his arm with his mother's, walking down the street to their own home. His frame, stiff and uncomfortable and everything he wasn't when they'd kissed, disappeared into the darkest night of the season. It was as if his body knew what was to come, even if his mind wouldn't let him accept it.

And just like that, Madhuri was left with nothing but the fading memory of her first real crush.

CHAPTER SEVENTEEN

arjun

Arjun's mother dropped his arm once they'd made it into their house, and she fell onto the uncomfortable couch in the corner of their living room, the one they saved for guests who didn't know any better. Her blanket sat forgotten on the rug.

"I'm so sorry," his mother whispered, unable to make eye contact with him. Arjun wondered if there were tears sparkling in her midnight-colored irises, the same shade of his own. Then again, his mother was never one for emotions.

"For what?" As soon as the words left his lips, he knew how naive he sounded. He'd had this conversation two years ago. He should have known why his mother was apologizing, the same way he should have known what was going through her mind the minute she picked him up from Madhuri's front porch. His mother's decay into her past self was rapid this week. The signs were all there. She started skipping family dinners again, sometimes cutting him off midconversation to answer an urgent email. She missed his last game, and already said she couldn't make it to the next. The habits that she'd promised to leave behind resurfaced like a plague, and even though his mother was physically with him again, Arjun felt alone as ever.

He should have seen it coming.

A stiff silence wafted through the air. He wished his mother would get to the point. She was wasting so much time like this, apologizing and waiting and apologizing again. Why was she delaying the inevitable?

"For making promises I couldn't keep." His mother finally looked at him. Her voice didn't waver. "I need to leave, Arjun."

"Your company needs you again, doesn't it?" He nodded, trying to mirror his mother's stoic expression. He willed his eyes to stay dry, for his breaths to stay even. He couldn't show any weakness, not yet. Not until she left for good. "You should go. That's your priority."

His mother rose from the chair. Her hair fell into coarse waves, much like Madhuri's. Arjun spent most of his life comparing the two women in his life. They'd broken his heart and put it back together. They could be distant and chilly, but they could also smile so brightly that he'd feel himself light up from the inside.

The stars knew that his mother would return and ask him for his forgiveness, for a second chance. His prophecy was the only reason that he let himself love her again after promising himself that he never would. He was guaranteed the best in all aspects of his life, but if that were the case, why was his mother saying her goodbyes? Why was she leaving again?

"You will always be my priority." She placed a hand on his cheek, her thumb catching the tear that he couldn't stop from falling off his dark lashes. "But my career is what saved me after the divorce. I can't bring myself to let it go. I hope you can understand that."

He pulled away from her touch. His heart froze over, numbing his nerves until he couldn't feel anything anymore. Was this what it was like to be his mother? He didn't like the cold sensation rumbling through his body, but it felt safer somehow. It was as if nothing could ever hurt him again, as if he was finally protected from the danger that came with loving the wrong people.

"I understand." Arjun's eyes remained focused on the paint-ing behind his mother's head. It was a family portrait, taken three days before his first day of second grade. His parents didn't smile in it. "I only wish you'd given *me* the chance to save you instead."

"I couldn't put the responsibility of my sadness on you, and especially not at such a young age. You didn't deserve that." His mother took a step back and wiped at the corners of her eyes, smudging her eyeliner into a sharp wing. He didn't know why she was crying when she'd made the decision to tear their family apart. It was so performative, so fake, so pseudo-maternal. "I'm hoping to be back for your game next month, so don't worry. I won't be gone for long."

The last time his mother said that, she hadn't returned from work until she absolutely had to—when Auntie Iyer called to inform her that her son was in the hospital with a lacrosse-induced concussion. His mother used to guarantee him a quick return, telling him exactly what he wanted to hear. She even hired the very best housekeeper money could buy, hoping that it would heal the rippling hole in Arjun's heart while keeping Auntie Iyer's suspicions at bay. Over time, her promises shifted, instead convincing anyone who'd listen that Arjun was mature and independent well beyond his age. That Arjun could handle himself while she pursued her career, that she'd only be gone for a few days at a time. But the days turned into weeks, the weeks into months, and Arjun would always end up alone again.

"Did I deserve to be abandoned, then?" Arjun asked, and if his mother had known him better, she would've noticed the way his voice cracked.

Instead, the room fell silent. She didn't have an answer for him.

The suitcases cluttering the entrance to his home disappeared, as did his mother. Arjun didn't cry when she left. He knew it wouldn't bring her back. Tears worked on people who recognized the way their actions hurt others, and his mother never would, not when she was chasing her so-called destiny and running away from the memories of their old life all at once.

He had been so optimistic that his mother was the woman who would fulfill his prophecy. She'd hurt him in the past. She offered him an opportunity to forgive her, and it was up to him to decide if she was too late or right on time. If it was the correct decision, he'd find love in her. That was all he ever wanted—what Madhuri had with her parents from the minute she was born.

His life wasn't like Madhuri's, though. He would forever be the boy with absent parents, trailing after a girl who wouldn't have chosen him if it weren't for an ulterior motive and a family that would never truly be his. Arjun was tired of the confusion, of the women in his life constantly putting themselves before anyone else. Before him.

The window beside his bed creaked, and before he could reach over to make sure it was shut, Madhuri cracked it fully open. Her unruly hair flew in the wind while her teeth chattered like dancing skeletons. When he noticed her chapped lips were almost gray in color, Arjun felt the distinct urge to pull her into his arms and kiss her until she was warm again.

He didn't want to make a move, though. Not like this. He didn't want to use her love, platonic or otherwise, to make himself feel better. She was worth a lot more than that, and he'd never be able to quantify just how much Madhuri meant to him.

"Arjun, could you please help me in?" Madhuri's sarcastic drawl hit his ears like tiny bullets. "Not only am I freezing to death, but I also think I have a tree branch stuck up my ass."

If his mother hadn't left just a few minutes ago, he would've laughed. "Sorry." He stumbled out of bed, his hand finding hers within seconds. He could've found it if he was blindfolded in the middle of the snowstorm, which was pretty close to what they were in right now. By Southern California standards, that was. "What are you even doing here?"

"I had a bad feeling when your mom stopped by. Thought I'd check in to make sure you were okay, but you definitely don't seem like you are." She threw herself onto his bed and pulled one of his pillows to her chest. It was navy blue in color, plain in comparison to the decor of the rest of his house. Arjun styled his room the way Auntie Iyer modeled everything—minimalistic with an emphasis on the people occupying the space rather than the space itself. It was a nice statement to frame their lower-middle-class economic status, but he'd prefer that to the elevated status he was born into. "What's going on? Do you want to talk about it?"

Arjun sat on the floor beside her, crossing his legs as if he were having his chart read again. "Mom left the way she always does when she gets bored with me." He shrugged, twirling a discarded, chewed-up pencil between his fingers. "Nothing new."

"Are you serious?" Madhuri's eyes grew so wide that he could see his reflection in them. He wondered why she was sitting with him, staring at someone as broken as him. Madhuri must have seen the dark circles beneath his eyes, the unkempt hair that went from woke-up-like-this sexy to haven't-showered-in-three-days depressing, and somehow decided to stick around anyway. His own family didn't even do that for him. "Why didn't you tell me?"

"It happened ten fucking minutes ago," he snapped. "Did you want me to FaceTime you during it or something?"

"Listen, you don't need to yell at me. I'm just trying to be here for you." Arjun had heard Madhuri have countless breakdowns, but he'd never heard her voice turn so cold when she was speaking to him. He'd never seen her shrink into herself the way she did just then, pulling his matching comforter around her until it threatened to swallow her whole.

"I'm sorry," he whispered. "I want you to stay. I'm just not in the best headspace right now." If they hadn't kissed that night, he'd have squeezed her hand the way he always did. Something felt awkward between them, though. He wasn't sure if it was his mother leaving or their undefined relationship, but every step felt like he was breaking through thin ice and into freezing, churning waters underneath. "You understand, right?"

"I don't, but I want to." Her lashes fluttered ever so slightly. He couldn't quit looking at them. "Help me understand, Arjun."

No one had directly asked him about his living situation. Most people assumed that Indian families like his were always perfect. Even Madhuri's parents never tried to figure out exactly how his family broke apart. It wasn't their business, so they kept themselves out of it.

Madhuri, however, always felt entitled to know everything about everyone. Normally that would annoy him to no end, but it was different now. He needed someone to care enough about him to want to know more.

He'd never been loved like that before.

Maybe that was why he told her everything, from the countless goodbyes and empty dinner tables to all the forgotten lacrosse games. Maybe that was how he ended up on the floor, lying on his stomach as if he were retelling Madhuri a childhood story laced not with warm memories but consistent pain. She watched him from her spot on his bed, the pillows long forgotten beside her.

The last thing Arjun thought before he fell asleep, most likely in the middle of a sentence, was how years of one-item Christmas lists and blown-out birthday candles had landed him in front of her at last. How he'd lost his mother's attention mere hours before he finally gained Madhuri's.

CHAPTER EIGHTEEN

madhuri

"On the topic of Hamlet's relationships, have y'all ever considered what exactly Horatio means to him?" Josie mused aloud during their AP English Literature Socratic Seminar. She leaned across her desk, balancing her weight on her elbows. "I mean, they're the literal definition of a friend zone gone wrong."

Madhuri was at the mercy of the emotions swimming through her brain ever since the night of her first kiss with Arjun, swept away by the image of his smile. It was a welcome change from her typical thoughts—Stanford Early Action results, her AP Chemistry grade, the crumpled experiment sitting patiently at the bottom of her unpacked suitcase. Even participating in a nonsense Hamlet debate with her best friend in front of her eavesdropping classmates was more appealing than the stressful alternatives.

Madhuri raised a questioning eyebrow at Josie when their teacher wasn't looking. "I'd be inclined to disagree. Every friendship doesn't result in a love story."

"Sure, but that doesn't mean that some aren't meant to be," her best friend shot back.

Their teacher interrupted with an instruction to focus their seminar on a specific subject rather than a literary free-for-all, and Madhuri immediately zipped her lips into a thin line. Josie muttered a disgruntled complaint under her breath as their teacher moved on to another seminar group.

"Did you really use the homoerotic subtext of Hamlet and Horatio as an allegory for my relationship with Arjun?" Madhuri ran an impatient finger over the edge of her phone, willing it to buzz. Many late-night Reddit rabbit holes had confirmed that the Stanford Early Action acceptances were mere hours from release. It was only a matter of time.

"You bet I did. Team Madjun for the win." Josie flashed her a playful grin. "Plus, it's fun to watch you flail under pressure every now and then, especially when it keeps your ego in check."

"First of all, that is the most pathetic ship name I've ever heard. Secondly, you should consider being nicer to me when you know I'm freaking out over Stanford as it is." She sent Josie a pointed look before her peripheral vision detected two girls listening in on their conversation. It wasn't difficult to identify her ex-best friends, Olivia and Brynn, not when their childish whispers hadn't changed in tone or technique since freshman year. Madhuri had managed to avoid having a class with them since their falling-out, when their group of four disintegrated into an exclusive circle that didn't reserve any space for her, but AP English Literature ruined her track record. She was forced to see them every morning, sitting no more than a foot away from her own desk, whether she liked it or not.

Josie followed Madhuri's heated gaze, elevating her voice enough to guarantee the two girls heard. "I was hoping I wouldn't have to hear that laugh again."

"Leave it alone." Madhuri's hand left her phone so that she could elbow Josie into silence. Her mood slowly decayed into a combination of fear and jealousy, pain and insecurity. The memories of their ex-friend group flooded through her brain with incredible force, threatening to transform her love for Josie into bitter caution. "If you want to say hi, go for it. I'm sure they'd love to catch up with you."

"Why would I want to do that?"

Madhuri thought back to the harsh bullying she'd endured, the tears she'd hidden in Josie's shoulder as they walked away from their toxic clique together. At that moment in time, she'd unknowingly imprisoned Josie in a friendship strained by the ghosts of their past, chained in the shackles of unpopularity. And now, as she and Josie whispered between seminars, Madhuri couldn't help but wonder if there would come a time when her best friend would leave her, too.

"Do you ever think you made the wrong decision in choosing me over them?" Madhuri whispered, almost afraid to hear the answer.

"I can't believe you asked me that. Don't you know why I left with you back then?"

When Madhuri shook her head, her eyes cautiously tracking their teacher's movements around the classroom, Josie continued with a small smile, "You're my person. No matter who tries to pull us apart, I will always stand by you."

Josie's words were sparse, yet carefully chosen, like the ripe lemons that swung from the trees in Arjun's backyard. Every spoken syllable destroyed her worst memories, forcing an undeniable warmth into her chest. Madhuri restrained the urge to smile back at her best friend as she considered a response that would hold even the smallest candle to Josie's.

Her phone buzzed before she could speak, vibrating toward the edge of her desk with a sinister purpose. Madhuri lunged for the device before it tumbled to the ground and swiped at the home screen until she found her email, where a red icon flashed at the corner of the app. The sender address jumped off the notification center.

Stanford University Office of Admissions.

"Ms. Iyer, do you have something you'd like to share with the class?" her teacher asked with a disgruntled sigh. "If you're willing to interrupt our seminar to be on your phone, I'm sure it must be the result of absolutely riveting news."

Josie must have taken note of the speechless squeal that left Madhuri's lips, because she jumped into fix-it mode immediately. "Actually, I think she was notified of a family emergency," Josie lied through her teeth, her mouth set in a terrifying grimace. "Would you still like for her to read the message out loud?"

Their teacher blanched at Josie's tone. "Is that so, Madhuri?"

Early Action results were out, and Madhuri couldn't help herself. She had to open the email and see her acceptance letter for herself before the excitement burst out of her like a definitive pop of confetti, before she transformed into a blinding ray of sunshine in front of the judgmental gaze of her classmates.

Her eyes scanned the email multiple times, looking for the specific keywords that she memorized before falling asleep every night. Instead of a hearty congratulations, she found the phrase she'd prayed she'd never have to see.

We regret to inform you…

She never planned on digesting the burning pain that came with a rejection. She never expected to heal from a breakup with her dream university, a breakup she had no choice in deciding.

Josie sneaked a peek at Madhuri's phone before turning back to her teacher. She wiped her face of any trace of emotion, but Madhuri noticed a strong sense of pity in the way Josie squeezed her hand beneath the desk. "I think she's in shock. Can I please take her home?"

The classroom fell silent as their teacher sighed, signed off on a pink slip, and handed it to Josie as she packed Madhuri's bag for her. "Drop this off at the main office before you leave."

Josie pulled Madhuri to her feet by the elbow and steered her away from the curious eyes of their former friends. As they left the classroom, Madhuri heard Olivia whisper to Brynn, "God, she's such a drama queen. Some things never change, huh?"

"Ignore them," Josie whispered to Madhuri, who walked beside her in silence.

Everyone told Madhuri that she was a shoo-in for Stanford, from her guidance counselor to her teachers to her friends to her family to Arjun. She had everything—the perfect grades, essays, letters of recommendation, and SAT scores. She worked her whole life for that one acceptance, for the school she'd dreamed of since she visited exactly ten years earlier.

They rejected her with a distant, chilling letter. Without a care for her or her feelings.

"Do you want to talk about it?" Josie deposited the pink slip in front of the attendance building and made a beeline for her Toyota, where she tossed their bags into the trunk with no thought for the contents within. "It can't be easy, losing Stanford and all. You've been talking about that school since forever, and I know—"

"Take me home, Josie," Madhuri interrupted. She clenched her fingers into two solid fists, hoping that the action would ground her until she could collapse into her mother's arms. "And no, I don't want to talk about it."

Josie flinched before setting her expression into nothingness yet again. She revved the car engine and sped off toward their neighborhood, the air between them brimming with a tension that Madhuri couldn't bring herself to disrupt. After what seemed like months, Josie finally pulled into the Iyer driveway with a squeak of her tires.

When Josie shifted into Park, Madhuri cleared her throat. "I'm sorry for snapping at you. You deserved better than that, but I hope you know that I didn't mean to hurt you. I don't know what I would do without you."

Unable to maintain eye contact, Madhuri searched the front yard and found her mother watering the flowers in front of their door, stopping every so often whenever her lack of energy winded her, a side effect of her lifelong Crohn's disease. She placed one hand on her stomach while she waited for the pain to subside and waved at Josie with the other. If her mother was confused by their early arrival, she didn't show it—after all, Madhuri wasn't someone who skipped school unless she absolutely had to.

Josie tugged at the seat belt tightly wound across her chest. "I'm sorry for pushing you to talk, but I only do that because it scares me when you shut down like that, when you lock me out without any warning."

Madhuri's mind stormed into war, one side fighting the Stanford rejection while the other wielded Josie as a shield against the bullies of her past. Somehow, her best friend forgave her for her festering, illogical doubts. Josie saw Madhuri for who she was, a flawed girl who never stopped trying to be anything but, and chose to stay, even when she didn't deserve it.

Madhuri swallowed the lump lodged in her throat as she hopped out of the Toyota, her feet barely making an impact with the ground. Her driveway, stained with chalk drawings and rain puddles, swayed beneath her. She took a moment to find her balance before offering Josie a smile that she desperately wished were real.

"Thank you, Josie."

"Of course."

The minute Josie left their driveway, Madhuri crumbled.

She let out a scream, a heartbreaking sound that ripped through her vocal cords without mercy. It turned into a sob and then another, threatening to destroy her from the inside.

It felt like her world was ending, like the Earth had fallen off its axis.

Her mother dropped her watering pail into the exposed dirt and ran to her daughter, who'd curled up in the center of their driveway with her knees hugged tightly to her chest. She pulled Madhuri into a hug, eyeing the phone that had fallen out of her pocket. Her mother read the email quietly as Madhuri lost herself in her embrace. It smelled like that night's dinner and henna, which her mother had used to dye her own hair that morning before school. The red highlights in her otherwise black hair gleamed in the soft light of the setting sun.

Her mother dropped the phone after a nervous pause. "Oh, Madhu," she whispered.

"You were right, Amma," she cried, holding on to her mother for dear life. "I was destined to lose and even Stanford knew it. They'd never accept a failure like me."

"That's wildly incorrect. You weren't destined to fail. You were destined to have your arrogance catch up to you. You were destined to be disappointed because you've constantly expected perfection from yourself."

"That's the same thing." Madhuri glared at her through teary eyes.

"No, it's not." Her mother sighed. "If you were meant to fail this year, Arjun would've left you. You would've been rejected from every college you applied to, not just Stanford."

"It's only December. For all we know, I could get rejected from the other colleges in the next few months."

"Don't be so negative." Her mother held Madhuri's face in her hands, greeting her with an intense stare. "Madhuri, you have to understand that your horoscope isn't meant to ruin your life. You're only destined to learn from your mistakes this year, something you've never had to do before. You never allowed yourself a second to breathe until now, when you let Arjun into your life. Some things are going to slip away in the process and that's okay. There's more to life than a snotty Ivy League education, you know."

Madhuri's eyes welled up with a fresh ocean of tears. She'd applied to countless other extremely competitive universities like UC Berkeley and Cornell, but none of them felt like Stanford. "I wanted Stanford, Amma. I wanted it more than Arjun and our silly relationship."

"What we want isn't always what we need." Her mother kissed her on the cheek. "Regardless, one rejection doesn't mean a lifetime of them. I have a feeling that you'll be accepted into the school you're best suited for. You have an incredibly bright future ahead of you and you don't need Stanford to achieve that."

Madhuri felt the pain of her rejection ebb slightly as her mother held her close.

"Promise?" Madhuri offered her pinkie to her mother.

Their fingers interlocked. "Cross my heart and hope to die."

CHAPTER NINETEEN

arjun

Arjun Mehta was a lot of things, but traditionally successful was not one of them. Sure, he was a nationally ranked lacrosse star and a self-proclaimed wannabe aerospace engineer, but he didn't expect Stanford to see that in him. Even his guidance counselor told him that it was a long shot. Amid a sea of applicants spanning from the future Beyoncé to the reincarnation of Gandhi, he didn't stand a single chance.

Madhuri had always been supportive of their coinciding dreams. They grew up loving Stanford together, begging their parents to take them to visit simply so they could watch the students in awe. As a result, they'd agreed to not discuss their application process until they'd been accepted. It was a well-known fact that Madhuri would get in, while Arjun was a wild card.

And yet, despite it all, Arjun was officially accepted into Stanford University.

He should've known from the way the school's lacrosse coach trailed after him, sending him a cryptic email months ago about his potential for the school's athletic and academic departments. About how the coach had already spoken to the School of Engineering about bending their class schedules to better fit future games and practices. The undertones of the message were clear. They wanted him to apply Early Action.

Even so, Arjun had never expected anyone to notice his potential. It didn't matter if he aced his ACT on the first attempt or managed to snag straight As throughout his senior year. If his own mother couldn't pay him a passing glance, how could he expect a school like Stanford to?

Especially when there were applicants like Madhuri, the perfect Indian daughter and the child Arjun was always second best to, shining from the top of the pile.

She must have gotten her decision by now, but considering she hadn't called him to freak out, he could only assume the worst.

He made it into Stanford, but Madhuri didn't.

He couldn't stop the shiver racing down his spine of toe-curling, heart-surging euphoria. He could make his mother understand that the hours he spent at practice while Madhuri studied weren't in vain. He could throw a party and invite everyone who ever doubted him, just so they could watch him click that coveted enrollment button. He could do so many things, prove so many people wrong.

But he never actually would. Not when Madhuri was likely sitting at home, devastated at the loss of her childhood dream.

His eyes flicked to the clock beside him, standing tall against the dark blue walls of his living room. It was nearly five in the afternoon, almost three hours since the results were posted during their final class period. He couldn't stop thinking about Madhuri's face and how she must have graduated from sobbing into her mother's shoulder to screaming at God, the Universe, and everything in between. He didn't want his happiness to come at the expense of the person he cared about the most, so he decided to keep the news quiet. No one, not even his mother, would know until he'd made sure Madhuri was okay. Besides, he didn't think he could inform his mother even if he wanted to. His anger had yet to subside after their last fight.

Arjun looked around his house, empty and cold once again, and he sighed. He might've grown accustomed to his loved ones casting him aside, but that didn't stop him from wishing that one day he might have someone to celebrate with.

Someone who wanted him just as much as he wanted them.

The happiness from his Stanford acceptance faded into nothing, and he resigned himself to his original plan—to check in on Madhuri before she left him, too.

Arjun's finger hovered over the Iyers' doorbell as he waited for a sign, anything that would offer him insight into the moment ahead of him. Madhuri had always been the one with the upper hand, the universal deck perpetually stacked in her favor, and he didn't know how she'd respond to his success. He didn't want to risk finding out.

The front door opened with a dramatic swish, and Raina watched him carefully, leaning against the wall with a casual hand on her hip. Her lips erred toward a grimace more than a grin, an expression that seemed so foreign to the trademarked Iyer family features. "Looking for my sister?"

Arjun noted the energy radiating off their house, electric in a way that could kill. He inhaled a deep breath and nodded. "If she's busy, I can come back later."

"Even if she is, I think she needs you right now. She told me that she wants to work twenty hours at Tillys this week, and as much as I understand her desire to distract herself, I can't keep covering for her with Amma and Appa." Raina offered him a soft smile. "You always have the most perfect timing, Arjun."

His body warmed ever so slightly. The thought of Madhuri, a girl who scorned the assistance of her friends as if it were a curse, needing *him* sent his heart into a flurry of hope. Perhaps he'd successfully manifested their meeting today, a turning point of emotional vulnerability that sent Madhuri into his arms forever.

He stepped into the Iyers' familiar foyer. "I owe you McDonald's for this, Raina."

"All I did was let you into a house that's pretty much yours at this point, but I'm in no position to deny fries." She perked up slightly and pointed up to the second floor. "She's upstairs. Follow the scent of teenage disappointment."

He rolled his eyes. "You better pack that sass away before Madhuri punches you."

Raina laughed out loud, and Arjun saluted her in a silent goodbye. He remembered the phone in his back pocket and the congratulatory email stored in his inbox as he climbed up the staircase, and he realized he hadn't even thought of what to say. It was obvious now that Madhuri hadn't gotten in, so was it moral to scream his success at the same time? Was he allowed to celebrate when she was falling apart?

Before he could answer his own questions, he was distracted by the softest sniffle. He could recognize her voice anywhere, even when it was soft and pleading, barely audible to anyone outside of her immediate embrace. Arjun followed the sound. He knew he had the courage to face her at her worst, for he could never see her as anything less than a warrior.

And yet, when he rounded the corner onto the second floor, he froze in his tracks.

Madhuri was balancing on a spinning white desk chair, reaching for an enormous book on top of the dusty book-shelf in her mother's study. Her hair had lost its shine, frizz-ing out into a million dry tendrils. Her body sagged like a dying palm tree, and he heard the sound of her cursing her dreams, her hopes, and her expectations out loud. If he took one more step forward, he'd be within inches of her, the first victim of a ticking grenade. He moved closer, compelled by the stubborn nature of her appearance. A particularly angry floorboard creaked beneath him right when Madhuri's fin-gers latched on to the leather-bound book. Her foot slipped off the chair as she heard the sound and she hugged the book to her chest, squeezing her eyes shut as she prepared for an impact with the ground.

Arjun lunged for her flailing frame in an attempt to catch her. Instead, he softened her blow as he fell with incredible force onto his back. Madhuri landed on top of him, pressing the book between their bodies as if to create a barrier. Within seconds, her eyes locked on to his. He witnessed the shock in her irises turn to flames of anger before withering into nothing.

"Uh," Arjun started, a soft blush creeping onto his cheeks. He was slowly losing control, falling prey to his aching heart. He wanted nothing more than to rip the book out from under her, pull her closer and closer until their breathing became one. "Hello, there."

Madhuri sputtered a few times before regaining her composure. She wiped at her red-rimmed eyes with the back of her palm, but she didn't immediately move away. Arjun wished they could stay that way forever—her lying on top of him like the closeness of their bodies brought her more comfort than anything else. "What are you doing here, Arjun?"

"I wanted to see you." He rested his head on his forearms, if only to stop his fingers from running over her sharp edges. He was acutely aware of her legs draped over his and the way her rose perfume infiltrated his senses like a love potion. Much to Arjun's dismay, Madhuri eased herself onto the floor beside him, the book tucked into her lap. "It's Stanford day, remember?"

"Right," she said slowly, and shifted her gaze to the book. Her fingers toyed with the frayed edges, opening it only to close it again. Arjun noticed the tremor in her limbs, the sudden loss of confidence in the Madhuri he knew so well. "I'd rather talk about anything else, though, if that's alright with you."

He lifted a curious eyebrow. "Can we talk about that book, then?"

"Do we have to?"

"Madhuri, you're holding our astrological charts in your hand right now and we both know that's forbidden." Arjun pulled himself into a sitting position opposite from her. His anxiety had all but dissipated. "What's on your mind?"

"Amma was right. I was destined to fail and now I am." Madhuri's eyes welled up with crystal tears again, but she shook them away before they could spill over her lashes. "I wanted to read my chart so that I'd better understand the anonymous force that set out to ruin my life, but then you showed up and shocked me out of my own scheme."

So, this was Madhuri's version of vulnerability—a combination of hopelessness and last-ditch attempts to shift the past. A desperate delusion that an antique book, one she once scorned, would be her saving grace. Arjun wanted to snap her out of her disappointment, but she'd have to recover on her own. All he could do in the moment was steer her away from Auntie Iyer's horoscopes, for the sake of her own future regrets.

"What if that's a good thing?" Arjun asked. When Madhuri sent him a confused stare, he cleared his throat and clarified, his voice shaking slightly. "I mean, what's the benefit of knowing the ending to your own story? Wouldn't it be better to see how it plays out?"

"I tried that with *The Kismat Experiment*. I wanted a concrete, scientific way to understand my romantic future and if any abstract forces would have a say in it. The thing is, trying to control nature makes everything so complicated." She set Auntie Iyer's book to the side and leaned into his space. Her eyes ran up and down his frame as if she were trying to confirm if he was real or not. "It would be so easy to know how everything ends. All I'd need to do is open the book and the answers would be right there, at my fingertips."

Arjun couldn't help himself. His body inched toward hers, and an electrifying shiver of lightning ran up his spine. There was something special about the way Madhuri watched him, as if their conversation had adjusted one of the gears in her ever-active brain. "Promise me you won't spoil our story yet."

"I don't know if I can do that." She leaned in even closer, so much so that her whispers sounded like sirens. His senses were suddenly overwhelmed by the static white noise buzzing away at his nerves. "Give me a reason to wait it out. Give me something to hope for."

"Do you trust me?"

"I do."

"That's your reason." Arjun pulled her hand into his, running his thumb in a circle over the back of her palm. "As long as you trust me, I'll make sure that nothing ever hurts you. Not the girls at school, not your family curse, and not even the Universe."

Madhuri hesitated for a brief second before she spoke. "Thank you, Arjun." She squeezed his hand twice. "For everything."

"Always."

CHAPTER TWENTY

madhuri

"Do you really think you can keep secrets from me, Madhuri?" Josie asked, snatching Madhuri's blanket from her hands. "You've been suspiciously quiet about your relationship with Arjun for too long, and I just *know* something's happened that you haven't told me yet."

"Nothing happened!" Madhuri dangled her head off the edge of the bed. Her long hair barely scraped her carpet, swaying with the draft that sneaked in from her open window. Madhuri stuck her tongue out at her best friend. "I'm being serious."

"You kissed him, didn't you?"

A moment of silence passed between the two girls before Madhuri forced a smile, more for Josie's sake than her own. As much as Madhuri wanted to see if her friendship with Arjun could be translated to romance, the rejection from Stanford put an end to her daydreams. Her prophecy was coming true right before her eyes—she'd failed academically, and it was only a matter of time before the rest of her life fell apart, too. And now, the one way she could course-correct her destiny was with the experiment. If Madhuri could end her relationship with Arjun the way she'd originally hypothesized, she'd finally regain control over her own life.

"How'd you know?"

Josie let out a happy squeal, making no effort to maintain her composure. "Lucky guess."

The thought of never kissing Arjun again entered her mind, and suddenly, Madhuri's smile began to fade. "Tell me the truth. What gave it away?"

"Well, there's the very obvious fact that you blush when I mention his name." Josie rolled her eyes. "But what really solidified my theory was the way you keep touching your lips like they're tingling and you're unsure of the feeling. Am I right or am I right?"

Madhuri rolled off the bed with a groan. "You're right."

Before Josie could tease her to death, Raina bounded into her room with a burning fire in her eyes. Her eyeliner was drawn into a perfect wing amid glittering eye shadow, and she was wearing Madhuri's lipstick, a red that bordered more on purple than cherry. Her Bharatanatyam jewelry and costumes typically suited her well, but when she stood in Madhuri's door frame with her mouth curled into a snarl, she looked more scary than gorgeous.

"We're late, Madhuri!" Raina threw a half-filled plastic

bottle into her duffel bag while glaring at her sister. "Stop chitchatting like Aunties and start the car!"

"I was waiting for you." Madhuri grabbed her keys from the nightstand. "I've been ready for over an hour."

Raina paused, looking her up and down with a judgmental lift of her eyebrows. "Are you really coming to the workshop in that?"

Madhuri turned her attention to the mirror, where she could see her navy blue sweatshirt and black skinny jeans. She wasn't wearing any makeup and her curls were brushed out and frizzy. She seemed normal, which was the whole point. Madhuri would never understand how Raina could wear her dance costumes out in public with pride. Didn't she understand how ridiculous she looked to their neighbors? Didn't she consider the people who'd stare at her as she walked past, tearing her appearance apart within the silence of their own mind?

"You know, you should be nicer to me, considering I'm giving up my Saturday to drive you because your boyfriend got a flat tire." Madhuri rolled her eyes. "Besides, what's wrong with what I'm wearing?"

"I don't know, Madhuri," Josie started. "I'm going to take Raina's side on this one. Y'all are heading to an elite LA Bharatanatyam workshop and you're pulling up like you're going to the grocery store to pick up toilet paper."

"Well, I don't have the time to figure out Madhuri's poor clothing choices. I already had to call AAA for Aditya this morning and I cannot handle another intervention before I even make it to the workshop." Raina shook her head, throwing her bag at Madhuri as she bounded down the stairs. "There's an extra salwar in there, if you want to change once we get there," she called out behind her, muttering something about being the more-prepared sister under her breath.

Madhuri lugged the bag onto her left shoulder, spinning her keys on her index finger. "Raina, you are such a pain!" she screamed. She turned her attention to Josie, who was smiling at them with a weird glint in her eyes. "What is it?"

"I just kind of understand why Arjun spent his entire life here now. It's like we're all part of the same family." Josie waved her off and picked up her stickered Hydro Flask. "We should get going, though. Raina seems to be more of a monster than a sister today."

"Yeah, we need to hustle before she eats us alive."

"You know, I wish she would. UC Berkeley Regents is speculated to come out by the first week of February, and I am not ready to tell my parents that their only daughter couldn't make it into their alma mater." Josie visibly flinched at the thought. "I even asked your mother to perform a reading to soothe my nerves, but she didn't mention any universities. The only thing she can guarantee is that I'll end up in the right place for me."

Madhuri's shoulders tensed as she imagined Josie sitting on their orange rug, her mind absorbing the Tamil language scrawled across the charts like a desperate sponge. She chose to ignore the second part of Josie's statement and offered her a kiss on the cheek instead.

"You've been working on creating the first student-run, statewide high school talent show in California history, and it's finally taking place in February. If Berkeley is going to accept anyone, it'd be you. Talented, creative, the whole package."

"I mean, you were rejected from Stanford despite your

research on influenza strains. I'm not even doing anything beneficial for the scientific community. I'm just a theater girl with a dream of making it to PA school one day."

"We both know that schools don't want the cookie-cutter applicant. I'm proof of that." Madhuri bit her lip, drawing blood from the chapped corners. "Listen, I know you're going to get into Berkeley. I also think our little trip to LA today will be good for you. You need a break."

"Don't I know it." Josie smiled again, but its familiar sparkle wasn't there anymore.

Madhuri didn't know what else to say, so she made her way down the stairs with Josie behind her. She felt guilty for not recognizing Josie's anxiety about Berkeley right away, but she'd been occupied with Arjun and Stanford for days now. The mass of her excuse weighed down on her as Madhuri cursed herself for letting Josie's emotions come as a surprise. She wasn't going to let her horoscope ruin her relationship with her best friend, too.

Driving at seventy miles per hour in LA's crowded streets was not the greatest idea, but considering that Raina would kill her if they were late to the workshop, it was the only option. Madhuri wove through the congested highway with a series of well-timed swerves, ignoring her sister's shrieking as much as she could. She turned the radio up a few decibels until Taylor Swift's voice overwhelmed Raina's, and she wondered how Aditya dealt with her unsolicited driving advice whenever they went out on dates together.

Josie sat in the back seat, making eye contact with Madhuri through the rearview mirror on occasion. A wave of silence washed over all three of them, and Josie was never one to sit through awkwardness, so she piped up. "Do you think you'll dance at the workshop, too, Madhuri? It's been years since Olivia and Brynn bullied you about it, and you're obviously in a much better place now. Maybe it's time for you to put yourself out there again."

Raina snorted. "You really think Madhuri's over what happened?"

Josie's eyes found Madhuri in the mirror again. "Isn't she?"

Before Raina could answer for her, Madhuri swiftly punched her sister in the shoulder. She remembered the day she quit dancing like it was yesterday, but Josie didn't have to know every single detail. No one needed to.

"What happened, Madhu? Why are you crying?" her dad had asked, his soft voice floating through her locked bedroom door. Madhuri heard her mother pushing an eavesdropping Raina back downstairs, an exasperated sigh leaving her lips.

"Go away!" She wiped her tears away with the back of her palm, willing herself to be strong, distant, cold. Girls like that were the only ones who survived high school.

"It's her friends at school," her mother whispered. "How many times will we let this happen? Shouldn't we teach our daughter to stand up for what she loves?"

Madhuri was the youngest girl in her studio to ever complete an Arangetram, a four-hour-long solo that expert Bharatanatyam dancers performed at the end of their formal training. She was never prouder than when she achieved her dreams, when the curtains closed, and the roaring applause smattered throughout the room. Her hair was stuck to her sweaty forehead and her makeup was starting to smudge, but she didn't care. She was a professional dancer at last.

But Arjun ruined everything when he posted that Instagram photo of her. She was smiling onstage, baring her sparkling teeth like a hungry Rottweiler. In the caption, he congratulated her on all of her hard work. Her first reaction when she saw the post was total glee. Arjun, her best friend, took the time to share with the world how much he admired her.

That feeling quickly faded when she realized that everyone at school would see the photograph. And sure, that wouldn't have been that bad if she went to a different school. If her parents had raised her in Edison, New Jersey, or Fremont, California, where her traditions didn't feel as foreign.

Instead, in their extremely small town, she faced the wrath of Olivia and Brynn, the same girls who thirsted after Arjun's brown skin while discarding her with scorn. The same girls who snickered about how she looked like the Joker in Arjun's photo. It only took a matter of minutes before the comments were flooded with hurtful remarks by scores of her classmates.

"I don't love Bharatanatyam," Madhuri corrected in a scream, eyeing the framed photo on her desk of her at her first dance recital with disdain. "I'm never going to dance again."

"You worked so hard to finish your Arangetram so that you could teach the other girls at the studio. Are you really going to let some uncultured, mean kids stop you from achieving that?" Her mother hit her fist against her bedroom door twice.

"It's not because of the girls. Bharatanatyam isn't even a real dance form. It's dramatic and dumb, and I should've known that sooner." Beside the frame was an album stocked with her pre-Arangetram photos. Madhuri thumbed through the pages, disgusted at how happy she used to be. Didn't she see how ugly she looked? "I shouldn't have wasted my time."

"Now, wait a minute—"

"No, Mom." Madhuri threw the album across the carpet. It hit her abandoned cup of tea, its contents spilling onto the beautiful embroidery. "I quit."

The distinct blare of a car horn snapped Madhuri out of her memory. She turned her gaze to the speedometer and saw that she was ten miles under the speed limit. She flashed Raina an apologetic grimace and floored their car, merging onto the nearest highway exit ramp. Taylor Swift blended into The Band CAMINO, and for once Madhuri wished she were listening to the Bollywood playlist long forgotten in her Spotify account.

"I'm not going to dance again, and that's final," Madhuri said, eyes focused on the winding road ahead of her. Raina and Josie quieted down at last—they knew well enough not to press Madhuri when she turned cold.

Some dreams were better left buried.

CHAPTER TWENTY-ONE

arjun

Arjun rose from his bedroom floor when the rays of January sunlight streamed through his window, eyeing the empty space Madhuri occupied the night before when they'd worked on their take-home AP Chemistry exam together. Every trace of her was gone, from her rose-scented perfume to the strands of curly hair she always seemed to shed, except for a single green Post-it. An act as small as a personalized note was enough to coax his heart to ease, especially when his mom had never thought to offer him the same.

Dear Arjun,
I'm so sorry I left without saying goodbye—I had to shift plans last minute to drive Raina to a dance workshop in LA. If you'd

like to accept my apology in the form of blueberry pancakes and coffee, it's waiting for you in the kitchen. It'll likely be cold by the time you're reading this, but I hope it's enough.

Madhuri

A slow head-over-heels smile crawled across his lips as he read her note. Madhuri could not cook to save her life, and she never planned on learning how to get better, so he was sure he'd be poisoned if he actually tasted her breakfast turned apology. What mattered were Madhuri's kind words. He wasn't sure when her heart thawed out for him, but her love was powerful enough to dim the pain his mother had caused when she left. He couldn't begin to thank her for the relief she brought him.

Arjun reached for his phone as he climbed down the stairs, hoping to message her before the workshop started, but an email with a glaring Stanford.edu domain distracted him. Arjun spent no more than ten seconds scanning the single paragraph of text and understood exactly what the notification was really asking him: Why hadn't he accepted their offer?

A vision of his mother sitting proudly beside him while he submitted his Statement of Intent to Register flashed before his mind, and Arjun realized that was why he couldn't bring himself to commit just yet. He hated that he needed his mother to make this decision when she was absent for all the smaller choices that led to this moment in the first place. He had navigated the NCAA recruitment schedule and the regulations regarding walk-on athletes on his own, despite being the first in his family to even attend a university in the United States. He signed his own registration papers, sent in his own equipment and varsity team fees. He knew nothing and learned everything because no one else would do it for him. He should've been able to say yes to Stanford, but he couldn't when his mother's face, cold and unmoving, was rooted in his brain like a sticky weed.

"Arjun Mehta, you better not delete that email." Auntie Iyer's stern voice hit his eardrums like tiny bullets as she unlocked the Mehta front door with her emergency key. Her hawk eyes had lasered on to his phone screen within seconds. A motherly threat was hidden in her words, daring him to disobey her.

If he were actually her son, he'd probably have screamed at her for interrupting him, arguing until he ran out of breath. He would've slammed the door in her face and sulked in his room, hoping she'd call him back down for dinner as if his outburst never even happened.

Thankfully, he wasn't her son.

He dropped his phone and flung his arms around Auntie Iyer, burying his face in her shoulder. He was fully aware that he was clinging on to her like a monkey, but he didn't care. Auntie Iyer, with her warm hugs that smelled like mirchi and maternal wisdom, was a gift from God.

"Oh, Arjun," she whispered, dropping the duffel bag in her hands to the floor. A definite clunk of metal hitting marble resonated through the air. "I'm sorry again about your mother. I know she left a little while back, but Madhuri mentioned that you're still not feeling like yourself. How are you doing, beta? Honestly?"

"Don't be sorry. And I'm doing much better now that you're here." Arjun pulled away, offering her a curious smile that he hoped would mask the chill of his empty house. "What's in the bag?"

"Another week's worth of meals." Auntie Iyer offered him a similar grin, though hers seemed worn down and tired. "I hope you're not tired of my cooking yet, because I plan to keep up with my delivery services for as long as you need it."

Arjun's eyes widened, darting from the heavy duffel bag to the anxiety-induced wrinkles in Auntie Iyer's forehead. "Please tell me you didn't stay up all night to do this again. I told you not to put so much effort into feeding me. I'd be perfectly fine with a stale pizza and half a bag of chips, you know."

"Whether I stayed up or not is none of your business. Besides, you've got another thing coming if you think I'm going to stand by and let you eat junk food for three meals a day." She grabbed a box of idli and coconut chutney from the bag and shoved it into his hands.

Before Arjun could thank her, Auntie Iyer moved on to her next thought. Her mind churned out ideas faster than most and her verbal execution was even quicker. Once she got started on fixing the people around her, there was no stopping it.

Auntie Iyer picked his phone off the floor, scanning over the email in a brief moment of silence. It was the first time he'd seen her near speechless, but of course that didn't last long. "Congratulations, beta. Stanford must see something great in you."

"I don't know about that—" he started before Auntie Iyer quickly shushed him.

"You need to learn to own your accomplishments, especially if it's a Stanford acceptance." She tried to hold back her smile. "Does your mother know? Madhuri?"

"I'm still too angry at my mother to speak to her, and as

for Madhuri, I didn't want to hurt her feelings." Arjun shoved his hands into the pockets of his gray sweatpants with a shrug. "I don't even know if I'll accept their offer, so why would I tell people?"

A bright flip-flop flew toward his head halfway through his sentence. He ducked in time for the chappal to hit the wall behind him, sliding to the floor with a thump. "Seriously, Auntie?"

"I can't believe this!" Auntie Iyer shook her head, wielding her other shoe like a weapon. "This is the opportunity of a lifetime and you're letting it slip through your fingers."

"I know that, but I feel like something is holding me back from accepting the offer. I think I need my mother here for this." He averted his eyes to a copy of *The Kismat Experiment* sitting patiently on the living room coffee table, waiting to be the next target of Auntie Iyer's disapproval. He wanted to run their experiment through the shredder after their kiss, but something had changed in Madhuri since her rejection from Stanford. She still didn't seem ready to commit.

To Arjun's horror, Auntie Iyer followed his line of vision to the bound paper, the wind from his cracked window ruffling its edges. Before she could pick it up, Arjun swiped it into the nearby trash and flashed her an innocent smile. The paper fluttered in the air for an extended pause, taunting Arjun with its mere existence, before it was laid to rest.

A beat of silence passed between them before Auntie Iyer responded. "When is your Statement of Intent to Register due?"

"Soon." His heart rate picked up as Auntie Iyer eyed the trash can. "Why?"

"You need to figure out if your mother is the real problem here."

"What's that supposed to mean?"

"You know, Arjun."

"No, I really don't."

"Think about it. Who could hold you back from Stanford besides your mom?"

Madhuri's face appeared in his head instantaneously. Her laughter spun through the space between his ears, and he envisioned the glimmer in her smile, the same shine he saw reflected off her eyes that night on The Beverly Hills Hotel rooftop. Every single memory they made together, from the dying pumpkins and deleted Instagram posts to their first kiss, played through his mind like a movie.

Stanford rejected her and accepted him, placing yet another divide in their relationship. He convinced himself that he hadn't told Madhuri about his acceptance yet because he wanted to be there for her in her sorrow, but he knew the truth—that she'd use it as an excuse to clutch *The Kismat Experiment* closer to her chest. A part of him always knew they'd end up here, choosing between their relationship and their destiny. Ignoring their expiration date, written both on paper and in the stars, wouldn't delay the inevitable.

Auntie Iyer flashed him a sympathetic grimace as if she could read his mind. "That's what I thought."

CHAPTER TWENTY-TWO

madhuri

"Not after Stanford, Josie. Me and Arjun cannot happen as long as I have a prophecy to prove wrong—and after the rejection happened, I know that I need to follow through with my plan more than ever." Madhuri shook her head, her gaze focused on her sister's form. Raina danced with ease, like it was second nature to her. She was the center of attention at the workshop without even trying. Madhuri sighed as she thought back to her past, how it used to be her stealing the spotlight instead. "That's why this relationship, as happy as it makes me, can only ever be an experiment. I can't let myself fall in love with what my family curse and every single Indian stereotype expects of me."

Josie clicked a photo of Raina on her phone before turning

back to Madhuri. She pasted an excited GIF above the image, tagged Raina in the corner, and posted it to her Instagram story. Aditya immediately liked it, and a series of hearts flew across Josie's screen. Meanwhile, Madhuri watched the situation unfold with a cautious lift to her brow. She knew her sister wouldn't have a problem with the post, but how could Raina feel so comfortable exposing her culture on social media like that? Wasn't she worried about the passive-aggressive comments, the well-meaning confusion, the overwhelming questions?

Josie stuffed her phone back into her pocket before looking back at Madhuri. "Does Arjun know that?" Madhuri opened her mouth to respond, but Josie waved her off. "Yes, he signed the experiment, and yes, he knows what he's getting into. Does he know that he shouldn't have any hope, though? That you'll date him and kiss him and confide in him like a real girlfriend, but you have no real intention of ripping up that piece of paper at all?"

When Madhuri told her best friend the story behind *The Kismat Experiment*, Josie wasn't surprised in the slightest. She'd heard about it in passing from Raina, who'd promised to keep it a secret from their parents but didn't quite follow through when it came to anyone else. Once Josie knew the truth, she immediately took Arjun's side, just like Raina had.

Madhuri averted her attention back to her sister, who clasped her hands together, bending at the waist while maintaining stern eye contact with herself in the mirror. She pressed her fingertips to the wood floor as an offering to the Goddess of the Earth before rising to her proper height. Madhuri licked the stinging taste of jealousy off her tongue.

"I don't know why I should tell him when that would ruin my only chance at proving my prophecy wrong." Madhuri waved Raina's water bottle at her, trying to catch her attention. "Plus, Arjun and I are finally starting to have fun with this relationship. Shouldn't we get the chance to experience that before I cut it off?"

"No one said anything about cutting it off. That's not the same as telling him the truth about your intentions." Josie shook her head with a sigh. "He's expecting you to rip up that experiment and you're holding it even closer to your chest. That isn't right and you know it."

Raina bounded up to them with flushed cheeks, sweat dripping down her forehead in a way that made her hormonal acne glisten like diamonds. She pulled the water bottle from Madhuri's hands, closing her eyes as she made obnoxious slurping sounds with her mouth. The last drop of water fell down Raina's chin, which she deftly wiped away. "You're going to dance the next choreography with us, Madhuri."

Madhuri snorted. "You're hilarious."

"I'm being completely serious." Raina lasered her focus on her sister. "I want you to dance with me. I asked the choreographer and she's all for it. She thinks the other girls could serve to learn from someone who completed their Arangetram at such a young age."

Josie's interest piqued at the mention of the unfamiliar word. "What's that?"

Raina grinned. "It's a four-hour-long solo dance recital done by Bharatanatyam students who've completed their training. Madhuri performed hers before she started high school, which is extremely rare."

"I remember seeing the beautiful pictures Arjun posted about it, but I didn't know how important the performance was." Josie leaned forward, while Madhuri stiffened at the mention of Arjun's Instagram post. After she shook off the painful memories, she noticed Josie's arm was wrapped protectively around her shoulders. It was like she could sense that Madhuri needed her to bring her back down to Earth, to reassure her that everything was okay with a simple touch. "You know, I'd love to hear more about your Arangetram one day. It sounds like such a life-changing event."

Raina nodded enthusiastically. "Well, Josie, what if I told you that you could witness her dancing firsthand rather than hearing about it after the fact? Madhuri, you wouldn't want to let down your best friend, right?"

"What do you not understand? I haven't danced since my Arangetram, and I don't plan on starting now." Madhuri readjusted her pottu, the tiny ceremonial dot placed on the center of her forehead, in front of the wall-length mirrors. She was wearing a simple black-and-orange salwar, her dupatta draped casually over her shoulder, but the clothes stuck to her like a prison jumpsuit. She was an impostor in her own body.

Raina snatched the dupatta and tied it around Madhuri's waist in a sharp knot. The pressure felt familiar, as if she'd never stopped tying the scarf in typical dancer fashion. "Look at how that fits you. It's natural. You can't ignore it."

Before Madhuri could distract her sister with another excuse, Raina grabbed her by the braid and pulled her into the center of the room. Curious students watched as the four counts of a song Madhuri knew by heart started, accompanied by a soft violin. It was an easy piece, the Alarippu, but every Bharatanatyam dancer had to learn it before moving on to more complicated dances. Raina and Madhuri had mastered it when they were seven, which left them ample time to relearn it with their own technique.

The blood in Madhuri's ears throbbed against her skin and sweat trickled down the curve of her heaving chest, even though she hadn't attempted a single move yet. Madhuri turned to her right and saw Raina flashing her a smile. When they made eye contact, the Alarippu suddenly felt doable. Madhuri offered her thanks to the Goddess of the Earth and gently touched her fingertips to the ground. A surge of energy electrocuted her limbs and her hands landed on her hips, right above the scarf tied around her body. Her face was set, her braid swinging down to her waist.

She looked like herself. All she needed to do next was dance like it, too.

The singer's voice wasn't merely familiar. It sounded like her grandmother whispering the lyrics under her breath as she watched Madhuri and Raina rehearse. It felt like the tears that rolled down her face every time her teacher chastised her for not practicing enough. Years of drilled choreography and smudged makeup floated through her brain.

Madhuri descended into the uncomfortable murumandi position, which required her to balance on the tips of her toes with her heels lifted completely off the ground. She didn't dare waver as her hands formed a cuplike shape, meant to resemble the bloom of a new spring flower, and she steadied her breathing to the rhythm of the music. Madhuri watched herself in the mirror as she maneuvered in and out of murumandi as if she'd never lost her connection to dance in the first place.

As she leaped into the next set of steps, Madhuri couldn't help but be reminded of the last time she'd performed for an audience, at the wedding. She'd never forget the way Arjun extended his hand to her, twirling her around in a circle as her skirt fanned out around her. Dancing with Arjun ushered her toward a future with everything she thought she'd left behind—Bharatanatyam and Tamil food, salwar suits and dupattas.

When the music softened to silence, so did the room around her. Madhuri squeezed her eyes shut as she held her final pose, worried that she'd somehow made a mistake in front of a class of talented dancers like her sister. Would they laugh at her behind her back or to her face?

Josie was the first to snap to her senses. She lifted her fingers to her lips and blew the loudest, most obnoxiously Indian whistle she could muster. Madhuri's father must have taught her that trick. The dancers around her started clapping, Raina the most enthusiastic among them. Her smile seemed brighter, as if she were hiding sisterly pride behind the sharp edges of her incisors.

And then, like every one of her dances, the moment ended.

Madhuri's body filled with dread. She was a talented dancer, evidenced by the roaring support of those around her, but she couldn't finish what she started. Dancing meant finding the spotlight and holding on to it. It meant opening herself up to the pain of judgment, even if she didn't like the people who were critiquing her. She'd promised to never put herself in that position again, which meant giving up Bharatanatyam, the same way that dating Arjun for real meant destroying her own free will.

Suddenly, Madhuri couldn't handle the intensity of the spotlight. Her heart was pounding, and her breathing came out in shallow, fast pants. She couldn't keep pretending that she was strong enough to move on, that all of her trauma surrounding Bharatanatyam had disappeared overnight. It was way too much, way too fast.

"I'm so sorry," she gasped, and sprinted out of the room. Madhuri ran until she made it to the parking lot, where she squatted in front of her car Asian-squat style and tried to process the last ten minutes. There was no plausible explanation for what came over her by agreeing to dance. Any other day, Raina never would have been able to convince her, even with physical force. Madhuri wasn't sure what made her risk the safety of her invisibility, but she wouldn't let it happen again.

"Hey," Josie whispered as she squatted beside her. "What are you doing over here?"

Madhuri picked at the dangling beads on her dupatta. "I'm taking a break."

"Do you think I can interrupt it with some very intrusive questions?"

"My lack of permission isn't going to stop you."

"You know me well." Josie smiled, easing herself into a more comfortable sitting position. She stretched her exposed legs out in front of her and leaned her head back against the hood of Madhuri's car. "Why'd you stop dancing?"

"I told you what Olivia and Brynn said to me. What more of a reason do you need?"

"That's not the whole truth. I want to know how you felt, why it's still so painful for you to talk about Bharatanatyam so many years later." Madhuri averted her eyes to the concrete. The similarity of Josie's words to Raina's at the wedding was too much for her to bear. When Madhuri continued to remain silent, Josie sighed. "I don't know why you hide that side of yourself. In fact, I don't know why you hide anything. There's nothing embarrassing about your Arangetram or idli and sambar or Arjun."

"You're never going to understand why I hide myself, because you've never had your identity mocked. You've never been told that your culture is over the top or that your food smells weird or that your crush is too predictable simply because the color of your skin matches his, whatever that even means." Madhuri's hands clenched into fists.

"Help me understand, then," Josie pleaded. "There's nothing I wouldn't go through for you, Madhuri. If I have to relive your most painful memories with you a thousand times, I would in a heartbeat. I only ever wanted to learn a little bit more about who you are—the real you, not the person you think I want you to be." A contemplative silence passed between them. "Do you really think I'm going to act like Olivia and Brynn?"

Madhuri wished she could take back her words when she heard the quiet disappointment in Josie's voice, but the damage was already done.

"It took me years to come to terms with the hatred I'd internalized because of my friendship with those girls. The fact that I can't even dance without having a mental breakdown shows that I still have a long way to go." Madhuri pulled her best friend's hand into hers.

Josie squeezed Madhuri's hand back. "I know how important your culture is to you, so all I'm asking is that you give me a chance to know the side of you that you've been pushing away for so long—the art, the food, the traditions, and everything in between."

"I will." Madhuri leaned her head on Josie's shoulder, and her best friend relaxed into her touch. "And I'm sorry I didn't do it earlier."

"Thank you. And while I'm at it with the requests, promise that you won't run from me again," Josie said after a moment of silence.

"I won't."

"Promise that you won't run away from Arjun, either," Josie added with a gradual smile.

Madhuri crossed her fingers behind her back, her heart rate slowing to a cold rhythm. The experiment was all she had left anchoring her to her free will, and she couldn't give up on it when she was so close to proving her family curse and the Universe wrong.

She had no choice but to lie.

"I promise."

CHAPTER TWENTY-THREE

arjun

"Are the stars still in my favor?" Arjun flashed Auntie Iyer a good-natured smile that he hoped would hide how seriously he took that question.

His Statement of Intent to Register stared at him expectantly from his laptop on the kitchen table. Even though he lived most of his life in this empty house, it felt especially quiet without his mother cooking omelets at the stove or watching her serials at an astronomical volume. Arjun's heart ached—he wanted to hate his mother for leaving him again, for being absent from such an important moment in his life, but he couldn't. He loved her too much.

Auntie Iyer eased herself into the seat beside him with an exhausted sigh, her hand resting on the top of her stomach.

She'd been with him since Madhuri left that morning, and even now, as the red of the sunset streamed through their translucent curtains, Arjun wanted her to stay longer. He cast the chart Auntie Iyer had brought with her a sideways glance as the draft escaping into the kitchen rustled the loose-leaf papers and stacked manila folders.

Auntie Iyer, as always, picked up on his emotions. "I'd say that the stars have always been in your favor. They're simply setting you up for a future you didn't quite expect."

"Expect? I didn't want any of this," Arjun muttered, dropping his head onto his keyboard with a deafening thud.

"There are so many teenagers who'd kill to be in your position. You need to be grateful for what you have, even if it isn't what you necessarily want."

Arjun didn't understand that mentality. His mother never taught him to be grateful. She didn't believe you should be grateful if that meant stagnating growth.

And how could he blame her? The moment she was satisfied with her surroundings, with her husband and her son and the tiny little world they'd built together, it all came crashing down. Arjun knew she'd rather die than have something like that happen again.

"Tell me more about this unexpected future of mine."

Auntie Iyer flashed him a sympathetic smile. "That's not how astrology works, beta."

Arjun flipped through his chart in a nonchalant manner. If Auntie Iyer saw his trembling fingers or chattering teeth, she'd lecture him on the negative effects of stress, especially the self-inflicted kind. There was only so much maternal wisdom he could handle.

He focused his eyes on the page he'd been looking for, the one highlighting his horoscope. Planetary alignments, influential constellations, and various scribbles filled the page. Most of the chart was written in Tamil and needed to be translated by Auntie Iyer, hence their annual meetings. As he thumbed to the next page, a crumpled note with a singular paragraph written in English fell onto the table. It was dated two years ago.

Arjun Mehta will succeed well beyond his wildest dreams throughout the next year. In the field of academics, he will be accepted into Stanford University on an athletic scholarship. He will study Aerospace Engineering with a considerable amount of struggle, but his hard work will come to fruition by his sophomore year of college. Athletically, he will surpass the expectations of himself and his teammates, but only once his superiors allow him to leave the bench. His patience will be tested immensely. Regarding love, he will find a family he can trust. He will pursue an unconventional relationship with his childhood best friend that has the potential to break his heart. However, if done properly, this may be Arjun Mehta's first and last romantic relationship.

Arjun tore his eyes away from the paper. "What is this?"

Auntie Iyer snatched the book from him, holding it tightly to her chest. "You weren't supposed to read that until August, before you and Madhuri leave for college."

The concrete kitchen tile beneath his feet churned like a ship rolling through high tide, and Arjun swore he saw his laptop sliding off the mahogany dinner table. Auntie Iyer shoved the papers into her bag with a disgruntled huff, her hair flying in the air as if she was stuck in a zero-gravity chamber. He leaned into his chair, and slowly, the dizziness faded away. He knew he wasn't experiencing another concussion, even with the bursts of light exploding in the black expanse of his vision. After all, it wasn't a body check that sent him into a spiral.

Auntie Iyer cupped his face in her hands, whispering his name as if it would bring him back to reality. "Are you okay? Do you want to talk about what you saw?"

He was not okay, and he did not want to talk about what he saw. Those sentences disintegrated on his tongue like sticky salt particles, rendering him speechless. Auntie Iyer had predicted everything a year in advance, from Stanford to Madhuri, and she hadn't told him. And if she was so accurate, that meant that his senior-year prophecy was correct as well. That meant that Auntie Iyer knew all along that it was Madhuri, not his mother, who would offer him an opportunity to find love. This whole time, she knew that his faith in his mother was futile, and she hadn't even warned him. She watched Arjun's heart break from the safety of her house a few streets over, silently picking up the pieces in the aftermath.

"How could you hide this? If I'd known, I never would have forgiven my mother when she came back all those months ago. I never would have been hurt."

"I never expose my readings prematurely, not to you or Madhuri." Auntie Iyer lasered her gaze on him. "Even if you had known in advance, nothing in that prophecy absolves you from pain. Heartbreak happens whether you can see it happening or not."

"I know you say that your prophecies aren't one hundred percent accurate and all that, but you predicted everything from my Stanford acceptance to my relationship with Madhuri months in advance. Shouldn't you have also known about my mother, then? Don't you think I deserved to be warned?"

Arjun turned his attention back to his Statement of Intent to Register, his mouse hovering over the submit button. The stars had already decided that he would study Aerospace Engineering at Stanford. There was no reason to delay the inevitable.

Even though his mind should've been stuck on himself, he couldn't stop thinking about how Madhuri would've reacted to what he'd read. She'd probably burrow herself in the blankets of her four-poster bed, hiding from the Universe until she had no choice but to face her own prophecy. He wondered if he should do the same. Neither of their perspectives on fate seemed to contain the right approach. They both kept getting hurt.

"I knew about your mother because we used to be friends, not due to my experience with astrology," Auntie Iyer whispered, lowering her vision to the floor. "We would have dinner together three times a week. We'd throw combined birthday parties for you and Madhuri. We'd plan them months in advance, the same way we'd plan our vacations to India every summer."

Arjun cocked his head to the side. "What changed?"

"Your mother's priorities did. After the divorce, she stopped coming to our house for chai because she feared that we would judge her the way the rest of our community did, and in all honesty, I don't blame her. She'd suffered through the pain of leaving her husband, and if the divorce on its own didn't break her trust in the world, the awful rumors from her former friends and family probably did." Auntie Iyer sighed. "I crafted so many excuses for her, trying to convince myself that she was still trying her best with you, even if she wasn't always present. But I think our families broke beyond repair when you landed in the hospital with your first concussion. I couldn't understand how your mother chose to leave me in charge of her only son at his weakest, when he needed her most."

The memory was fresh in his mind. He was bound to his dreary hospital cot, but he could still hear Auntie Iyer screaming into her phone across the hall. She paced up and down the freshly mopped floors, her heels clicking loud enough to cause a scene on their own. Arjun remembered Auntie Iyer hurling warnings and threats at his mother as if that would incentivize her to leave the office for him. It hadn't worked.

A week later, he received a Get Well Soon card in the mail. The address of his mother's office in New York was stamped across the front. That was the only personalization he could find in the envelope. The inside of the card featured a quick message written by Hallmark. And he realized he would have to be satisfied with just that. Pathetically enough, the card was tacked to the corkboard above his desk to this day.

"She asked me for my forgiveness, and you didn't stop it," Arjun said. "I trusted her after years of staying strong on my own because of *your* goddamn prophecy, and you let her break my heart anyway. Why?"

"It's not my place to interfere. Besides, you needed to learn from your experience with your family. If I'd stopped you, would you have understood the true meaning of your prophecy? Would you have become the man that you are today?"

Would Arjun have realized what Madhuri meant to him if his mother had never left? He used to be convinced—*delusional* was likely the better word—of his relationship with his family despite everything they'd been through. Maybe he needed to be hurt in order to understand their actual place in his life.

For the first time, Auntie Iyer answered the question for him. "You're the strongest young man I know, Arjun, and I'm so grateful to have seen you grow into your potential over the last few years." She offered him a soft smile. "I'm proud of you."

Arjun had never heard someone say that to him before. He never believed that an adult, especially one with no blood relation to him, could be proud of him. How could he expect that when his own mother refused to acknowledge him?

In that moment, Arjun realized that Auntie Iyer was wrong about one thing—Madhuri wasn't what was stopping him from submitting his Intent to Register. It was the lack of approval from an adult he admired. All he needed was an affirmation of the dedication and resilience that led him to Stanford in the first place, and Auntie Iyer, whether she knew it or not, gave him that.

The choices Arjun made after his realization happened so quickly that they blurred together in a mosaic of buttons clicked and signatures signed and fees paid. He felt Auntie Iyer's arms snake around his shoulders, and when she hugged him to her chest, the anger inside his heart slowly began to fade. Auntie Iyer was the closest thing he had left to a family. He couldn't let her go even if he tried.

"Done," Arjun whispered, his eyes locked on the message plastered to his laptop screen.

Thank you for submitting your Statement of Intent to Register for Stanford University.

CHAPTER TWENTY-FOUR

madhuri

"I'm sorry I'm late!" Madhuri exclaimed, incredibly out of breath.

Arjun clicked his tongue the way her mother did when she was upset. "A simple apology isn't going to cut it. I've been waiting here for twenty minutes, hoping you didn't stand me up on our first real date outside of the experiment."

Madhuri took a puff from her bright red inhaler. She'd just run up a two-mile-long dirt path in her brand-new black Vans and was mourning the loss of their color and the resurgence of her asthma. It was entirely her fault for parking down the hill to the Griffith Observatory, but the congested Los Angeles traffic left her no choice.

She caught Arjun grinning, no doubt because he found her lack of lung capacity amusing. That was what she got for dating a varsity lacrosse player. "Mom's sick, okay? I was taking care of her, and I lost track of time."

The smile was wiped clean off Arjun's lips. "Is it Crohn's again? I thought it went dormant a few months ago."

"That's what we thought, too, but she ended up with another flare-up her doctors never saw coming. Amma's been out of it for some time now." Madhuri sighed. "I've been feeding her thayir sadam, and I think that's helping her stomachache. All we can do now is wait it out."

"Madhuri, I'm so sorry," Arjun whispered. "I wouldn't have teased you if I knew."

Madhuri stuffed the inhaler into her bag. "Don't be. You're a welcome distraction."

Arjun slipped his arm around her waist, pulling her into his chest. His signature scent overwhelmed her senses, and all she could think about was how she'd be able to smell him on her clothes after they parted. Her heart leaped against her will when he leaned in, brushing his nose against hers.

"Is this distracting enough for you?"

Madhuri couldn't find her voice, so she settled for an affirmative grunt. She must have sounded like a caveman, because Arjun started grinning again. Something about the way Arjun teased her rendered her absolutely useless.

"How about now?" he whispered, his lips mere inches from hers. A cloud of cold air passed between them, and Madhuri wished she had the self-restraint to push him away—to lie and say that she didn't want him to lean in even closer. She wanted to feel her temperature skyrocket until the air around her boiled as if it were a pot of simmering chai.

"Mmm-hmm," Madhuri responded with a scratchy croak. "It's almost too much."

Arjun's fingers dug into the crook of her hip. "Almost?"

Madhuri had a very strong feeling that if Arjun didn't kiss her at that exact moment, her body would split into smithereens, cutting through the January sky like glass shards. She knew better than to lose sight of her end goal, of the Stanford rejection and her prophecy and *The Kismat Experiment*, but she couldn't deny the power of Arjun's magnetic field any longer. She stepped into his warmth, taking a mental note of his smile and the way it encapsulated her like the blanket Josie knitted for her sixteenth birthday.

A charged silence passed between them before Madhuri regained control over her breathing, just long enough to say, "Arjun, if you don't shut up and kiss me in the next thirty seconds, I swear I'll—"

Arjun, with the gentle motion of his thumb against the base of her chin, tilted her head up to meet his gaze. His eyes searched hers for a fleeting moment, so quick that Madhuri questioned if she'd imagined it completely, before he pressed his lips against hers.

Every kiss with Arjun was like the first—an all-encompassing touch that spoke leagues beyond their silly arguments and whispered conversations. She felt herself melting into him, and it took all her strength not to go completely weak at the knees. Arjun must've noticed her body language, because he tightened his arm around her waist, and suddenly the only force keeping her upright was his strength. He smiled against her teeth as if he knew exactly how much he affected her, and Madhuri wondered when the gentle boy next door had become so confident, so charismatic, so charming.

God, she loved it.

Arjun slowly broke their kiss, and Madhuri noticed a foggy haze in his eyes.

"Hi," he said.

"Hi." She beamed up at him, and reluctantly twirled herself out of his grasp. "That was…"

"Perfect," he finished with a good-natured laugh. "You know, the longer I'm with you, the more I realize how hopeless I am."

Madhuri returned his laughter, but her stomach sank as she processed his words. She remembered the day they heard their prophecies like it had happened an hour ago, the gentle September breeze wafting through her kitchen windows and ruffling Arjun's unkempt hair. Even months ago, Arjun supported her with unwavering faith while she ran away, faster and faster until there was no one left to chase her. Calling him hopeless back then was easy. The word fell off her tongue without hesitation, the last syllable hissed as if it were a warning. To see him internalize the insult over time was one thing. To fall for him because of it was another.

She was as hopeless as him.

Arjun snapped her out of her thoughts when he slipped his hand into hers, leading her toward the dome when she didn't respond. After pushing through multiple tourists and a steep flight of stairs, they made it to the ledge of the building. Arjun had already set up a picnic blanket and a steaming plate of parathas for them, and as he pulled her up, Madhuri understood why he'd brought her there. Beneath them was a sea of people funneling in and out of the Observatory, clicking pictures of every inch of Los Angeles architecture. That'd always annoyed her—how the world would marvel at her home like it were a zoo. To Madhuri, the Observatory was the first place where she truly understood her father, an aerospace engineer who wanted nothing more than to share his passion for the stars with his daughters. She'd found a genuine purpose to this building that stretched far beyond the cheap telescopes and metropolitan skyline. Los Angeles wasn't a tourist destination to her, and Arjun knew that, which was why they were sitting on a cement ledge with nothing but a blanket and Indian comfort food.

It didn't take long before both of their mouths were filled with flaky parathas, and Madhuri noticed a stray cilantro leaf stuck to the corner of Arjun's upper lip. She reached out to brush the crumbs away, her thumb hovering over his cheek. "I wish we could do things like this more often," Madhuri whispered. "I'm always so preoccupied with school that I seem to forget how much I love spending time with you."

Arjun covered her hand with his as he took a moment to think. His thumb ran a small circle over her knuckles and Madhuri just about melted. "Why don't we come back to the Observatory once you're committed to a university you love? That'd take away the edge, right?"

"Consider it a date." Madhuri flashed him a grin powered solely by his touch, the bolts of electricity snapping from his neurons to hers. Her heart warmed when she admired the way Arjun understood her so effortlessly, how they'd become one over the course of time and space.

He swallowed and ran his tongue over his teeth as if he were suddenly insecure of his eating habits. Once he regained his composure, he changed the subject. "Do you know why I brought you here, Madhuri?"

"If I had to guess, I thought it was because you know how

much the Observatory means to me. How a lot of my favorite memories with my family start and end right here." She searched his face for a sign of affirmation, only to stumble upon his motionless, cleanly wiped expression.

"That's one reason, but it isn't the most important." Arjun fiddled with the belt loops on his jeans. "You know how I'm majoring in Aerospace Engineering, right?"

"How could I not? My dad pretty much molded you into a younger version of himself."

Arjun let out a chuckle. "Exactly. Your dad and this observatory helped me realize my passion. I can't imagine not working with the stars in some way or another in my future, especially considering that I may not be able to have my chart read as frequently as I can now."

Madhuri wasn't sure what he meant, but she didn't have a good feeling about it. Their futures were creeping up on them quickly and Madhuri had always expected Arjun to be beside her in some way or another, even when they were pursuing their careers. If Arjun couldn't get a reading from her mother, though, it implied that he was leaving.

"Why wouldn't you be able to?" Madhuri cocked her head to the side, feigning ignorance. If he could read her mind, he'd hear the voices in her head screaming for the world to hit Pause, if only for a second. She felt the distance growing between them already, the way it did that night on The Beverly Hills Hotel rooftop. This time, though, she wasn't letting Arjun leave without a fight. "You're not going anywhere, right?"

Arjun grabbed the backpack that was sitting beside him and unzipped it, avoiding eye contact with her the whole time.

"I've been meaning to tell you this for a while, but I didn't know how you'd react."

"Arjun, if you don't get to the point right now, I'll murder you."

He smiled at her. "It'd be an honor to be murdered by you."

Madhuri wanted to roll her eyes at him for being cheesy and for dodging the question and for being the textbook definition of annoying, but all she did was smile back. She couldn't help it. "Tell me! I can't wait any longer."

Arjun fished a cardinal-red sweatshirt out of his backpack and tossed it to Madhuri. The fabric was soft against her fingertips, and although it smelled new, Arjun's scent was unmistakably present. She turned the sweatshirt over in her hands, only to see a bright Stanford Lacrosse logo staring her in the face.

Madhuri forced her gaze away from the sweatshirt to her experimental boyfriend, who seemed to be interested in watching everything but her. It didn't take a genius to understand why he hadn't told her earlier. He must have been scared that she'd make his incredible accomplishment about her own loss, but Madhuri didn't feel a hint of sadness or jealousy toward Arjun. Her heart brimmed with immense pride.

She slipped the sweatshirt over her body, curling the sleeves into her fists. And then, with her arms open wide, she threw herself at him. "Congratulations, Arjun," she whispered into his neck. "No one deserves this more than you."

Madhuri felt Arjun stiffen at her touch, probably due to surprise, before relaxing into her. She felt his chest press against her, his breathing reaching an equilibrium with her own. "Thank you," he said, his words murmured like a prayer. "You're the only person I've wanted to tell."

"Then why didn't you?" Madhuri pulled away, staring at him expectantly. "You made it into your dream school to play your dream sport and study for your dream career. I would've been shouting it from the rooftops if I were you."

"I didn't want to hurt you. If I ever believed that my success might hurt someone I cared about, I'd rather just keep it to myself." Arjun sighed.

Madhuri's heart dropped when she saw Arjun turn away, his eyes glued to the cement walls. She cupped his face in her hands, desperately searching for an answer in his eyes. "Were you afraid I'd leave you, too?" He didn't say anything, and Madhuri understood his silence. She might be at the mercy of their prophecies and her family curse, forever bound by the restraints of her experiment, but she knew without a doubt that they'd always be a fundamental part of each other's lives. "Arjun Mehta, I will never leave you. Saying goodbye to you would be like ripping out a piece of my own heart. I couldn't do that in my wildest dreams."

Arjun finally made eye contact with her, and she swore she saw a tear glistening on his dark lashes. "Thank you. I don't think you know how much it means to me that you like me enough to stay."

"It's more like I like you too much to ever leave." Her fingertips curled into the thick coils of hair at the nape of his neck. She noticed the way his dimples carved themselves into his cheeks like sparkling moons. "There is no Madhuri Iyer without Arjun Mehta."

He smiled at her, slowly and then all at once. "And there is no Arjun Mehta without you."

CHAPTER TWENTY-FIVE

arjun

The clinical scent of vodka suffocated him. Empty plastic cups littered the shiny wood floors and drowned underneath pools of sticky alcohol. The bass of a popular hip-hop song echoed from his speakers, threatening to destroy the foundation of his house. His phone lit up every few seconds, and most of the notifications were from Instagram, where he'd posted a story of the winning scoreboard from their State Championship game. Hidden beneath all the likes and comments, though, was a single missed call from his mother, which he had no intention of returning. He wouldn't let her ruin one of the best nights of his life. Eager to forget his mother, Arjun searched the party, a Winter Formal pregame turned last-minute State Championships celebration, for a specific girl.

Madhuri had been at the game hours ago, where their team won in a landslide. Her hair was tied into two ponytails, blue and white ribbon swinging alongside her curls. Madhuri's scream had found its way into the field, bouncing against the metal constraints of his helmet. His heart softened whenever she cheered his name. He'd never get enough of it.

"Arjun," Josie yelled over the blaring hip-hop. Her fingers were wrapped around a chilled beer that was open, but unused. He had a feeling she was holding it to fit in with the stumbling athletes around her. "Congratulations on winning State Championships!"

"Thanks, Josie. How are you liking the pregame?"

"You know you can't call it a pregame if it's the night before Formal, right? That goes against the very definition of the term." When Arjun playfully rolled his eyes at her, she continued her train of thought with an amused chuckle. "It's amazing, as always, but think I'd enjoy it more if I had someone to get drunk with. I had to run off to answer a phone call about the talent show, and in that time, my usual drinking partner took matters into her own hands. Miss Madhuri is already far too gone, and I have no chance of catching up to her tonight."

A siren went off in Arjun's mind. Madhuri was the human version of a chemical reaction—she processed her rumbling thoughts and searing emotions at a snail's pace until a bottle of alcohol intervened as her personal, explosive catalyst. The last time she'd taken it too far, she'd been mourning the end of her dance career. It was the summer after their freshman year, after she'd forgotten their fight and finally came back to him. She'd stolen a vodka bottle from her parents' cabinet, waving it in Arjun's face like it was a trophy. Three measly shots later, Madhuri was hopelessly crying on the floor with her head in his lap.

He couldn't let that happen again.

Arjun's eyes flicked to Liam, his best friend. Lean muscle and a face to rival Adonis, Liam was the easiest and safest way to distract Josie. He was the party's damage controller, the kind of boy who would play beer pong with his friends, but all his cups would be filled with sparkling water. Arjun nodded his head toward him, offering Josie a knowing smirk. "Why don't you find a new partner?"

Josie followed his gaze and snorted when she saw Liam's broad frame. "Yeah, right. How's Mr. Caveman over there going to be able to hold a conversation with me for more than five minutes? I don't speak in grunts, you know."

Arjun laughed out loud. "You're forgetting that I'm an athlete, too."

"Yeah, well, you're different."

"Listen, you never know what could come of it." Arjun gave her a light push in Liam's direction. "Didn't you say that you needed to expand your friend circle beyond Madhuri and I anyway?"

"I know you're shaking me off so that you can sneak away to find your girlfriend." Josie's eyes raked over Liam's body again as if she were committing it to memory. "I will not complain, though."

When Josie approached Liam, a glint in her smile, Arjun released a lengthy breath. His heart rate skyrocketed when he imagined what might have caused Madhuri to lose herself.

Was it their prophecies again, or perhaps her second-semester transcript? Of course, there was the possibility that Josie was exaggerating the truth. Maybe Madhuri was tipsy, but if that was the case, why hadn't she come to find him yet?

Arjun set his teeth into a tight line, his jaw ticking like a bomb. He didn't have much time to spare, nor did he want to risk it. His girlfriend could take care of herself, he was sure of it, but he needed to make sure that she was safe first.

He threw his cup into the nearest trash can, the leftover Jungle Juice sloshing into the bag, and thought back to Madhuri's various hiding spots scattered across his house. She'd spent most of her childhood sneaking into his laundry room, sitting in the tight space behind the rumbling dryer whenever she needed a moment to herself. Soon after, she'd upgraded to the guest room—the only one with a functioning lock. Madhuri's final not-so-secret getaway would be the half-finished tree house in their backyard. Arjun's father had never gotten around to completing it, so it was essentially a roofless wooden plank stuck in the center of a towering oak tree. The ladder swinging from the base was mangled at best, and yet Madhuri managed to climb up the splintering worn-out rope. With one look outside his window, Arjun was able to spot her sitting at the top with her legs spread out in front of her. She was an accident waiting to happen.

"Madhu," Arjun called out as he ran toward the tree house, craning his neck back so he could see her better. "Do you want to get down from there?"

She didn't respond. Instead, she flashed him a grin that said nothing short of *make me*.

"If you don't come down in the next minute, you leave me no choice but to call your mother."

Madhuri's eyes suddenly focused on him, her fingers gripping the edges of the wood plank tighter. "You wouldn't." There was a slight slur to her words, but she was generally coherent. Josie must have been exaggerating.

He crossed his arms over his chest. His stare met hers and he felt his stomach drop. Madhuri's hair had gained two sizes in volume, the curls frizzing into nothingness. Her cardigan was stuck to her body, attempting to protect her from the chilly February night but failing miserably. He wanted nothing more than to wrap his arms around her, to allow the electricity coursing between them to shock her back to life. "Want to bet?"

That did it. Madhuri stuck her tongue out at him and began her dismount from the tree. Her frame wavered slightly, but she carried herself well enough. Regardless, Arjun was there to catch her, even though it would never actually be a necessity. Madhuri was in complete control of her actions at all times. She didn't need anyone but herself.

She stumbled as her right foot hit the ground, sending her straight into his arms. A sickeningly sweet aroma of alcohol and rose-scented perfume overwhelmed his senses. Madhuri relaxed into his chest and looked up at him with wide eyes.

"You caught me."

"Why are you so surprised?" Arjun pressed a gentle kiss to her forehead, and Madhuri smiled to herself as if she was content to simply be there with him. He'd held Madhuri during their date at the Observatory the night before, but it still felt like an eternity had passed since then. His hand found hers without hesitation. "I've been catching you since we were kids."

Madhuri straightened her spine, attempting to stand up straight without swaying. After two failed attempts at regaining her balance, she sat down in the grass with a disgruntled sigh. "I'm not surprised. I keep waiting for you to fuck up, and when you don't, it pisses me off."

Arjun lifted a brow before sitting down beside her, pushing their conversation into a kinder territory through comedic relief. "Does the nice-guy act not do it for you? Say the word, and I could always turn into an asshole."

"That's not what I'm saying." Madhuri's gaze moved to the sky. A gray fog had clouded over earlier that evening, foreshadowing a lightning strike in the near future. "My prophecy said I would fail in all aspects of my life, romance included, and somehow, you're way too good to be true. I guess I'm just waiting for the other shoe to drop."

"Those prophecies aren't always accurate." When Madhuri scoffed at his unhelpful response, Arjun continued. "And even if it is correct, you're underestimating your own power."

"What do you mean?"

"I mean that your destiny doesn't rule you. Free will exists, Madhuri. You have the innate ability to rewrite your past, present, and future. If it feels like your path is set in stone, I promise you that it isn't. Nothing ever is."

While Arjun enjoyed knowing exactly where he was going, he was starting to understand Madhuri's love for self-determination. If he hadn't known about his prophecy, he would've thought he'd accomplished Stanford on his own, not because of the arbitrary luck of the Universe. He wasn't sure who to thank anymore—

himself or the stars. Maybe that trade-off was what Madhuri was looking to avoid all along.

"How can you be so sure of that?" Madhuri dug her finger-nails into his open palm, and Arjun weathered the pain the way he always did when it came to her. "I created this relationship out of my own free will to prove my curse and my family wrong. I promised myself that I would never fall for you, that the Universe was wrong about us, and look at where we ended up."

"What is that supposed to mean? Aren't you happy where we ended up?"

"We only ended up here because of you." Madhuri turned to face him, her eyes rimmed with a tired shade of red. "If free will existed, then you and I were never supposed to work. I wouldn't have allowed us to. The success of our relationship proves the power of your destiny, whether you'd like to admit it or not."

Arjun didn't know how to respond. His brain was falter-ing, wondering why she'd phrased that last sentence like it was a bad thing.

"And if your destiny exists and we're meant to be together," she began, her voice choking on each syllable, "then why are you leaving for Stanford? Why is the Universe pulling us apart right when we've finally decided to make it work?"

"It's my dream. You would leave if you had the chance, wouldn't you?"

When Madhuri hissed, Arjun knew that he'd struck a nerve. He hadn't meant for the words to come out so harshly. He was trying to stand up for himself, to reflect Madhuri's own hypocrisy back to her. Still, his anger continued to mount. Their confrontation was long overdue.

"I wouldn't know," she gritted out. "Listen, I'm trying to be supportive, but I keep thinking about how much it's going to hurt to be away from you when you're at Stanford. I don't know how I'm going to survive missing you that much."

As much as the second half of Madhuri's response warmed his heart, Arjun was more focused on the bite to her words, the subtle hint that she wasn't as happy with him as she claimed to be. "It doesn't sound like you're being supportive. Did you expect to always be the one that succeeded? Are you upset that, for once, I beat you at something?"

Arjun was being immature, and he knew that, but so was Madhuri. She threw tantrums on a daily basis. Whenever her life didn't go the exact way she wanted it to, she'd lash out at anyone in her path. Why couldn't he have the same luxury?

Madhuri faltered. "That isn't true. I want you to succeed, I really do. I just wish I could succeed with you."

A gentle silence passed between them. The tension was beginning to dissipate, evaporating like a puddle in the summertime. Arjun wasn't angry with Madhuri. He was definitely irritated, but he understood where she was coming from. They were just figuring out how to be together and the world was pulling them apart again. They couldn't catch a break.

Her hand squeezed his twice. "I don't think I'm ready to say goodbye to you yet, Arjun."

"Then don't."

Arjun leaned in, his lips locking with hers. It was only their third kiss, but something about it seemed more adult. They'd lost the childish innocence that came with knocking teeth and public displays of affection. This time, Madhuri kissed him like he was about to disappear—like she couldn't waste any more time fighting with him, not when their expiration date loomed over their heads like a curse.

CHAPTER TWENTY-SIX

madhuri

Madhuri was covered in sparkles, quite literally. She'd spent the better half of the day scrubbing the white shimmer (and the vodka hangover) off her body, using a little over half of the products under her bathroom sink. She was ready for Winter Formal, wearing a conservatively short silver dress. It hugged her body the way Arjun did, soft and gentle and wholesome. Her hair was pulled into a high ponytail, but her makeup was much less dramatic. She would've done more, but the fact that she was shining like a disco ball took priority.

Arjun would be at her house in under five minutes and her skin was horrendously sparkling. Maybe he'd be into it. Vampires were still a fad, weren't they? He could be the Bella to her Edward.

Her mother rushed into the room, cheeks pink with excitement. A Nikon camera swung from her arm and Madhuri hissed when she thought of the flash that it would emit. She'd never been the model type, especially not when she was sparkling. "Are you not ready yet? We need to take pictures, Madhu."

"Do you not see me right now, Mom?"

Her mother squinted at her. "You look beautiful, as always."

"Put your glasses on."

She did so, muttering under her breath about how demanding her daughter was. When she properly looked at Madhuri, her eyes widened into a black hole. "What happened to you?" she screeched, her fingers inspecting the glitter just above Madhuri's lip line.

Madhuri motioned to the plastic bag lying on the tiled bathroom floor. "When I took my dress out of the bag, the sparkles from another dress in the store fell all over me." Madhuri sat on the sink counter with a dejected sigh. "What should I do?"

A glint suddenly sparked in her mother's expression. "Coconut oil will get rid of it."

Madhuri's heart flipped. Fire burned within her chest, an arson with flames that blew dangerously close to her mother. She felt a sudden bout of anger festering inside her, years of pent-up insecurities triggered by something as simple as the mention of coconut oil. She wasn't sure why she was still so affected by it—all the popular girls used coconut oil to treat their hair now. Why was Madhuri so worried, then? With her culture normalized at last, she should finally be able to be herself.

"What's wrong?" her mother whispered, placing a gentle hand to her face.

Madhuri had gone red with fury, a feat that occurred once in a lifetime due to her dark brown skin. Her breath came out ragged and torn, worn out from the memories flooding through her brain. "Do you remember sixth grade, Mom? When you massaged my hair with coconut oil before school?"

Her mother offered her a tense grimace. "I remember you yelling at me to never touch you with coconut oil again."

"That's because the girls at school said they wouldn't sit with me until I showered. I apparently smelled weird. Foreign. Like an FOB." When her mother cocked her head to the side, obviously confused, Madhuri clarified. "It stands for Fresh Off the Boat. They were making fun of me for being an immigrant."

"Why does that matter now, though? You haven't been bullied in years."

"They don't bully me anymore because my culture became a trend, not because they learned their lesson. The minute henna and turmeric and coconut oil go out of style, I'm fucked."

Her mother ignored her colorful language and silently grabbed a bottle of coconut oil from the bathroom cabinet, setting it in front of Madhuri. "I'm going to leave this here for you, okay? You can decide if you would prefer the sparkles or the coconut oil." She placed a gentle kiss on Madhuri's cheek. "I love you."

Her eyelids fluttered shut. "I love you, too, Mom."

The coconut oil bottle seemed to have grown fangs over the span of their conversation, golden venom dripping from its teeth, but Madhuri knew she didn't have anything to lose by trying it. She wasn't about to waltz into Winter Formal looking like a disco ball, and it wasn't like she didn't know how to mask the smell now that she was older and sufficiently traumatized by the past. Still, there was a menacing quality to the oil that Madhuri couldn't quite shake. Moving on may only require her forgetting everyone who'd mistreated her, but facing the memories, whether that be through Arjun or Bharatanatyam or a godforsaken bottle of coconut oil, was much more difficult.

Her fingertips trembled as she filled a transparent dropper with the rich oil. Her phone rang on the granite counter, vibrating until it fell onto the carpeted floor with Josie's name flashing on the screen. Madhuri ignored it. Just about anything could distract her from her newfound courage, and she wasn't willing to risk it.

Madhuri touched the dropper to her cheekbones, and the sparkles fell off her body one by one, leaving behind nothing but a trail of glitter on the bathroom floor and the sight of her glowing brown skin in the mirror.

"You're absolutely radiant," Arjun whispered all in one breath. He wore a black dress shirt and pants, a silver tie hanging from his neck in a bold statement. His muscles rippled under the fabric, but what really caught Madhuri's attention was the way he smiled when he saw her. It was barely there, no more than a quirk at the corners of his lips. And yet it was like he was smiling for her, as if he knew that she'd be the only person to recognize it for what it truly was.

She ran her hands down her dress, feeling the fabric beneath her fingertips. "Thank you."

They'd spent the past hour taking photos, her mother gushing over the two of them like her life depended on it. Madhuri could tell that Arjun wanted his parents there, too, but that wasn't stopping him from enjoying the night. He was being himself, goofy and adventurous and effortlessly charming, and she was the lucky girl who got to experience him at his best. She was the one who held his hand as he drove them to their high school, who had the honor of dancing with him under the reflected light of a hundred hanging paper snowflakes.

Arjun parked his Range Rover in front of their school. She could hear the pounding bass through the walls of the car, but she didn't feel like pulling Arjun into the center of the room just yet. She wanted to stay a little longer with him.

"How are you feeling?" she asked. "Do you miss your mother?"

Madhuri worried she was being too blunt, but when Arjun leaned forward, she knew they'd be okay. "You know, my mother actually video-called me before Formal to see my suit. I know she probably had good intentions, but I didn't pick up. It would've made the start of what should've been an amazing night feel bittersweet." His hand moved to Madhuri's cheek. "So yes, I do miss her, but not enough to want her back in my life just yet. I think I need some more time before deciding that for sure."

"I'm glad she didn't hurt you any more than she already has. You deserve to have the very best night," she murmured, feeling her body gravitate closer to his. She struggled to stomach the urge to kiss him. "Plus, my family and I will always be there for you, no matter what happens."

Arjun offered her another one of his soft smiles. "I—"

The shrill sound of her phone ringing interrupted their train of thought. Madhuri scrambled out of his grasp to pick it up, suddenly remembering the missed calls Josie had left for her over the course of her night. She could tell that Arjun was a little irritated, so she kissed his cheek, saying, "I'm so sorry. Give me one second," before picking up the call.

Josie screamed through it, rendering the speakerphone absolutely useless. "Madhuri, Madhuri, Madhuri, Madhuri," she chanted, choking on her own breaths.

"Slow down, Josie," she responded. "What's going on? Are you at the dance yet?"

"I'm inside with Liam." Madhuri heard Josie excitedly thumping her feet against the sleek gymnasium floor, and she felt herself start to smile. "You need to check your email right now."

"What?"

"Trust me, Madhuri. I have a good feeling about you."

A few clicks later and a burst of confetti erupted on the web page. The blue and gold virtual streamers slowly fell off the screen, revealing a message underneath that immediately sent a fresh set of tears to Madhuri's eyes.

Congratulations! I am delighted to offer you admission to the University of California, Berkeley. You have been admitted to the College of Chemistry.

Arjun leaned over her shoulder with a curious expression. His arms snaked around her waist as he rested his head in the crook of her neck, reading the message on her phone. When the realization slowly dawned on him, he screamed out loud, peppering kisses to the sharp line of her jaw. Madhuri heard him congratulating her over and over again, but she couldn't quite process it.

She was rendered speechless, her heart rate skyrocketing. She couldn't stop staring at the email from UC Berkeley, her father's dream school. He used to tell her stories of when he was a kid, sitting on the balcony of his bungalow in India and dreaming of a future in America. He was the one who pushed her to apply, even though it wasn't her own dream school. It was as if he always knew that Berkeley would be there for her when Stanford wasn't. Her parents did have an awful knack for predicting the future.

All Madhuri could think about was her parents and the pride they'd feel when she told them the news. She couldn't stop imagining the way they'd tell everyone they knew that their very own daughter was selected as a Berkeley Regents Scholar. At the end of the day, Madhuri knew that every single choice she made in high school was for them. From working at Tillys to gaining an acceptance to one of the most prestigious schools in the nation, it was all for them. Madhuri would never stop trying to make them proud because she knew, even though they'd never say it out loud, that she was their American dream. Every single one of her accomplishments validated the countless sacrifices her immigrant family made to offer her these opportunities.

Madhuri heard her name being called from every direction, Josie's voice screeching from her discarded phone and Arjun coaxing her to snap out of it and celebrate with him. The weight of her endless failures slowly faded away, leaving behind the sweet taste of victory on her tongue, and for once, it felt like Madhuri didn't succeed because she was meant to. It wasn't a result of her inherited genetics or the will of the planets or arbitrary luck.

Madhuri knew she'd earned Berkeley with her willpower and nothing else.

CHAPTER TWENTY-SEVEN

arjun

Chicken had never smelled so good.

Ever since the grand opening of a Raising Cane's a mile away from their school, Arjun and Madhuri had decided that they'd eat at the fast-food joint after Winter Formal. They didn't actually end up going to the dance, though. After a quick phone call, Madhuri and Josie had decided to skip the event altogether and grab a celebratory "We Got into Berkeley!" dinner with their dates instead. Arjun definitely preferred it to the original plan—dancing in a packed gymnasium, trying to ignore the body odor of his classmates and the way his shirt was drenched with their sweat. Dinner with his girlfriend and two of his closest friends, even if it was at an over-glorified version of McDonald's, was a much happier alternative.

Madhuri was a strict vegetarian, so she dug into a heaping plate of steaming French fries and Texas toast, slurping an iced tea with vigor. Her smile seemed to tear through her face, and if Arjun weren't enthralled by her mere existence, he'd have noticed her resemblance to Pennywise the Clown.

Arjun's eyes followed the perfect trajectory of the fry Madhuri tossed at him, catching it in his mouth with a smug smirk. He wiped his mouth with the back of his hand before speaking. "We're really going to get tired of each other in the next four years, huh?"

Madhuri threw her head back with laughter when he caught the fry. There was something absolutely radiant about her, shining through every word she said, every breath she took. Arjun hadn't seen that side of Madhuri in months.

"I thought you said you'd never get bored of me, Arjun," she teased, leaning forward on her elbows. She watched him with a playful glint in her eyes. "At least I'll always have Josie if you decide to leave me behind."

That caught Josie's attention. She'd been previously engrossed in watching spotlight videos of Liam from their last game, smiling contentedly to herself. "Exactly. Madhuri and I are forever, no matter what." Josie extended her pinkie finger across the table. "Promise?"

Madhuri interlaced her finger with Josie's. "Promise."

Liam grinned at the sight of them. "Do you have anything you want to promise me, Arjun? Any wise words from our champion team captain?"

Arjun pretended to straighten his tie, setting his expression into a rock. "To my dear teammate Liam, the words I depart to you are simple: go Bulldogs."

Everyone at the table broke into another fit of giggles. Madhuri nearly snorted her tea, clutching her nose as if she were in urgent need of medical attention. Her dramatic flair caused Arjun to laugh even harder until he ended up losing himself in Madhuri again. He went silent, unable to stop staring at the way her dimples etched into her skin, threatening to become a permanent mark instead of an unexpected miracle. When her dimples flashed, Arjun knew that the girl he'd fallen for all those years ago was slowly coming back to him—the same girl who was effortlessly confident in who she was and wasn't afraid to let the whole world know.

Madhuri snapped her fingers in front of his face. "Where's your head at, mister?"

"I'm thinking about how far we've come." Arjun lasered his focus on Madhuri, who was confidently maintaining eye contact with him. "Especially you."

Josie swallowed a large gulp from her lemonade. "I noticed that, too, when you danced—remind me how it's pronounced again? I don't want to get it wrong." Madhuri whispered the word under her breath, and Josie nodded. "Oh, yes. Bharatanatyam. At the workshop."

Madhuri broke eye contact at last, averting her gaze back to the lukewarm French fries on her plate. "It's not that big of a deal. I only did it to make Raina happy. It's not much deeper than that."

"It absolutely is that deep." Arjun shook his head. "You haven't danced since…"

"Since our freshman year." Josie finished his sentence with

a firm nod, and she kicked Arjun's shin under the table. Madhuri watched the altercation with a soft look in her eyes, as if she knew her best friend was protecting her from a conversation she might not want to have in front of Liam. "Anyone want more iced tea?"

Liam cleared his throat. "I can leave if you need me to. This seems personal."

Madhuri shook her head, flashing Liam a weak smile. Arjun couldn't help but notice that her dimples were long gone. "No, you can stay. Can you keep everything to yourself, though?"

Liam saluted her. "Scout's honor, Madhuri. You have my word."

Arjun slipped his hand under the table and found Madhuri's. He offered her a squeeze, a nonverbal reassurance. He knew that the Bharatanatyam drama would be hard for her to talk about. Even when he apologized for posting that photo, their friendship nearly broke all over again. Time put Madhuri back together slowly, healing her wounds when no one else would. She forgave him eventually, but the tension surrounding her Arangetram never died.

Some things did change, though, like how she was finally surrounded by friends who didn't judge her. Arjun wondered if Madhuri knew just how much she could trust them.

Madhuri kissed his cheek, and he could hear the sharp breath she inhaled as she pulled away. She seemed to be stabilizing herself before telling her story, as if she feared that the past had the power to knock her down. After a moment of silence, Madhuri spoke. She told Liam about her former friends, the girls who did nothing but torment her for being herself after their friendship ended. Madhuri didn't cry, not even when she brought up the day she quit—the day she saw the Instagram photo he posted and all the chaos that ensued after it. Arjun caught himself marveling at her resilience.

Liam sighed when Madhuri's words slowly rolled to a stop. "I'm so sorry that happened to you, Madhuri."

"Don't be sorry." She shrugged. "I've moved on."

"I don't think you should move on, though," Josie said. Arjun exchanged a calculated look with her and saw the wheels turning in Josie's mind. In a flash, he understood exactly what she was thinking. "You seemed so happy when you were dancing again, back at that workshop in LA."

Arjun piped up once Josie had finished her sentence. "You know, Raina's performing in Josie's talent show. Why don't you join in on her routine?"

"Yeah, right. You want me to upend the choreography Raina's spent months working on just so that I can perform with her? In front of all the girls at school, plus their families and neighbors and literally all of Orange County? That's a funny joke."

Josie leaned over the table. "I agree with him. You should perform with Raina. What are you so scared of?"

"I'm scared of being judged again," Madhuri said. Her voice was monotonous, and it pained Arjun to see her lose the excitement that Berkeley had given her only hours ago. "Outside of Olivia and Brynn, the rest of the kids at school don't look at me like I'm an alien anymore. Why would I risk that? Why can't I just wait until college to dance?"

"Why are you procrastinating on accepting your culture?" Arjun responded. "There's not going to be an environment where it's easy to be yourself. One day, you'll have to move on for your own sake, but if you keep pushing that off, I'm afraid you'll never get there."

Madhuri's eyes moved back to her phone, where the Berkeley acceptance email shone proudly. She turned back to Arjun and Josie, her threaded brows twisted into a straight line. "You'll be there if I fail, right?"

"You're not going to fail," Josie whispered. "But we'll be there. That's a guarantee."

She looked up at Arjun and he felt his heart catch when their eyes met. "What do you think, Arjun?"

"I'll support you no matter what you decide." He offered her a smile. "All I'll say is that there's a reason Berkeley accepted you. They see what I see in you every day, and I think if you choose to dance at the show, you'd get to see it, too."

And just like that, Madhuri's dimples were back.

Arjun had been avoiding his home like the plague. He drove circles around the darkened windows of his room for weeks after his mother left, his Range Rover purring like their air conditioner used to. His family was the kind to leave it on throughout winter, while the Iyers had their fireplace running in July. Although he was sensitive to high temperatures, whether the heat came from the burning wood in the living room or the oven as Madhuri baked chocolate chip cookies instead of doing her homework, Arjun always found some excuse to stay in the Iyers' sauna. It was still better than the chilling loneliness drafting through the halls of his own home.

He'd do anything to avoid unlocking the Mehta front door with his rusted key from sixth grade, the first year he was left home alone for a consecutive twenty-four hours. He hated how the refrigerator, which used to be stocked with half-grade parathas his mother managed to buy at the last minute before she left, was suddenly empty. He was eighteen now. His mother didn't need to keep buying him food, not when he had all the tools necessary to do it himself.

Arjun's fingers tightened around his steering wheel as he drove down the winding path leading from Madhuri's home, where he dropped her off after the dance. Each house he passed grew in height and confidence, towering over him as if he were a little kid who didn't belong there.

Arjun tore his eyes away from his neighborhood. Everything about it resembled the opening setting to a horror movie, calm and silent before chaos ensued. He knew he wouldn't die—that was his overactive imagination talking—but he knew he wasn't entirely safe, either. Auntie Iyer always said that a human being could sense an unforgettable moment before it happened, simply by the unnerving wavelength of energy it gave off in the Universe, and he definitely felt that now. Something was different.

He continued to follow the streetlights, which turned darker with each consecutive flicker. The pit in his stomach became a heavyset bowling ball, sinking deep into his body and threatening to pull him down with it, when his eyes landed on his house. The lights in his bedroom were on for the first time in weeks. His mother's jet-black Mercedes sat in the parking space beside his. He turned his Range Rover into the driveway, and instead of parking, his hand hovered over the Reverse gear. He still had a chance to turn back around, to book it to the Iyers' in a fit of hysteria.

He wasn't sure what made him decide to set his car to Park, if it was the urge to take revenge, to win back the last word. Without another moment of hesitation, he slammed the door behind him and walked right through the front door without a care for the consequences.

Arjun was pulling a Madhuri—the walk-into-a-scary-situation-and-own-it tactic. She'd taught it to him when the school lacrosse coach wanted to make his son the team captain instead of Arjun, who deserved it more than anyone else. He hadn't pulled that card ever since. Rocking the boat wasn't really his thing.

"I was wondering when you'd come home, Arjun."

His mother clicked her tongue when he opened the door, disappointment etched in her voice. His eyes moved to the antique grandfather clock set against the walls of their foyer. He'd made it home a minute shy of midnight.

His mother stood beneath the well-lit chandelier in their living room, the television set to the Indian dramas she was addicted to. Her fingers held a glass of chilled wine instead of mango juice. Arjun didn't drink, but in that moment, he wished he did. The scene felt familiar to the fight that sent his mother packing. He needed liquid courage, too, if he were to relive it all over again.

"It's not really your business." Arjun hung his car keys on the coatrack beside the door, one of his mother's pet peeves. He wanted her face to show some kind of annoyance, but she remained unreadable. "You don't get to set a curfew if you're not here to see me come home."

She raised her glass to her lips and took a long sip before she refocused her gaze on him. Arjun noticed the dark circles under her eyes and the utter lack of makeup trying to hide them. His mother barely looked like herself. "I can't argue with that logic."

"Why are you here?" Arjun enunciated each word, punctuating his sentence with a gritty question mark. He couldn't find it in him to feign politeness, not after the way he'd been treated by her. He felt flames of anger pushing against his tongue, threatening to burst through his words. He wouldn't be silent any longer. "How many times are you going to leave and ask for forgiveness? Haven't you put me through enough?"

"I'm here because you got an athletic scholarship to Stanford and I had to find out from my colleague's daughter, who forwarded your commitment post on Instagram." His mother sank into the nearest chair. Her fingers pressed against her temple as if she didn't have the energy to process his silence. "Why didn't you tell me? Didn't you think I'd be proud?"

"Your pride doesn't mean shit. It doesn't erase all of the times you've disappointed me, the dinners you've flaked on, and the conversations you've ignored." Arjun bit his lip, trying to stop himself from tearing up. "You can't expect me to believe that Stanford is the only reason you're here. There's no way you bought a plane ticket to find out something you could've learned in a FaceTime call."

"I didn't think this was a conversation we needed to have virtually. Besides, I said I'd be here for the big milestones, like your graduation in May. This is pretty much the same thing, only a few months earlier." His mother squinted her eyes at him. "You don't believe me, do you?"

Arjun's mind was racing. He didn't understand why his mother hadn't considered Stanford beforehand, why she only planned on coming back for graduation. "Did you not think I would get in?" he asked, his voice softening. The anger was still rumbling inside his chest, but he felt a sudden sadness overwhelm him with greater intensity.

"I'll be honest. When Kamala told me that Madhuri didn't get in, I expected the same outcome for you. That doesn't say anything about your intelligence or skill set, but a school like Stanford is once in a lifetime and—"

"You don't think I'm a once-in-a-lifetime kind of kid."

His mother averted her eyes to her now-empty glass of wine, inspecting the dust collecting on the rim. If she'd been around, she'd know that Arjun hadn't vacuumed the place since she'd first left. He didn't see the point in taking care of a house that was nothing but a shrine to what could've been.

She shifted the topic with ease. "I want to be there for you, Arjun. Whether you were rejected or not, I thought I'd try to make up for my past mistakes now."

Her words were eerily familiar, a silent ask for forgiveness that he'd heard before. Every single time he let her in, trusted that she'd be there for him for longer than the parental obligation required, she let him down. His mother bargaining with him over a rejection that never even happened presented him with a crossroad—he could fall prey to her arm's length affection, or he could learn from their mistakes. He had the chance to offer his mother the freedom she'd always wanted while granting himself the peace he'd spent his entire life searching for. And maybe, just maybe, the space could heal their family at last.

Arjun's phone chimed with a text from Madhuri. He needed a distraction to calm himself down before he lost control. There was a part of him that wanted to hurt her the way she hurt him, but he couldn't let those voices overpower his conscience. He would never be the person to act out of spite.

Madhuri: You're coming over when I tell my parents about Berkeley, right? I know you're getting changed into something a little more comfortable, but it's past midnight and I can see they're getting tired. I don't want to wait too long if that's alright.

Arjun: I'm almost ready. I'll be there in ten minutes.

Arjun turned back to his mother, who watched his phone wearily.

"Your other family needs you?"

"Yes, but again, that's none of your business," he hissed. "I'm not leaving, though. Not until we finish this conversation."

His mother nodded and held on to her glass tighter. "Go ahead. What's on your mind?"

"I'm tired of you leaving and coming home as you please. I'm tired of how you've manipulated me into staying silent so you can avoid the consequences of the pain you've caused." Arjun picked his car keys up, spinning them around his index finger. "Most importantly, I'm tired of how much I've loved you these last eighteen years. That love made me trust you when you asked for my forgiveness. I'm done with it, and I'm done with you."

His mother ran her thumb under her lashes, almost as if she were wiping away a tear. It was the only hint of emotion he'd ever seen on her face. "I'm so sorry, Arjun."

"I'm not finished speaking," he said. "This is our house, so I understand that I won't be able to avoid you for the rest of my life, but I want to make a deal with you."

She took a cautious step toward the front door, mere inches

away from where he stood. Arjun could see a glimmer of hope in the way her hand trembled, as if she were deciding whether she should reach out for him again. He knew he wouldn't accept it even if she did.

"What's your deal?"

"I want you to stop trying to be my mother. I don't need you to come to my lacrosse games or catch me if I fall off the couch." Arjun inhaled a deep breath to prepare him for what he was about to say next. "And I never want to hear you say you love me. You don't, not in a way that matters, and that's okay. I've come to terms with it, and you should, too."

"Are you sure that's what you want? To be nothing more than housemates until you move out for good?" His mother stood frozen in place. "I can stay awhile longer, if you'd like. We could talk this through—that is, if you still want to give us a chance."

"I don't have any more chances left to give you." He sucked in a breath, willing himself not to cry when his mother asked to stay. He never thought he'd have to push his mother away for his own good, that he'd voluntarily choose solitude over her empty trust and broken promises. "I think you need to leave."

She stared at him for what seemed like forever and Arjun tried not to make eye contact. He knew that if he did, he'd find it hard to stick to what was best for him. Looking at his mother would remind him of their memories, good and bad. It would risk his already wavering courage.

"I understand. You need time to figure out how you feel." His mother stepped around him to open the front door. All she had on her shoulder was a sling bag, and Arjun could see a passport and a plane ticket shoved inside, peeking out over the zipper. The ticket had no return date, meaning it was a one-way flight back to California. A tear slipped from Arjun's eyes when he realized that his mother's actions were finally sincere, too many years too late. "But I hope you know that I'm doing this for you, beta."

"Thank you," Arjun whispered. He felt her lingering behind him, waiting for him to change his mind. If he were being honest, he almost did. If she'd stayed a few minutes longer, he might've turned around.

Before he knew it, the door closed, and he heard his mother's Mercedes turn on. He wondered what he'd see if he looked out the window for one last glimpse, one last sign for him to forgive. Would she be watching him from her car, sobbing apologies that would be muffled by the sound of the engine?

Arjun ran to the window, but when he wiped the fog and condensation away, he saw nothing but his Range Rover in the driveway. His mother was gone, and although the familiar pain of her absence stung, Arjun didn't regret his choice to let her go.

He knew he'd become used to the silence and to the friendship of his own mind in due time. After years of forced independence, Arjun would much rather be alone than have the ghost of his mother haunting his slowly healing heart.

CHAPTER TWENTY-EIGHT

madhuri

Madhuri couldn't wipe the cheesy grin off her face. It wouldn't budge, not even when she thought about performing in Josie's talent show. It didn't take a genius to know what put that smile on her face. Her acceptance to UC Berkeley filled her with more than simple happiness. She felt like herself again, like she could conquer anything standing in the way of her and her future. She'd felt similar feelings with Arjun or when she danced with Raina at the workshop, but it was never as intense as what she was experiencing now. Madhuri, for the first time in months, was unbreakable. Maybe that was why she agreed to dance in the talent show. Arjun and Josie picked the perfect moment to push her out of her comfort zone.

She knew that dancing again in front of such a large audience would be similar to diving into the deep end of the community pool, which wouldn't be that bad if she could, at the very least, doggy paddle her way to safety. The problem, though, was that she couldn't swim to save her life—just like she couldn't shake off the ruthless bullying she'd spent years of her life enduring. Fixing the tear in her heart wouldn't be as simple as learning to dance again, whether that be onstage or in the confines of her room. It would take an endless amount of time with the right people on her side, and it would also result in multiple mental breakdowns. Running away from it all would be so easy. She could create a new life for herself in San Francisco, surrounded not only by Josie and Arjun, but by countless other students who'd probably faced the same adversities.

Madhuri was jolted out of her thoughts when Arjun rang her house's doorbell over and over again, and she laughed as she swung the door open. "I'm coming, you heathen!"

Arjun smiled at her, although it wasn't as bright as what she'd seen at Raising Cane's mere hours ago, and her excitement faltered. "Are you okay?"

He stepped inside without an invitation and placed a kiss to her forehead. Madhuri swore that her heart would never stop skipping a beat when it came to him, no matter how long they dated. "Never mind, you seem pretty okay now," she teased, closing the door behind him with a bump of her hip.

Arjun offered her a stiff chuckle. "When am I ever not?"

His demeanor seemed forced, but Madhuri couldn't completely tell. She wanted nothing more than to read his mind, if only to understand him a little better. But it was obvious that he wasn't in the mood to discuss anything serious, so she'd have to follow his lead and feign normality until he was comfortable enough.

She was about to throw a punch to his bicep when her parents came rushing from the living room. Raina leaned against the wall with a smirk, her phone aimed toward Arjun and Madhuri in case she needed to capture a Snapchatable moment.

"Now that Arjun's here, can you tell us your news?" her mother asked all in one breath. "Josie called to tell us about how she's a Berkeley Regent and we've been screaming ever since. I need to know if we should be reacting in the same way for Madhu, too."

"You know, I'm surprised we didn't get a noise complaint from the neighbors," Raina called out, her tiny laugh muffled by the distance separating them.

Her father lifted a brow, wrapping an arm around his wife. "Is there anything you want to tell us, Madhuri?" he asked with a hopeful glint in his smile.

Being able to see her parents on the edge of their seats, waiting to celebrate her greatest success with her, was unforgettable. Even in a family like hers that was always ready to talk about their feelings, Madhuri didn't often see many sides of her parents' emotions. She knew them as responsible and strong, lighthearted and loving. They were always open, destroying boundaries with each dinner-table conversation. Still, as their child, Madhuri never saw the sheer amount of hope they had for her. She knew they'd kept it from her on purpose, so as not to put too much pressure on her, but watching her parents in that moment was eye-opening.

Madhuri paused, trying to commit every detail in front of

her to memory. She never wanted to forget the expression on her parents' faces, the smile that was practically glued to Arjun's lips, or the swagger in Raina's walk as she joined their parents in the living room. She knew, much like her first kiss, this would be a moment she'd be unable to shake, no matter how hard she tried.

"I got into Berkeley!" Madhuri screamed. She took a running start and jumped into her father's arms, crushing him in an all-encompassing hug.

Her father faltered, perhaps out of the initial shock of her words, before tightening his arms around her. For the first time in her seventeen years, Madhuri witnessed him cry. She didn't directly see it, but she felt the tears hit her bare shoulder as they held each other. Her mother joined them within seconds, shouting various forms of congratulations into the open air.

Raina and Arjun watched them with bright faces from the sidelines, waiting patiently for their own time with Madhuri. Being surrounded by the most important people in her life lit her heart up like a long-forgotten chandelier. Madhuri noticed how effortlessly they all complemented each other, whether that be in their happiest moments or in their saddest.

This moment just so happened to be both.

Madhuri felt her mother slowly pull away from their hug. She continued to cling on to her father with both eyes closed until she heard Raina scream in terror. By the time Madhuri turned to where her mother was standing, she had already fallen to the ground.

Her mother was hunched over herself, her body lurching as she attempted to throw up the substance that caused her such pain in the first place. Her father was beside her, rubbing her back and whispering comforting words.

Raina sprinted into the house to find their mother's medication, a heap of larger-than-life pills stuffed into an orange prescription bottle. She shouted orders over her shoulder, first to Arjun to find the car keys to their Honda Pilot. Everyone in her family had a purpose, a goal to achieve before her mother made it to the hospital and was under a professional's care.

Everyone except for Madhuri, who was frozen pathetically in place.

Raina threw a duffel bag into the trunk of their SUV. It was their emergency bag filled with spare water bottles, acid-reflux tablets, and solid food that didn't upset her mother's stomach—specifically idli and coconut chutney. They were on strict doctor's orders to destroy any citrus-adjacent foods from their family diet, such as oranges or pasta sauce, if they didn't want her mother to risk another flare-up. They'd been so careful for so many years, and her mother still became sick.

"Madhuri!" Raina shouted from the passenger seat window as Arjun and her father carried her mother into the back seat of the Honda. "If you don't get in this car right now, we're leaving without you!"

Madhuri couldn't bring herself to move. Her toes turned to magma, sinking deep into the ground beneath her. Her eyes darted around her surroundings, trying to make sense of how the happiest moment of her life could turn nasty within seconds—how the strongest person she knew, the woman who would walk to the ends of the Earth for her family, was punished for no reason. And just like that, gravity strangled her family out of Cloud Nine and sent them careening face-first into the dirt.

Her mother had been right all along. No matter how hard people tried to run away from their destiny, it would always catch up to them. Her mother could battle Crohn's with countless medications or diet lists, but at the end of the day, the disease was inevitably going to send her to the hospital. It was simply a matter of when.

Arjun left the steering wheel and stormed out of the car, his eyebrows furrowed into a haphazard line.

"You've left me no choice, Madhuri," he whispered before picking her up by the calves and swinging her over his shoulder like a fireman.

She'd normally fight with him to put her down. After all, she was a strong and independent woman. Surely, she could manage walking to a car on her own. But Madhuri didn't have the strength to move, let alone beat her fists against his back in an attempt to free herself. She allowed him to drop her in the car beside her mother and father without a word. Her silence continued as Arjun drove them to the nearest hospital, muttering random swears under his breath in Hindi.

Their eyes met in the rearview mirror and a shiver ran through her body. Judging by the creased stress lines in his forehead, Madhuri could tell that Arjun felt her deepest fear, too—that her family was not going to be happy again for a long time.

CHAPTER TWENTY-NINE

arjun

"Do you know anything yet?" Madhuri whispered.

Arjun studied the hospital waiting room with incredible precision, mentally noting every detail ranging from the color of the walls (a dull shade of bluish gray) to the unmistakable scent of bleach that wafted through the air. A pile of magazines was stacked in a tower on the table beside them. In the corner was a potted plant that Arjun believed would've been dead if it weren't plastic to begin with. The waiting room was decisively dull, a frustrating limbo between sickness and health, a seesaw that was always teetering toward the side of heartbreak.

The last time Arjun visited an emergency room, he was checked in as a concussion patient. At first glance, nothing had changed since that moment. He was still frightened by the environment, still missing a mother who would care for him at his most vulnerable. And yet there was one painful difference between then and now—Auntie Iyer.

If Madhuri could hear his thoughts, she'd call him a total dramatic. They'd done their research on Auntie Iyer's disease and it wasn't going to kill her. She might not be sitting beside him, comforting him the way she had after his brain injury, but that didn't mean she was gone forever. Still, losing his own mother no more than a few hours ago made Auntie Iyer's condition seem unnecessarily critical. He couldn't afford to lose her, too.

Arjun turned to his left shoulder, where Madhuri's head rested. She'd dozed in and out of sleep ever since they'd checked into the hospital, exhausted from the night's events. If he focused on the sharp edge of her brow, he could still see a line of sparkles.

"I haven't heard any updates, but the doctor should be out soon."

Madhuri sighed and slipped her hand into his, giving it a squeeze before she turned her expression back to stone. "I'm really glad you're here, Arjun. I don't know how I would've handled this situation without you."

"Well, I hope you'll never have to find out." He pressed his lips to the side of her head. "As long as it's up to me, I know I'll be here for good."

Madhuri pulled away from him, her eyebrows drawing into a thin line as if she was trying to understand his tone. The shift in her emotions happened so quickly that Arjun feared he'd suffer from whiplash. It was so similar to how she'd closed herself off after their fight in freshman year. "What do you mean by that?"

"I mean we're going to be in Northern California together after high school," he said, his eyebrows furrowing into a thick line. "We won't be separated anymore."

Arjun watched as a storm passed over Madhuri's face, a thundercloud brewing in the dent of her long-gone dimples. She chewed on the inside of her cheek as she fell silent again, deep in thought as she calculated a response. His heart screamed for her to take mercy on him, praying that she wouldn't use her words as a dagger, stabbing through his heart the way they always did. There were only a finite number of times he'd be able to heal from the wound.

"Why do you think we'll never be separated again?" Madhuri asked, her eyes boring into his with an unmatched intensity. "What's your guarantee?"

Arjun wanted to tell her that he loved her, and that feeling was his guarantee. There was no way Madhuri could fight something as extreme as his emotions, but Arjun would never forgive himself if he wielded his love against her as a weapon of self-defense. That would make him no better than his mother.

"My guarantee is us, Madhuri," he retorted. "Aren't we a real relationship? Aren't our feelings strong enough to anchor us through anything?"

She raked a hand through her hair and Arjun noticed the tremor in her fingertips. He wondered when he had gained the power to make the confident, unbreakable Madhuri shake like that. "I know our feelings are strong, but I walked into this relationship under the expectation that we would break up at the proper time. I wasn't aware that had changed in your mind."

His temper ignited. He'd been patient with Madhuri for years. Every single time he found a way to get over her, she pulled him back in. He felt like he'd become her unwavering safety net, always there but unused unless absolutely necessary.

And that was the catch. Arjun never was necessary. Not to Madhuri, not to his mother, not to anyone.

"Let me get this straight." Arjun paused, willing his heartbeat to slow down before he said something he didn't fully mean, didn't completely think through. "You're going to Berkeley and I'm going to Stanford. We're going to be thirty minutes away from each other, instead of hundreds of miles apart like we expected, but you're still breaking up with me after graduation? You're ready to lose everything we have because of an experiment? Because you'd rather have your hypothesis win over mine?"

"You agreed to that experiment!" Madhuri responded with a slight rise of her voice. When she received a stern look from the front desk receptionist, she settled back down into her seat. "I'm not in a position to carry our relationship into college, no matter how real it may be. I don't think I'm ready for that level of commitment at the age of seventeen."

Arjun crossed his arms over his chest. He was tired of letting Madhuri be the one girl who could walk all over him and suffer no consequences. His mother didn't even have that luxury. "What are you waiting for, then? If you know you're not ready to fight for the long run, why are you still stringing me along?"

"What are you insinuating, Arjun?" Madhuri asked, softening her tone. When Arjun looked at her closely, he could see a tear sparkling in her right eye.

Arjun knew that if he made one wrong decision, he might lose Madhuri forever. He'd already lost his mother, and Auntie Iyer might be following in her path soon. He wasn't sure if alienating his best friend, his last anchor to a family that wanted him as much as he wanted them, was the right thing to do. And yet Arjun wondered if that was exactly why he should break up with Madhuri. If he truly loved her, he wouldn't keep her around with ulterior motives.

"I'm asking you to let me go."

"Now?" Madhuri hissed, her fury evident in the way she met his gaze. He heard the betrayal in her voice a little too clearly, and he didn't blame her for it. He was abandoning her in a dreary hospital, forcing her to cope with her mother's sickness on her own. He'd hate him, too. "Do you really think we should break up when my sick mother is literally on the other side of this room?"

He saw a patient's family turn toward them with dirty looks. Arjun had to de-escalate the situation before Madhuri started to yell, so he pulled her into his arms, breathing in the scent of her rose shampoo as if it were the last time. She didn't struggle and, instead, relaxed into him. He heard her sniffle into the fabric of his flannel.

"You've never needed me in the past and you're positive that you don't in the future, either, so why do you need me now? If you let me go, I'll have the time to learn how to live without you. I think I deserve that."

"Is this why you were being so weird last night? Before my Berkeley announcement?" She rested her chin on his chest, staring up at him with those endlessly dark eyes of hers. A fresh set of tears sparkled on the edge of her lashes before falling onto the crest of her cheek. They sank into her skin until they disappeared from his sight for good. "You didn't seem like yourself."

"My mother came home and we had a pretty rough conversation. I was still processing when I got to your house." He hadn't talked about his confrontation with his mother yet, not out loud, at least. It was painful, a fresh wound that hadn't healed. "I promise, my sadness wasn't about you."

Madhuri pressed her forehead to his. Her eyes fluttered shut when she spoke again, her words beautiful in the most haunting way. "I'm so sorry, Arjun. About everything."

"Don't be sorry," he whispered to the tune of their breaking hearts, falling apart in silent unison. "You're always going to be my person."

"And you'll never stop being mine."

Auntie Iyer's doctor made her way into the waiting room. She rested a plain clipboard against her hip, identifying Madhuri as the patient's family within seconds. Raina and Uncle Iyer had gone back to the house to pick up a few things for Auntie Iyer once she was allowed visitors, leaving Arjun and Madhuri to hold down the fort at the hospital. He'd spent hours waiting for the doctor's update on Auntie Iyer's condition, but now that it was here, he couldn't concentrate.

The doctor's voice crumbled into static white noise. Madhuri sent Arjun a sideways stare, giving him a chance to speak up the way he typically did, before taking charge of the situation herself. She engaged in a conversation with the doctor, and even though Madhuri exuded confidence, Arjun could sense that her sudden onset of strength was mostly fake in the aftermath of their breakup.

Sitting back in his chair as Madhuri regained control of her surroundings, Arjun felt the exhaustion rumbling through his skeleton. Everything from their situation to Madhuri herself drained the energy straight out of his bones. He wanted to make excuses for her, to argue that she was hurting him because her mother's illness hurt her first. He despised how she kissed him as if they were the only two people in the world and how that was all it took to make him feel special—how they always found each other, whether that be a result of their hard work or the power of something much greater than them.

Most of all, Arjun Mehta hated how much he loved Madhuri Iyer.

CHAPTER THIRTY

madhuri

Madhuri didn't feel the pain of Arjun's absence until she was sitting on her mother's bed an hour after their breakup, watching her sleep in silence. She cast a wayward glance over her shoulder, hoping that her silent pining would manifest him back into their room. Save for a nurse scrambling from door to door, the hospital hallway was empty.

Arjun wasn't coming back.

It was downright exhausting to exist when he wasn't in her life. Everything reminded her of him, from the coffee Raina was drinking to the bright yellow friendship bracelet on her wrist. Arjun tainted each aspect of her life, forever branding his smile on the edges of her mind.

She was pathetically and utterly consumed by the ever-present memory of him.

Madhuri knew she was being selfish. She'd gotten exactly what she wanted: an experimental, fake relationship that ended without any real drama. She'd defeated the Universe and proved her hypothesis correct at the expense of Arjun's heart. And yet here she was, pining for a boy who she once guaranteed she'd never fall in love with, a man who'd slowly transformed himself from a best friend into something so much more. But Madhuri couldn't think about that now, not when her mother needed her the most. Her feelings for Arjun, whatever they were, would have to wait.

"When do you think she's going to wake up?"

Raina released a sigh from the thin space between her lips. Her phone buzzed with a missed call from Aditya, and her sister turned the ringer on silent, shifting her attention back to Madhuri. "I'm not sure, but it's not like she's in a coma or anything. I'm not worried."

Madhuri looked at her father, who was sprawled over the mangy brown couch in the corner of the room with his legs hanging off the armrest. Raina sat at the foot of their mother's bed, her shoulder grazing Madhuri's every few seconds. In both of their hands was a steaming plastic cup of coffee, bitter and nearly impossible to swallow.

"You're not scared?" Madhuri asked. "I've never seen Amma like this before, and honestly, I think I'll have nightmares about this hospital for a while."

"I'm terrified, but my feelings really don't change the situation." When Raina paused, Madhuri took the moment to admire her sister's maturity. "What Amma needs is for her family to be strong. Appa is going to be preoccupied with the emotional and financial burden of the hospital visit, so it's up to us to make this situation as easy as possible for them."

"You two don't need to do anything," her mother said, propping her body up against two hard pillows. Judging by the ghost of a smile dancing across her cracked lips, Kamala Iyer had been listening to their conversation the entire time. "In fact, nothing changes. Raina, you're still in charge of the dishes every night, and, Madhuri, you're on meal-prep duty for our lunches. Your father and I will manage the bills just fine on our own."

"I can get a job, Amma," Raina offered, returning her mother's stare with a pair of pleading eyes. "I think Target is hiring, and you've always said how I'm a naturally talented salesperson. Besides, once I perform at Josie's talent show and complete my Arangetram this summer, I'll be done with dance. Think about all the free time I'll have on my hands."

"Your only job is to focus on your education. There's no need to overwork yourself with a part-time job at this age, especially not when your father and I have a perfect grasp on our finances as it is." Her mother gave them a stern shake of her head. "Look at your sister, Raina. She didn't distract herself with a job and she was accepted into Berkeley. I wouldn't want you to compromise a similar future because of one little hospital visit."

Her father choked on his own snore and scrambled to his feet as he woke up, his attention immediately gravitating toward the hospital bed where his wife lectured his two daughters. A grin split his face in half as he pulled a chair up to them.

Madhuri lifted an eyebrow, contemplating the multiple

paths that their conversation could take. She could spill the truth about Tillys and suffer the immediate consequences, such as the risk of sending her mother to the hospital all over again—this time with a shock-induced heart attack. She could also continue her lie and anonymously donate her secondary income to her family when the hospital bill arrived in their mailbox. Either way, Madhuri knew that her mother would find out about her part-time job eventually.

"I have to tell you something," Madhuri said after a moment of consideration, drawing her words out like an incriminated toddler. "I've actually had a job since tenth grade."

Silence fell over the room like a suffocating blanket and a rush of adrenaline pounded between Madhuri's ears. The Iyer family was never quiet unless they were preparing to scream, and Madhuri was about to be on the receiving end of a volcanic eruption. Her father noticed the tension rising in the room and made a poor attempt to calm her mother by running his fingers through her hair, but she swatted him away. Her mother narrowed her line of vision on Madhuri, her chest rising and falling at a heightened pace.

"You've been lying to us?" her mom whispered, her fingertips digging into her husband's arm. When he yelped in pain, she retracted her claws and clenched them into a solid fist.

Madhuri exchanged a look of pure fear with Raina, who deftly avoided eye contact. She bit her lip, trying to string together a thoughtful explanation. "You two have been so determined to pay for my college education and I'm so thankful for that, but I wanted to lighten that financial burden as much as I could. Now that we have this extra bill to pay on

top of my Berkeley student loans, I think my secondary income will be helpful."

Her father cocked his head to the side as if he were considering her words. "What have you been doing with your
money all this time?"

Madhuri averted her gaze to the white wall behind her
mother, devoid of all color but a singular beige couch resting
against the plaster. "I had Josie's mother make me a savings
account when I received my first paycheck, and I will recover
full control over it on my eighteenth birthday. Every single
penny has been saved."

Her mother shot her father a pointed look. "Your financial responsibility doesn't change the fact that you directly
went against our only rule and lied to our faces for almost
three years."

"I'm not going to apologize for trying to give back to my
family. I don't think I did anything wrong in trying to help."

Her mother let out a frustrated groan. "I'm not taking your
money, Madhuri."

"I'm not giving it to you," she retorted. "I'm taking the
loan out on my own name."

Raina gasped when she heard Madhuri talk back to their
parents. Madhuri cut her eyes at her in warning and Raina
sank into herself, intensely focusing on her now-cold coffee.

Her father took Madhuri's hand in his. "I understand that
you want to help us, Madhu, and I'm so proud of you for
it." His voice cracked ever so slightly, an emotional tic that
Madhuri couldn't help but pick up on. She'd inherited the
same one. "However, you won't be taking the loan on your
own. Our job as your parents is to support you until you can

support yourself, and while you're on your way to stability, you're not there yet."

The bags under her mother's eyes bulged when she sighed. It was easy to see her body crying for rest, but she would always be an active person, whether that be intellectually or physically. Having an intense argument with her daughter offered a sense of normalcy to their lives, and for once, Madhuri was grateful for her mother's limitless energy.

"I've raised you well," her mother murmured under her breath, and Madhuri's face brightened at the rare sound of her praise. "That doesn't excuse the fact that you've been lying to us, though, so I'm grounding you for a week."

Madhuri grinned. "I'd love that."

Her mother laughed, and the entire room seemed to come alive. Madhuri watched as flowers sprouted from the medical emergency button hidden behind her mother's head, brightening the room with yellow petals. She knew it was a figment of her imagination, but it was the first burst of color she'd seen since Arjun left.

"What do you think, Dev?" her mother asked with a playful lift of her brow. "Should we channel a typical American-parenting style and stop her from seeing Arjun for a few days?"

The flowers lost their shine, wilting into the ground at the sound of Arjun's name. Their vines curled into the corners of her imagination and Madhuri's vision turned back to gray. Maybe that was what compelled her to invite yet another argument into their conversation, especially after she'd gotten off with nothing more than a warning when it came to her part-time job. Madhuri lifted her gaze to meet that of her parents, and Raina squeezed her hand as if she were nonverbally encouraging her to continue.

It was time to put *The Kismat Experiment* to rest once and for all.

"Actually, you don't need to worry about Arjun." Madhuri pulled her backpack into her lap and ruffled through it in search of *The Kismat Experiment*. Once she found the sheet of paper, crumpled up and stained with makeup from when Raina had confronted her at the wedding, she handed it to her mother. "We're not together anymore."

Madhuri watched as her parents read each page slowly, waves of betrayal passing over their faces. Her father whispered their hypotheses under his breath, testing each syllable as if he couldn't believe his daughter was the one to have written them, and her mother's eyebrows furrowed together the way they always did before she cried.

"You lied to us *again*?" her father asked, his fingers clenched around the paper. "Don't you feel any shame for your actions? For experimenting at the expense of a boy's heart?"

"I'm sorry. I was so lost in wanting to prove *you* wrong—" Madhuri nodded at her mother "—that I didn't realize how badly I'd messed up. I wanted to take charge of my own future, and I thought that I could do that by destroying my prophecy with this experiment," Madhuri said, and she wondered if Arjun knew that he had succeeded in making her fall for him despite all her schemes. "I didn't think I'd ever like Arjun as more than a friend, either, but after our date at the wedding, I knew I couldn't keep this up any longer. I planned to abandon the experiment, but then Stanford happened."

Her mother shook her head. "I don't understand. What does Stanford have to do with your relationship with Arjun?"

"When Stanford rejected me, I realized that my prophecy had come true—you predicted that I would fail academically, and I did. I felt like I was at the mercy of my destiny, like my free will was completely nonexistent in the grand scheme of the Universe. In that moment, I decided that the only chance I had to disprove my prophecy was through my relationships, which were still unharmed by your predictions. I also realized that I could use *The Kismat Experiment* to end our family curse as well. Two birds, one stone."

"For the love of Krishna, not this curse business again!" her mother exclaimed, her face turning a furious shade of red. Madhuri knew her mother wasn't messing around, because for any kind of pigmentation to show on her dark brown skin, she'd have to be incredibly emotional. "You cannot use an innocent human being to disobey your family or your destiny. There's no way for you to escape what is meant for you, no matter how hard you try to fight against it."

Madhuri's eyes brimmed with tears, and she willed herself not to let them fall down her cheeks. "There has to be a way," she whispered, gripping on to the covers of the hospital bed with every ounce of strength she could muster. "Free will has to exist. What's the point of living if I'm not the one in control?"

"It does exist. You chose how to react to your astrological reading, and your decisions are what proved it correct. You single-handedly manifested my predictions into existence, especially those regarding your relationships, when you decided to hurt Arjun for your own advantage and when you chose to lie to us for months on end." Her mother sighed. "I expected more from you, Madhuri. I expected that whenever you were overwhelmed by your place in the Universe, you would come to us. That would always be better than concocting a high-strung dating experiment to spite the entire Iyer lineage."

She sniffed, letting her head fall into her mother's lap. After a moment of hesitation, she felt her mother's fingers in her hair. "Well, it's over now. I lost Arjun, I broke your trust, and I've learned my lesson. I'll never fight the Universe again."

A stiff silence passed through the room before her mother spoke up. Her voice was so quiet that Madhuri wasn't sure if she'd heard her correctly when she said, "But you don't know Arjun's destiny. It may counteract yours."

Madhuri picked up her head, and a spark of hope passed through her heart. "What do you know about his prophecy, Amma?"

"That's confidential." Her mother placed a kiss to her forehead, and Madhuri calmed back down, knowing better than to push her mother's patience any further. "I'm glad you finally decided to confide in us. While there might not be any way to fix this mess of yours, I hope you know that we're always on your side."

"You're still grounded, though," her father added, before turning to Raina, who'd conveniently gone silent over the course of their conversation. "And you're grounded, too."

Raina cried out in dismay. "But I didn't do anything!"

"I know you knew about the experiment, too." Her father chuckled to himself as if he were more so amused by his youngest daughter rather than actually upset with her. "You aided and abetted your sister, so you'll have to suffer the consequences."

"Thanks a lot, Akka." Raina cut her eyes at her, but Madhuri didn't have the energy to bite back with a snarky response of her own.

Madhuri desperately wanted a moment of peace, a moment to dream of Arjun—his smile, his laugh, and everything in between. She knew he wasn't coming back, but for some reason, she couldn't manage to get him out of her head. And while it was a breath of fresh air to not be lying to her parents anymore, it didn't help her come to terms with the breakup.

Her heartache didn't seem like it would ever fade.

CHAPTER THIRTY-ONE

arjun

"You don't have to hide in the hallway, you know," Auntie Iyer said. "I'm alone."

Arjun stepped into the light, leaning his tense back against the door to Auntie Iyer's room. He cringed when the combined scent of hospital Jell-O and Clorox reached his nose.

Auntie Iyer lifted a brow at his facial expression. "Do I smell that bad?" When he responded with only a half-hearted chuckle, Auntie Iyer spoke again, this time with concern replacing the teasing lilt to her voice. "What's wrong, Arjun?"

"Nothing. I'm worried about you, that's all." Arjun took another cautious step into the room. He searched the area for any sign of Madhuri, waiting for her pastel-pink scrunchie to hit him in the face out of nowhere. Once he'd guaranteed his safety, he settled onto the brown couch beside Auntie Iyer's bed, pulling his legs to his chest like an anxious six-year-old.

"Yeah, right." Auntie Iyer snorted. "I know you and Madhuri broke up. You don't have to hide that from me because I'm sick."

Arjun thought he'd become used to Auntie Iyer's deadly combination of mind reading and brutal honesty, but she continued to catch him off guard every day. His childhood was spent running around her home, stealing desserts from the pantry and tormenting her daughter, and he still remembered the way she'd stare as he narrowly missed the ugly vase standing beside their staircase. If he could withstand all those years under Auntie Iyer's watchful eyes, it was no surprise that she knew him better than anyone else.

"How are you feeling, Auntie?" Arjun asked, forcing a smile to his lips. He couldn't talk about the breakup yet. It still didn't feel real. "How's your stomach?"

"I know you're changing the subject and I'll allow it for now, but don't expect me to let it go completely," Auntie Iyer warned. "I'm okay, beta. I've dealt with much worse."

"Just because you've had worse doesn't mean this hurts any less."

"I could say the same to you."

Arjun's heart slammed out of his chest. It was only a matter of time before Auntie Iyer pried the full extent of his post-breakup emotions out of him. "What is that supposed to mean?"

"It means that you don't have to stay strong for me or for Madhuri or for yourself. You're allowed to be hurt by the breakup without comparing it in significance to your parents leaving you." Auntie Iyer's eyes held a distinct emotion in them that he couldn't figure out.

"I know you're a psychiatrist, but you don't need to turn me into one of your patients."

Auntie Iyer clicked her tongue. "I'm trying to be there for you, Arjun. Trust me, the last thing I want to be is your stand-in mother, astrologer, *and* therapist."

The *M* word sent a pang of pain through his chest. He clutched the fabric of his shirt, trying to make the images of his mother disappear from his brain. When her frowning face stayed firmly in place, Arjun knew he'd have to kick her out with another *M* word, one that was possibly much worse.

"How'd you find out about the breakup? Did Madhuri tell you?" Arjun asked, his voice cracking over each syllable of her name. He looked over his shoulder, trying to calm the rapid uptick in his heart rate as he thought about what he'd do if he saw Madhuri walk into the room. "Speaking of, where is she?"

Auntie Iyer pulled herself up so that she was sitting on the bed with her legs crossed. Arjun noticed the dark circles under her eyes and the wrinkles rippling through her forehead. For the first time, Auntie Iyer didn't seem invincible. There was something painfully human about her, so much so that Arjun could see Madhuri's reflection in her.

"Cafeteria. Poor girl hasn't eaten for hours on end." Auntie Iyer held her hand out to him, a silent invitation for him to sit beside her. Her fingertips wavered slightly, weakened by her illness and the dreary white walls she was subjected to. Arjun squeezed her hand as he settled into a space at the foot of her bed, his legs dangling off the edge. "She did tell me about the breakup, but even if she hadn't, I would've known what had happened the minute she sat down in the spot you're sitting in right now."

"And why do you say that?"

"In the past seventeen years, I'd never seen Madhuri handle a problem without you there to glue her back together." Auntie Iyer sighed. "She was sitting alone for the first time today. That's enough proof, don't you think?"

Arjun tried to imagine Madhuri sitting by herself at the foot of her sick mother's bed, but his mind wouldn't let him. He was left there to wonder if she'd had tears in her eyes, or if she wished they could take back everything they'd said if only to be there for each other now.

It'd been hours since the breakup, and Arjun couldn't envision Madhuri anymore. He didn't know what he'd do if Madhuri became a stranger to him after all these years, and he couldn't imagine a world where he couldn't remember the exact pattern in which her hair curled or how her eyes would darken seconds before her temper flared.

He wanted to tell Auntie Iyer everything, if only to bring Madhuri's face, a beige canvas of sharp lines and jagged edges, back to the forefront of his mind, where it belonged.

"Madhuri told me the truth. She doesn't want to continue our relationship into college." Arjun shrugged, twirling his fingers through the hospital sheets until they bunched into an uncomfortable pile. Auntie Iyer swatted his hand away with a stern expression. "I couldn't handle it anymore. I'm tired of chasing after her and never getting anything in return. I feel like that makes me selfish, but maybe it's a sign that we're better off as friends."

"I understand exactly where you're coming from. Madhuri

played with your emotions for years, and it doesn't make you selfish to want more than that."

"I can't believe you're on my side. Isn't that a conflict of interest?" Arjun's voice softened as he thought back to his own mother, who'd believed Madhuri's rejection from Stanford meant he'd have the same fate. His own mother, who never supported him unless it was out of guilt. How was Auntie Iyer so different?

"I love Madhuri endlessly, but that doesn't mean I can't tell right from wrong." Auntie Iyer smiled at him. "You're choosing yourself, Arjun, and you can't do that if you let my daughter control you. I think she and I both understand that. We won't hold it against you."

"If you knew that she'd end up hurting me and I'd have to let her go, why'd you let her date me in the first place? Aren't you supposed to protect me?" The *like a mother* at the end of his sentence was implied, a ghost of a phrase that died on his lips before it could be spoken. Arjun knew that nothing he could say would pressure Auntie Iyer into a title if she didn't want it herself, so there was no point in even speaking it into existence.

"Sadly, I wasn't privy to this so-called experiment until a few hours ago." Auntie Iyer sighed. "And even if I had known in advance, there's only so much a mother can do if her words go in one ear and out the other. I know my daughter, and she tends to learn her lesson *after* she's hurt herself and others, never before."

Arjun's resolve crumbled. He didn't have the strength to continue untangling Madhuri's complicated actions, nor did he want to keep finding someone else to blame. They were broken up for a reason. He'd have to cut his losses and move on.

"You know, I'd always thought falling in love would be this beautiful thing, like how Shah Rukh Khan breaks into dance when Kajol reciprocates his feelings. I thought I deserved a Bollywood romance like that, a happily-ever-after for the rest of my life."

"You're in love?" Auntie Iyer responded. Her eyes weren't wide the way they would be if she were surprised. Arjun knew that Auntie Iyer had known his feelings long before he had, but even so, saying it out loud didn't seem right. If he admitted that he loved Madhuri, it would only make their situation that much more real—the girl of his dreams was gone, and he was the one to let her go in the first place.

"You don't have to say anything you don't want to. But if you're worried about being too late, please listen to me carefully. Love is never on time, and that's exactly what makes it worth fighting for. You can't predict when it'll happen or how, but once it does, you owe it to yourself to embrace it."

Arjun sighed. "How am I supposed to embrace a love that ended before I even had a chance to see it through?"

"You don't know if it's ended for good. You and Madhuri both have a lifetime of experiences ahead of you, so who's to say that the love can't come back again in the future?"

"That's awfully optimistic, you know."

"If there's one phrase I would use to describe you, it's 'awfully optimistic.'" Auntie Iyer placed a gentle hand on his cheek. "Don't let this experiment or my daughter or even my readings—which are perfect, by the way—make you forget who you are, beta."

Arjun laughed, and for the first time in a long while, it didn't feel forced. "Alright, Auntie Iyer, you've convinced me. I love Madhuri, and that, too, in the most hopeless, awfully optimistic sort of way."

Auntie Iyer tried to stay serious, but Arjun saw her lips twitch. Slowly, she started to grin, and it seemed like she was proud of him—for choosing to love even if it wasn't reciprocated, for being fearless even if Madhuri wasn't. Maybe that was Arjun's wishful thinking, but he really did believe Auntie Iyer appreciated him and all the ways in which he was the polar opposite to her daughter.

"You know, you've truly redefined what it means to experience an unrequited love."

"Was that a joke?" Arjun asked, withholding the urge to playfully roll his eyes at her. He had to remember that Auntie Iyer wasn't his real mother. He couldn't treat her the way Madhuri did, not when Auntie Iyer could kick him out of her life at the drop of a hat. He had to remember that he needed the Iyers much more than they needed him, especially now that he and Madhuri weren't together anymore.

Auntie Iyer's facial features softened. Her eyebrows curved down instead of forming a tightly threaded arch. "You're right—that was insensitive of me," she whispered. "I guess I wanted to see that smile of yours again."

He flashed his shining teeth at her on an impulse. It was more of a mockery of her request than a true smile, and Auntie Iyer had to have known that. Nevertheless, she let it slide.

"Happy?" Arjun teased, still grinning wildly at her.

She shook her head. "No. I'm not going to be happy as long as you're hurting."

"You don't need to worry about that anymore. Once you're discharged, I think I'm going to stay at my house for a while. I should give Madhuri and your family some space to heal together."

"Your timing has always been the absolute worst, Arjun."

"What is that supposed to mean?"

Auntie Iyer clicked her tongue, her face turning smug. She reached for her bag, which was sitting atop the nightstand beside her bed, and Arjun nudged it toward her.

"It means that you need to have a little more faith in the people who love you," Auntie Iyer said. She dug around in her bag and Arjun's ear picked up the distinct sound of metal clinking together. After a few agonizing seconds passed, she pulled a singular silver key out of her bag and held it out to him. "This is for you."

Arjun gingerly accepted the token, turning it over in his palm as he inspected every inch of it. Etched into the metal of the key was his name written in cursive followed by a star. He ran his fingers over the engraving as he tried his best to contain his excitement. Did the key represent what he thought it did, or was it more of a sorry-my-daughter-led-you-on-for-years gift? He tore his gaze away from the key and faced Auntie Iyer, who was smiling at him.

"Thank you," Arjun started slowly, drawing out his words as if he weren't quite sure how to continue their conversation. "What's this for? Did Madhuri tell you about what happened with my mother?"

"No, she didn't. It seems that I'm damn good with lucky guesses." Auntie Iyer tossed her bag to the side. Her energy seemed to be coming back to her one sentence at a time. "To answer your question, this is a key to our home. We should've made this for you years ago and I apologize for that, but I thought I'd give it to you now."

"I really can't accept this. I can't live with your family after Madhuri and I broke up." Arjun sighed, willing away the guilt etched into his bones. "And even if you didn't know about my mom and I, this seems like a pity gift, and that's the last thing I want."

Auntie Iyer's eyes shone, neon beams of light reflecting off her irises. "No matter what happens between you and Madhuri, you will always be one of us—and I promise you, that's not out of pity. This key only ensures that you'll never be on your own again. You don't have to use it if you don't want to, but you deserve to have it regardless."

A tingling sensation coursed through Arjun's fingertips. Every inch of his body was telling him to let go, to celebrate the moment he became a part of the home he'd always admired from afar. His heart broke the restraints of his chest, glowing like a thousand stars in the sky. His eyes filled with tears, the kind that shone with pure emotion, and for once, he wasn't trying to stop them from falling.

"I've never had a family like yours before," Arjun whispered. "What if I ruin it?"

Family. The word felt so foreign to him. By definition, his family consisted of his mother, his father, and him, and the Iyers didn't fall into that description. They might have been the only people who were always there for him, but it wasn't like they shared the same blood. There was nothing concrete tying them together, no biological proof or ulterior motives, which meant that the Iyers *chose* him. For some unknown reason, they made the choice to accept him into their family despite his baggage, to love him unconditionally as if he were one of their own.

"How could you ruin something you've been a part of your whole life?" Auntie Iyer responded with a soft smile. "Our family isn't complete without you."

He remembered when Madhuri would let him into their

home to sleep because his heater had conked off, turning his bed to ice. He remembered making Maggi noodles with Uncle Iyer after every driving lesson they had together before his exam. He spent a lifetime wasting their precious resources and consistent love, and he didn't think he could justify the strain any longer. Besides, he'd finally grown used to the silence of his own home, to sudden appearances and disappearances, to only caring about himself because that was the only way to survive. Was the key worth risking another lost love at the expense of his hard-earned security?

Auntie Iyer closed his palm around the key, patting the top of his hand with the lightest touch. "I understand that this is a lot to think about, so take your time. I'm not expecting an answer from you right away, but whether you accept the key or not, never forget that you'll always have us in your life."

Arjun wanted to thank Auntie Iyer, but he couldn't quite find the right words. For the first time, he loved that she could read his mind so effortlessly. It saved him the anxiety of asking for time himself, of wondering if his request gave her another reason to leave him.

"Promise?"

"Cross my heart and hope to die."

"You better not," Arjun warned. "I need you around."

Auntie Iyer grinned. "The feeling's mutual."

CHAPTER THIRTY-TWO

madhuri

Madhuri's mother had a talent for spinning words into powerful sentences as if she were handling delicate thread. Each syllable slipped through her fingertips, weaving in and out of each other to form one colorful masterpiece after another. That magic string contained the stories of her parents, new immigrants finding their way in the United States, and the rest of her ancestors who'd created lives for themselves in India.

Sometimes, Madhuri would listen to the story of her grandmother and how she'd left her family behind to pursue a career in the culinary arts, succeeding despite all the odds stacked against women in that time period. She was only ever told that story when she was at her worst, demotivated and drowning under the pressure of a teenager with too many dreams to achieve in too little time. And when night fell, when she was tired and in need of reassurance, Madhuri listened to the story of how her parents fell in love, a lullaby that put her to sleep with a smile tugging at her lips.

Today, a week after they'd been discharged from the hospital and a week since she'd seen or spoken to Arjun, her mother wanted to tell their family a new story, one Madhuri and Raina had never heard before.

The Iyer family sat in front of their roaring fireplace, the wood crackling with dancing orange embers. Madhuri leaned forward until the heat wafting off the glass case of the fireplace hit her face. For the first time since the breakup, she didn't feel like she was seconds away from breaking into tears. The warmth of the fire numbed her, allowing her a minute to breathe without the absence of Arjun pulling her back into place.

Her elbow was balanced on her knee, propping her lifeless head up. She leaned in a little more with her eyes closed. Just as she felt the heat overwhelm her, an unknown source of wool scratched against her cheek. When she cracked an eye open, she saw Raina's sock-covered feet in her face. Her little sister let out a witchy cackle as she wiggled her toes, a stray lint ball falling off the fabric of the sock.

"Ew!" Madhuri screeched. She scrambled to the empty spot on the couch next to her mother, as far away from Raina as possible. "Amma, can you please tell Raina to not be so disgusting?"

Her mother ran her hand over Madhuri's hair, and that featherlight touch was all it took to calm her temper. "Will you focus on the story rather than your sister? I told you that you don't know this one yet."

Her father threw a pillow at Raina, who was still laughing to herself, and he tried to conjure up a stern glare to his face. "Both of you need to get it together. Let your mother speak."

"You're right—I should've been listening." Madhuri snapped herself out of the trance her mother created. She crossed one leg over the other, watching her mother with an intent gaze. "What's this about?"

Her mother offered her a soft smile. "I know you disagree with a lot of astrology, and interestingly enough, I was just like you as a child. I believed in hard science, not predictions made by a pandit who barely knew me."

Raina looked up from her phone with wide eyes. She dragged her chair into their makeshift circle, suddenly interested in the story. "I can't imagine Madhuri ever changing her mind, and she's less stubborn than you, Amma. What changed for you? What made you believe?"

"When I was sixteen, I was first sent to the hospital with Crohn's disease. No one in our family had ever had it before, and it was a genetic disease, so you can assume what kind of worry this stirred in your grandparents."

Madhuri watched her mother fidget with the edges of her kurta pants. She'd never seen her so restless. In fact, the nervous tic made her mother seem truly human. Madhuri would kill to catch those glimpses more often, if only to assure herself that she wasn't the only imperfect one in their family.

"During this time, your grandmother turned to the planets to help us. She'd spend the morning praying to Ganesha and the nights stargazing with your grandfather, trying to find a solution in my astrological placements. I didn't understand why she'd become so invested in something that was nothing more than an illusory correlation. I'd spend hours fighting with her, trying to convince her how ridiculous she looked to the world and, worst of all, to me."

Madhuri felt her heart drop. Was this what she'd subjected her own mother to over the years? Had she really humiliated her mother for her beliefs, for her unwillingness to accept reality at face value?

"I didn't understand her until we'd fought our most painful fight. I'd made the both of us cry, me from the exhaustion that came with my hospitalization and her from heartbreak. I'd called her names, questioned her methods, told her to spend her time elsewhere. At that point, your grandmother had just about had it with me. She wasn't going to waste her breath, so she tossed a booklet at my feet and stormed out of the house."

Madhuri heaved a heavy sigh. "Don't tell me..."

Her mother nodded, her lips thinning into a straight line. "It was my astrological chart, made for me at birth and painstakingly updated every month by my mother, who'd tracked the planets for me just like her mother had done for her. The chart predicted the major events of my lifetime, as well as a timeline for which they'll occur. I'd later come to realize that every single word written in that booklet came true, no matter how hard I tried to run away from it."

"What did it say about the Crohn's?" Raina asked.

"It told me the exact day I'd get hospitalized, as well as every hospital date following it."

Madhuri couldn't believe it. "You knew you'd fall sick on the night of Winter Formal?"

Her father covered for her mother, who seemed to be taken by a sudden wave of emotion. Perhaps the memory of their grandmother and the generations of women before her hurt her mother more than expected. "We knew. That's why our bag was packed ahead of time and why your mother needed to hear about Berkeley as soon as possible. She didn't want to be admitted without knowing."

"The reading is very clear that my Crohn's disease is a chronic condition, one that won't kill me but will definitely make my life a little more challenging. Anyway, that's not the point of this story," her mother said. "The point is that you can't run away from your destiny. Trust me, I tried. I did everything I could to prevent the next hospital visit once I'd read the booklet, and I only ended up pushing your grandmother away in the process."

Madhuri tried her best to control her temper, but there was no stopping the eruption once she'd heard her mother speak. "That is such complete bullshit!"

Her father opened his mouth, about to warn his daughter to watch her tone, when her mother waved him off with a stony expression. "Let her be. She needs to let her emotions out."

While her mother's condescending tone was hard to ignore, Madhuri pushed forward. She felt a flood of tears enter her eyes. Her true feelings were moments away from crushing her after being bottled up for years. She couldn't hold her tongue any longer.

"Just because it's meant to be doesn't mean it actually will be." Madhuri's voice edged its way to a scream as the first of many tears fell onto her cheek. "My chart told me that Arjun and I were written in the stars and our family curse promised me a happily-ever-after with him, but look at where we are now. I pushed him away too many times until I left him with no choice but to break up with me." Madhuri hesitated, unable to stomach just how vulnerable she was being. "This so-called destiny you're talking about? It might've worked for you, but it completely let me down. The Universe failed me."

Her mother placed a hand against Madhuri's cheek, letting her thumb catch the next tear. "Why are you so upset that your relationship with Arjun didn't follow our curse? Isn't that what you wanted from the very beginning?"

Madhuri wanted to explode. Her mind was overcome with a range of answers to her mother's question, all of which were important enough to be considered if it weren't for Arjun's gorgeous face. His smile shone through her brain like a ray of summer sun, distracting her from any kind of rational thought.

"Madhuri, do you love Arjun?"

Madhuri didn't know how to respond, not when she felt so lost in her own mind. Instead, Madhuri did what she knew best. She deflected. "That's not the point. I'm upset that you preach how correct our astrological readings are when they've never been right for me."

Her mother let out a sharp laugh. "You don't remember your chart, do you? You were destined to a year of mediocre grades, misunderstood emotions, and complicated relation-ships. Tell me that wasn't the case for you."

Madhuri groaned. "That's way too general to believe and you know it."

"Don't believe it, see if I care," her mother bit back. "If the stars have nothing to do with your life, you might as well try to understand what you can control and use that to fix what's gone wrong."

"Arjun doesn't want me back. Even if I wanted to change

things, I wouldn't be able to. It's too late for us, and no amount of planetary intervention can fix that."

Her father spoke after taking a back seat for much of their conversation. "Khanna, I need you to listen to me. If not to your mother, listen to me."

Madhuri hadn't been called *khanna* in years. The word meant *child* in Tamil, but despite its simple definition, there was something so protective about it. In the past, her father used the endearment when he needed her to feel comforted by more than a hug. If he was saying it now, it meant that her father thought she was about to break, and he was trying to soften her fall.

"You know the answer to your mother's question, Madhuri. You've always known." Her father placed a kiss to her cheek. "Even if it's too late, you need to tell Arjun how you feel. Even if you cannot love him in the sense you expect, he's your best friend and he deserves the truth."

"What if he hates me, Appa?" Madhuri asked quietly, trying not to hiccup on the force of her own tears.

"Arjun could never hate you. He's family."

"Also, if you tell him how you feel, you can finally say that you broke the family curse. There's no way Arjun's going to marry you after all of this drama," Raina added with a misplaced grin on her face.

Madhuri gasped. "Take that back right now."

Raina stuck her tongue out at her and hid behind their mother. "Never."

As she chased Raina around their house, their parents close behind them, Madhuri felt the tears slowly dry off her face. She wasn't any less heartbroken over Arjun or betrayed by

the influence the Universe had in their lives, but those feelings were suddenly easier to bear. In that moment, Madhuri
knew that even if she lost Arjun forever or failed miserably
at the talent show a few days from now, she'd have her family by her side.

That was more than enough.

Madhuri never thought she'd be here, standing outside of
Arjun's house with a box of Insomnia cookies in her hand and
an apology locked and loaded on her lips. She'd prepared her
words in advance, scripted on ruled note cards that were cur-
rently clipped together in the back pocket of her skinny jeans.
Her index finger hovered over the doorbell, buzzing with
anxious energy at the thought of seeing Arjun's face again.

The sharp edges of his jawline, and the way his eyes crin-
kled at the corners when he smiled, and how could she forget his hair—messy and unkempt and in desperate need of
styling. God, she'd happily volunteer her hands to the cause.

Madhuri was down *bad* for Arjun, and she couldn't help but
wonder if this was how he'd once felt about her. How did he
survive in the limbo of she-loves-me and she-loves-me-not?
They'd wasted so much time with her running away and his
second-guessing, and now Madhuri wanted nothing more
than to return to the beginning. She wanted a chance to see
Arjun for all he was before the Universe ripped them apart,
a do-over without the hypotheses and the variables.

"Please, please, please," Madhuri whispered, her eyes squeezed
shut as if she were offering a prayer. She pressed the doorbell
and faintly heard a dull chime echo through the house. The
sound of Arjun's feet scuffling toward the living room reached

her ears, and for a fleeting moment, Madhuri let herself hope that he had been waiting for her the entire time.

Arjun cracked open the front door, and his eyes immediately lasered on to her own. Madhuri felt herself go up in flames when she met his gaze, jolts of lightning zapping down her spine and through her veins. It had only been a week since their breakup, but seeing him again was enough for her to almost drop the box of cookies in her hand. Arjun made a move for the box, which teetered on the edge of her fingertips, but it toppled forward before he could catch it. Instead, his hands connected with hers, and she gasped at the immediate effect of his touch.

Her apology cookies tumbled out of the box, and a heap of crumbs littered his porch. Madhuri stared at the disaster surrounding them, her bottom lip quivering slightly. "Oh, Arjun, I am so sorry. I didn't mean to make such a mess."

"Why do I feel like the mess you're talking about isn't these cookies?" Arjun bit back a smile, and waved his hand toward his house. "Would you like to come inside? I've made a fresh pot of ginger chai with no elaichi."

"My favorite," Madhuri mused as she stepped over the carnage and entered his house. The hanging chandelier in the foyer was turned on, and the natural sunlight that streamed in through the windows reflected off the glass. She took note of the golden haze that fell over the room, forming a soft halo over Arjun's head.

"I know. I'm not sure what compelled me to make it, but maybe I had a feeling you'd show up today." He shrugged, walking over to the kitchen to strain the chai into two patterned mugs. Madhuri pulled herself up so she could sit on the edge of the marble island behind him. She swung her legs back and forth, hoping to release her anxiety through physical means, and when Arjun saw her, a sad expression passed across his face. Before she could comment on it, he turned back to the chai. "So, what brings you over?"

"Yes, well, I wanted to talk to you about… Wait, that's not how I planned to start this conversation. One second." Madhuri fished around in her pockets to find her note cards, and once her hands latched on to the stack, she held it up in the air triumphantly. "Aha! Let me flip through this real quick so I can figure out where to start."

Arjun leaned against the opposite counter with the two mugs in his hands, and her heart skipped a beat at the sight of him. He was so casually cool, while she was flailing around like a toddler thrown into the deep end of the community pool.

She returned her attention to the script she'd prepared for this very moment, but she barely made it to the third flash card before she dropped the entire stack like she had with the box of cookies. The cards shuffled among themselves, decidedly out of order now that they were on the floor, and she heard Arjun let out a loud laugh.

"Fuck." Madhuri stared at the cards in disbelief. "That wasn't supposed to happen."

Arjun took her right hand, which was frozen against her side in utter humiliation, and wrapped her finger around one of the mugs. He settled down on the island beside her, and offered her an understanding smile. "What's going on, Madhuri? We both know you don't need flash cards to talk to me."

She brought the mug to her lips, the steam of freshly brewed chai washing over her face. "I'm nervous, okay?"

"The Madhuri I know would never admit something like that." He playfully bumped his shoulder with hers. "What happened to the girl who had the nerve to fight the Universe and *win*? The girl who broke a generational curse with a scientific experiment she crafted herself?"

"That girl is gone." Madhuri placed the mug down on the counter and turned to face him. She resisted the urge to place her hand against his cheek, to run her fingers over the edges of his jaw. "And she's never coming back."

"Why do you say that?"

"Because that girl hurt you, and I'll never forgive her for it," Madhuri murmured, her eyes filling with tears. "I'll never forgive *myself* for prioritizing a piece of paper over you, for trying to destroy my destiny simply because it had your name written all over it."

"I forgive you, Madhuri. You don't have to punish yourself on my behalf." Arjun sipped his chai, calm as ever. She wondered if this new demeanor of his was a way to protect himself, and as much as it hurt to be on the receiving end of it, she understood where he was coming from. Madhuri had been the same way not too long ago, closed off and incapable of vulnerability. He continued, "Our destinies do seem to be woven together, though. I don't think we could get rid of each other if we tried, but what we can decide—you know, with our free will—is how we want to be in each other's lives. Any thoughts?"

Madhuri looked up at him from beneath her eyelashes, and in that moment, she knew she had to tell Arjun the truth. As scary as it was, she couldn't avoid her feelings for him. They ran deep, infiltrating every corner of her mind like swirling vines of ivy.

She was tired of pushing him away simply because their relationship was predictable. So what if her feelings for him were prophesied months in advance? So what if everyone, from the girls at school to her mother's readings, predicted this moment?

None of that could change the fact that she loved him with her entire being.

"I want to be in your life forever," Madhuri began, testing each syllable as if the weight of her words were too much to bear. "I want to be there for every birthday, for New Year's Day and Diwali. I want all the moments, big or small, and I want them with you. Not as your best friend, not as a stranger you used to share a childhood with, but as someone who absolutely adores you." She placed a hand over his. "Arjun Mehta, you're my destiny, and I love you."

Madhuri noticed Arjun's breath hitch in his chest, and a charged moment of silence passed between them. He let her hand go and eased himself off the counter, his gaze jumping from the long-forgotten mugs of chai to the flash cards on the floor. He couldn't even look at her, and her heart sank once the realization struck her—Arjun didn't have any second chances left to give, and even if he did, Madhuri was much too late to ask for one.

After what seemed like hours, Arjun finally spoke. His voice cracked with every word as if it broke his heart to break hers, but honestly, Madhuri believed she deserved the punishment. She'd done the same to him for years on end. This was nothing in comparison.

"Can I take some time to think on this?" Arjun asked, his lips curving into a subtle frown.

Madhuri swung herself off the island and swiped her flash cards back into a haphazard stack. Once she was eye level to him, she nodded. "Take as much time as you need. I'll be here whenever you're ready."

"Thank you." He followed her to the door, holding it open with an unreadable expression on his face. "You have no idea how much I appreciate you finally telling me the truth."

Madhuri didn't know if she could ever come close to describing how she felt when she let Arjun go again. She could only hope that he'd come back to her when he was ready, whether that was as her friend, her boyfriend, or something else entirely. And if he didn't come back at all, Madhuri didn't think she'd ever be the same. A piece of her would always be missing, and she feared she would spend her life searching for it.

Madhuri forced herself to smile as she stepped outside. "Thank *you* for being my person."

The door closed, and exactly as her prophecy had predicted all those months ago, Madhuri was left hopelessly and utterly alone.

CHAPTER THIRTY-THREE

arjun

She loved him.

Madhuri Iyer, the queen of the friend zone and the keeper of his heart, loved him.

And instead of admitting his own feelings for her, instead of being grateful for finally getting exactly what he'd wanted for the last four years, Arjun decided to ask her for time to think. No, that wasn't right—he'd more or less kicked her out of his house, physically incapable of saying anything else to her in the moment.

Ironically, it didn't take more than forty-eight hours for him to land back in front of her house, holding a silver key in his hands. He turned it over in his palm, eyeing the star carved into the metal wearily. He'd spent days considering the consequences of his actions, of what it truly meant to accept the key from Auntie Iyer. He knew this would be the ultimate betrayal against his mother, and yet another complication in his relationship with Madhuri. And now that Madhuri loved him, Arjun knew he couldn't keep the key. He wanted to be invited to the Iyer household because their eldest daughter truly wanted him there, not because her mother promised him a spot on their couch.

Arjun stared at the mahogany door in front of him, the sides of which were framed by a series of colorful elephants looped through a strong golden rope. A cheap-looking plastic wreath hung off the center of the door—a result of Madhuri's influence, no doubt, in a last-ditch attempt to balance the sheer Indian-ness of her front porch with something more American. She probably didn't take it down for that same reason, despite Christmas being over two months ago.

Arjun tore his eyes away from the entrance and pocketed the key. He inhaled, trying to feel his pulse against the walls of his rib cage. He'd come to the Iyers' home with the sole intention of giving the key back, but he felt his feet grow cold. He wondered if he'd made the right decision, if he needed more time. Two days to think seemed like more than enough until he was standing at their door, about to reject the only family who'd ever accepted him.

He took a step back and then another. "I need more time," he whispered to himself as the front door flung open.

"More time for what?" Madhuri stood on her porch with her arms crossed over her chest. Her eyes were painted with a thick black liner, her lips bleeding red. The messy curls of her typically untamable hair were wrangled into a waist-length braid.

Arjun felt his breath catch in his throat as he took in the

sight of her maroon Bharatanatyam sari, the gold embellishments reflecting the rays of the setting sun. When she stood there in her costume, Madhuri looked natural. Her confidence radiated through the bells wrapped around her ankles, sounding her presence ahead of time. For the first time since their freshman year, Madhuri seemed comfortable in her own skin.

He couldn't tell her any of that, though. Not after their breakup, and especially not after she told him she loved him. Her confession sent shock waves through his heart, and while Arjun knew he'd finally gotten what he'd wished for, he couldn't bring himself to accept it yet. He wanted to decide what to do with the key before he said yes to Madhuri, if only to prove to himself that he didn't need her family in order to love her.

"Do you plan on saying something?" Madhuri asked. "I'm getting late for the talent show. Josie's going to pick me up at any minute."

Arjun snapped out of his senses and forced himself to take a step forward. The six feet of distance separating them felt unbearable. "Where's Raina? Isn't she performing with you?"

Madhuri ran a thumb across her bottom lip. She inspected the lipstick stain on her finger before smudging it onto the jacket hanging off her arm. Arjun noticed the quiver in her hand and hoped it was a clue to her emotions rather than a case of preshow jitters.

"She left a few hours ago to grab a snack with her dance team." Madhuri squared her shoulders, settling her blank expression into one that seemed a little more comfortable. "I'm performing a solo now."

Arjun's eyes widened. "That's huge! What changed your mind?"

"You did," she responded without hesitation. "Although our breakup was painful, it made me realize that nothing in my life is set in stone. I decided that if I'm only ever going to be able to rely on myself, I might as well accept every aspect of me, Bharatanatyam included."

"You know you're never alone, right? I guarantee that Josie and your family are going to stick around forever."

Madhuri shook her head, her earrings clinking like wind chimes. "That's not the point. I need to show up for myself when no one else does. I don't want to be weak anymore. I don't want to let go of the people—" She choked on her words, doubling over to catch her breath. Once she'd settled down, she continued, "I mean, the *things* that I love all because some girls at school made fun of me."

"You're right." Arjun took another step forward, close enough that he could smell Madhuri's token scent of Orbit gum and rose perfume. All of a sudden, he felt as if he'd been transported to Auntie Iyer's study the day that they'd first created *The Kismat Experiment*. "I'm proud of you."

Madhuri leaned into him, craning her neck upward to look at him. He wanted to say something, *anything*, that could destroy the tension rippling between them, but before he could put his thoughts into action, a sharp car horn rang out from behind them. Josie waved from the driver's seat of her Toyota, screaming about how late they were. Arjun turned around to say hi, only to have Josie send him a withering stare.

"Don't mind her. I told her about what happened these last few days, and she's been protective over me ever since." Madhuri placed a hand on his cheek, daring to linger her touch for a dangerous second. "Would you want to talk later?"

"Sure." His face tingled. "Good luck, Madhuri."

Madhuri's fingertips brushed over his chest as she slipped past him. A shiver raced down his spine, leaving him no chance to look over his shoulder in hopes of making eye contact with Madhuri one last time before her performance. Arjun heard the slam of a car door and the revving of an engine, followed by the smell of smoke fuming from the exhaust of a gas-guzzler.

Arjun stood and stared after the car's path long after it disappeared from view. He didn't know how long he was rooted in place, but eventually Auntie Iyer stepped through the front door, her husband locking it behind her. She watched Arjun with a curious expression.

"Shouldn't you be at the talent show, beta? If you're waiting for Madhuri, you should know that she decided to leave earlier with Josie to get a sense of the stage before her performance."

Arjun nodded to his car parked on the curb. "I plan on driving over any minute now. And I'm actually not here to bother Madhuri today."

"What are you doing here, then?" Auntie Iyer asked with a good-natured smile as she dropped her bag into her husband's arms. She sent Uncle Iyer a look that he understood immediately, leaving them alone to pack the car with any essentials that their daughters might need during their performances.

Arjun pulled the key out of his pocket and held it out to Auntie Iyer. His heart rate sped up as if each pump of oxygen was a warning for him to stop, to not push away the only family that wanted him without any strings attached.

"I'm returning this." Arjun offered Auntie Iyer a soft smile. "I don't need a physical symbol of our relationship in order to have faith in it, and I'd like to think you feel the same way. I guess this is my way of asking if I can continue to be the boy next door who annoyingly rings your doorbell every day."

Auntie Iyer picked up the key and slipped it under the front porch mat. "I would love that, Arjun. I offered it to make sure you knew that we'd be there for you even when your parents aren't, but I should've known you've understood that all along."

His smile transformed into a beam of light. "I love you."

Arjun had never told someone that he loved them out loud. Sure, he'd thought it before, whether that be in regard to Madhuri or his mother or Auntie Iyer. He'd wanted to say it to all three, but the timing never felt right. He was always scared of what would happen if they disappeared right after, if they couldn't handle the intensity of his emotions, but Auntie Iyer had proved herself. She had no intention of leaving him, whether Madhuri was involved or not.

Auntie Iyer lifted an eyebrow at him. "Do you plan on admitting that to anyone else?"

He laughed out loud. "I think that's my cue to head to the show. I've got to make a stop on the way, but I'll see you all very soon."

"We'll save you a seat."

Arjun turned toward his car, about to take a step forward when a strong feeling overwhelmed him. He couldn't quite place it, but it took charge of him like a matador controlling a bull. He spun on his heel and ran into Auntie Iyer's arms, pulling her into a tight hug.

She stiffened at the touch at first as if she were surprised by his actions. But then she wrapped her arms around him the way a mother would with her biological child—as if she never wanted to let him go.

"I love you, too, beta."

CHAPTER THIRTY-FOUR

madhuri

Madhuri didn't realize until this very moment that she had forgotten the terrifying nature of the stage, the harsh spotlight that threatened to drill a hole through her forehead. She squinted into the beam bleeding through the closed red curtains, trying to stifle the urge to block it with the back of her hand. Beads of sweat trickled from her hairline down to the curve of her neck. Her makeup melted, a result of stage fright, an incoming nervous breakdown, and the massive heat source she was standing under combined. She needed to stop her body from spontaneously combusting. She hadn't made it back onto the stage only for her to crash and burn. She was the ruler of her own destiny, and she would decide if she was going to fail or not.

"Madhuri," Josie whispered from backstage, and Madhuri

turned to face her, chewing on her lip with worry. Josie narrowed her eyes, a warning to stop destroying her makeup before the performance, and somehow sent her a megawatt grin at the same time. "Good luck."

As the curtains shifted to the sides, Madhuri smiled back at her, feigning confidence. "Thank you."

The fabric swished against the hardwood floors, exposing Madhuri to a crowd of hundreds. Josie had managed to rent out the UC Irvine Barclay Theatre for the talent show, an auditorium only minutes away from their high school. The Barclay could hold a maximum of seven hundred and fifty people and almost every single seat was filled. Josie had outdone herself and Madhuri was so proud of her best friend, but there was a part of her that hoped no one would bother showing up.

Madhuri searched the crowd for her family, identifying her mother and father in the front row. They waved at her like overzealous PTA parents, wild grins etched onto their faces. In her father's hand was their beat-up camcorder, which didn't make much sense, considering that he had the latest smartphone that performed the same function better.

Her gaze moved to the seat next to them, where Aditya, Raina's boyfriend, sent her a shy, almost bordering on hesitant, thumbs-up. The poor boy was more afraid of his girlfriend's sister than her parents, but Madhuri preferred it that way. Her Amma and Appa were quick to accept others into their inner circle, which meant that as the eldest daughter of her immigrant family, it was solely up to Madhuri to make sure that Raina was never hurt by the people she loved.

She scanned the rest of the row until she landed on the seat beside Aditya, and her heart sank when she saw the sheer emptiness of it. She hadn't expected Arjun to be there, not after everything she'd put him through. Maybe that was what it meant to love him, hoping that he'd be around even when she knew the odds were clearly stacked against her.

The MC introduced Madhuri, beginning with her biography and relation to Raina, who had performed before her. Raina's dance, a group number with the academy featuring her very own solo, was breathtaking. Madhuri watched the piece from her cramped position backstage and her eyes immediately gravitated toward her little sister, who stole the spotlight the minute her bells rang against her ankles. If Madhuri had seen her perform even a month ago, she would have felt the sharp sting of jealousy in her chest, but things were different now. For the first time, she wanted to dance, even if the whole world was watching.

"And now, let's offer a warm Irvine welcome to Madhuri Iyer as she performs her Thillana," the MC roared with unshakable energy, echoing her name through the auditorium speakers as he disappeared backstage.

The doors of the Barclay swung open and a stubby usher who seemed quite flustered by the last-minute arrival escorted a man down the aisle. The light didn't catch his face until he settled into the seat beside her parents and Aditya, a bouquet of sunflowers resting in his lap. Arjun looked up at her, his expression resembling one she hadn't seen before—thoughtful, yet somehow brighter than ever. When Madhuri continued to stare at him, he offered her a reassuring grin.

Madhuri shifted into her starting position as the stage went dark, an aramandi with her hands attached to the curve of her hip. She steadied her breathing the way her dance teacher had instructed her to before a performance, closing her eyes as she waited for the first notes to ring.

In that instant, Madhuri confronted the memories of her past failures, of all the times she'd run away from her love for Bharatanatyam. She'd brushed these thoughts away earlier, when she was backstage and could distract herself with touching up the sharp wing of her eyeliner or congratulating Raina after her brilliant performance. Now, though, she was faced with a choice—she could run again, or she could accept the moments that haunted her for exactly what they were.

A chance to learn, to grow, and to dance her heart out when it finally mattered.

And so, she did.

The music began, punctuated by the chime of a bell on every fourth count. After eight beats, the singer's voice reverberated through the auditorium. The language she once knew was foreign to her ears, and she tried to stop herself from imagining the confused looks on the audience's faces. The singer transitioned from her opening stanza to the timeless Thillana, a short dance known for its mastery of technique and beauty. Madhuri's eyes shot open when she heard the charismatic beat of the song, sending her vision from the left to the right for eight counts. Her right foot jutted out as she balanced on her heel, her arm creating a grand sweeping gesture as if her choreography was inviting the audience in.

The minute she'd grown comfortable with her place in the spotlight, her eyes met Arjun's of their own accord. She couldn't help but lock in their gaze, channeling the expressions that were meant for him into her own dance.

"Beautiful." She could read his lips, the whispers he shared with their connected minds.

Arjun's starstruck expression sent butterflies through her body and she smiled on instinct. It felt natural to dance when she was looking at him. It was as effortless as kissing him under the stars or laughing at his ridiculous jokes.

Her fingertips pressed against each other as they occupied the next position, over and over, until she'd settled into a steady rhythm. It was like freshman year once more, where she seemed to move without a single command on her part. Her legs had a mind of their own, sending her across the stage as she conveyed a story with nothing but her body.

As the Thillana grew to a close, the sound of a mridangam faded into white noise and Madhuri settled into her end position: her left leg crossed over her right as she balanced on one foot. She held a palm up to the audience, embodying the typical pose of a Hindu deity, her expression blank, save for a peaceful, all-knowing quirk of her lips.

The audience didn't make a single sound when the music ended. She was convinced she'd die of embarrassment if the silence continued any longer.

Her parents rose to their feet as they offered her a hearty round of applause. Her father blew a sharp whistle from the space between his lips and her mother bounced on the balls of her feet, despite being discharged from the hospital no more than a week ago. Madhuri could have been imagining it, but she swore she saw her parents tearing up. Arjun joined them with a celebratory shout of her name, and after him followed the rest of the audience.

"That's my little girl!" her mother screamed amid the applause, her voice cracking on the final syllable.

Madhuri noticed that not everyone was standing. Some of the girls from school, Olivia and Brynn included, clapped slowly, bored yawns stretching their mouths into an oval shape. None of that mattered when she saw the impressed looks on her teachers' faces or when she heard a mother in the front row praise the performance to her own daughter.

This was the moment she'd wanted years before she even quit Bharatanatyam. She wanted to be a part of a community that was often more judgmental than the voices in her head, for them to see what her culture meant to her and how its beauty transcended geographical boundaries. All she needed was for them to try, the way Josie did over the course of their friendship, or the way Liam did the night of Winter Formal.

The curtains closed after she took her bow. She searched for Josie the minute the audience disappeared from her sight, only to see her best friend running toward her with the sole intention of tackling Madhuri into a bone-crushing hug.

"You absolutely killed that!" Josie screamed into her ear. "I'm so proud of you."

Once Madhuri recovered from the shock of Josie's physical impact, a grin tore through her face. "I think everyone can hear us, Josie. Your headset is still on."

The green light on Josie's headset blinked menacingly, but Josie discarded it without a second thought. "Who cares? You conquered your biggest fear in front of seven hundred freaking people. How are you not screaming right now?"

"No clue," Madhuri said with a shrug of her shoulders. Within minutes, a stage manager approached them with a grimace and pushed them backstage, mumbling under her breath about their delaying of the upcoming acts.

When Madhuri flashed Josie an apologetic pout, Josie waved her off with a chuckle. "That's my aunt. She's very easily stressed, so making her the stage manager probably wasn't the best idea, but then again, her services are free."

A familiar voice chuckled from behind them. "You're rambling again, Josie."

The two girls turned around to see Arjun standing there, bouquet in hand. Josie rolled her eyes when she heard him speak. "I think you've lost your teasing privileges, Arjun."

Madhuri flicked the corner of Josie's ear with a pointed look. "You don't have to keep protecting me. Everything that happened between us is my fault, okay? Arjun deserves you to stick around for him."

"I know it's your fault, but it's easier to let your mistakes go. Call it a best-friend bias."

Arjun took a cautious step forward like he was approaching an easily spooked deer. "And that's completely valid. You can keep hating me for initiating the breakup as long as you'd like, but I do have one request. Do you think you could give Madhuri and I a few minutes alone?"

Madhuri nodded at Josie. "I'll meet up with you right after."

"You better," she responded, the snark slowly leaving her voice as she walked away.

Once Josie had disappeared completely backstage, Madhuri approached Arjun. She was suddenly conscious of her hair's frizziness or the smudge of eyeliner on her cheek or if there was any red lipstick on her teeth. She tried to mask the paranoia with a cool exterior, leaning against the stiff cement walls of the Barclay Theatre. "What's going on, Arjun?"

Arjun inhaled a deep breath and Madhuri knew exactly what was coming next. He was going to end their relationship, or at least whatever was left of it, once and for all.

"I know I told you to let me go, but in my defense, I didn't think I'd change my mind after we broke up. It seemed pretty clear to me that we were only ever better as friends. That is, until I realized that we'd been chasing each other in circles ever since we were kids, and I finally had the chance to break the cycle when you came to see me a few days ago." Arjun placed the bouquet of sunflowers on a stand beside him, taking another slow step forward. "Except I'm a fool, and I let you leave all over again."

He offered her a soft smile and continued. "I know without a doubt that I only want to be with you. That feeling is never going to change, whether we're hundreds of miles apart or right next door. It's set in stone even if you run away, even if you never talk to me again after this."

Madhuri's breath caught in her throat. This didn't sound like a breakup.

"What are you saying, Arjun?"

"I'm saying that I love you, Madhuri Iyer. I always have and I always will."

The world around her blurred like the fuzzy edges of a photo taken at the wrong moment. Time froze, as did the contestants and staff bumbling behind her. She only saw Arjun standing in front of her, his head cocked ever so slightly to the side. His eyes were turned downward like a puppy's, pleading for her to answer him, to put an end to their infinite push-

and-pull. More than his eyes, Madhuri noticed the way her name fell off his tongue. He had said it a million times over the years, but this time something was different.

She heard his proud Indian accent when he said her name, evident in the way he rolled the *r* without a beat of hesitation. Each syllable was foreign like the words of a traditional prayer, yet familiar like the stars sparkling above the crest of Griffith Observatory. She knew she'd never get tired of the way he said her name, even if he said it for the rest of her life. She couldn't imagine going a day without the sound of his voice.

Slowly, the world came into focus again. The people around her moved in streams of hushed conversation and stressed whispers, brushing past them without a care. Even as her environment came back to life, she could only see Arjun and his fading smile as the silence between them wore thin.

Madhuri closed the space separating them, her hand resting on Arjun's cheek. Even that action, one she'd performed a million times in the past, sent sparks flying through her fingertips. "I love you, too, Arjun. Always have, always will."

Arjun pulled her into his chest by the waist. Their noses briefly brushed against each other, and Madhuri wondered if he could identify the scent of her spearmint gum. As he leaned in, preparing to sweep her into a kiss, Madhuri heard him whisper a simple, heart-stopping word under his breath.

"Finally."

CHAPTER THIRTY-FIVE

arjun

Nothing had changed in Auntie Iyer's study since Arjun's last visit. The prophecies of years past continued to hover in the crook of his imagination, as if waiting to remind him of the trials he'd surpassed before this very moment. The bookshelves were made of the same sturdy wood, forever marked by a pair of initials embossed on two coordinated planetary charts.

The last time he'd been here was after a particularly intense lacrosse practice. He'd forgotten his pencil case and had to borrow Madhuri's colorful pens, chewing them to pieces to get a rise out of her. The intoxicating scent of her gum and the disgusted snarl on her face as his saliva dripped down her favorite pen's cap would forever be burned into his mind, a memory of where it all began. He'd always remember the experiment they'd agreed upon, the rules written like an objective, punctuated by an expiration date that he thought he could outsmart.

Arjun looked away from the carved initials when he felt Madhuri's leg nudge him under the table. He'd never thought he'd be sitting in the home he grew up in, playing footsie with the girl of his dreams. If he were to be honest, that was what had changed the most about this place—his relationship to Madhuri. They went from little kids playing tag between the rooms of the Iyer household to two teenagers locked in an experiment written at this very table.

"Josie should be here any minute," Madhuri said. There was a mischievous twinkle in her eye and Arjun knew by looking at her that they'd been thinking the same thoughts. "Better get that pink pen of yours out."

"You mean *your* pink pen, right?"

"I disowned that pen the minute I saw you slobber all over it in September. It's been a Mehta ever since."

"And what happens if I make you a Mehta, too?" Arjun asked, sending her a playful wink.

"Whether you're referencing stealing my last name from me through marriage or licking me to mark your territory the way you did with that poor pen, I strongly decline." She made a show of dodging his wink. "I know we're dating long-term now, but let's not get too ahead of ourselves."

"Leave it to you to burst my bubble."

Madhuri leaned forward, balancing on her elbows. Arjun noticed the way her dimple seemed to say hello to him, the way it shone proudly from the curve of her cheek. He was absolutely enamored of her. "I didn't say no, did I?"

Before he could come up with a witty response of his own, Josie slammed a heavy textbook onto the table and slipped into an empty chair. She narrowed her eyes at the two of them. "Please stop flirting before I smack both of you."

Arjun threw an arm around Josie, laughing as she feigned annoyance and tried to swat him away. "It's nice to see you, too, Josie."

"Don't get any ideas. We might be friends again, but that doesn't mean you can treat me as affectionately as Madhuri." Josie sent Madhuri a warm grin. "Watch your woman, Arjun. I might just steal her away from you."

"I'd like to see you try," Arjun teased as he found Madhuri's hand under the table and gave it a single squeeze. They hadn't used their double-squeeze communication method in a while. Maybe it was because their lives finally seemed to be going according to plan.

Madhuri rolled her eyes at them. "I promised Raina we'd be at her celebration dinner on time, so you two need to stop bickering before you make me late."

"How's Raina liking her victory?" Josie asked with heightened interest.

"Honestly, I think she's more excited about winning the talent show than the five-hundred-dollar cash prize. She's planning on donating all of it to her dance school, which makes sense now that she's been hired as an assistant teacher." Madhuri's voice progressively grew louder as she bragged about her sister. But then she took notice of the passing time and got down to business. "Josie, you're our witness, not our distraction. Shut up."

Josie threw her hands up in a protest, mumbling about

Madhuri being a dictator under her breath. Arjun saw the smile on their faces, the look they exchanged when they assumed he wasn't paying attention. He could only ever read Madhuri's mind, while she had an insight into the thoughts of Josie, her family, and him. He used to wonder what it was like to be so deeply connected to so many people, but now that he'd found his family, too, he didn't have to wonder anymore.

Madhuri pulled two sheets of paper out of her backpack and laid them on the table. One was her copy of the crumpled-up *Kismat Experiment*. The once-gleaming paper had decayed into a mess of tear droplets and accidental rips since its initial creation. "Arjun, would you like to help me do the honors?"

"Hell, yeah." Arjun pinched the paper and his fingers gently brushed against hers. A current ran through his hand on impact. By the way Madhuri looked straight at him, her shoulders squared into a straight line, Arjun knew she'd felt it, too. "I've been waiting for this moment since we first signed it."

Josie pulled out her phone to capture their memory. "Say 'kismat'!"

Arjun grinned at Madhuri before they ripped the experiment straight down the middle. The sound of the paper tearing was music to his ears, like the unforgettable burst of a cork flying out of a champagne bottle, and Arjun congratulated himself for managing to date the love of his life, get accepted into his dream university, and find his forever family all in one year.

Madhuri's fingertips found the collar of his Stanford sweatshirt, the one she stole from his closet every single time she visited his house, which, in her presence, had slowly become a home again. She was the yellow haze streaming through the streetlights outside his driveway, the heat wafting over his kitchen stove as she taught him how to elaborately burn his food for dinner every night. Even when his mother was back in town, a silent spectator per Arjun's request after he'd taken the time to reevaluate their relationship, Madhuri brought light into his life.

She pulled him close, flashing him a grin that showed all her teeth. "Here's to us, Arjun."

Josie groaned out loud as she stuffed her phone back into her pocket. "Can y'all please do that literally anywhere else?"

Arjun chuckled and kissed Madhuri's forehead, suddenly conscious of Madhuri's parents a mere floor beneath them. "She's right, Madhuri. You better learn how to control yourself."

Madhuri let him go with a huff, choosing to ignore their teasing. She picked up her pen and scribbled a title on the blank piece of paper. When her shadow left the sheet, Arjun saw the tilt of her cursive letters stringing together a familiar sentence underneath the bold title.

Disclaimer: this is not a fake relationship.

Arjun lifted a brow. "It better not be. I don't think I can handle another heartbreak."

"I promise, you don't have to worry about that anymore," Madhuri said before continuing to write, punctuating the end with two dotted lines. "If you sign here, you're agreeing to a very real relationship with yours truly. You're agreeing to trust in my love for you forever."

Josie crowed when she saw the new experiment, alternating between complimenting how cute they were and insulting

Madhuri for going soft on her. Arjun, on the other hand, was lost in thought as he watched one letter blend into the next.

Arjun picked his pen up, his thumb fitting easily into the notch his teeth had created in the plastic. He took a moment to think before he drew a large pink *X* across the front page. He looked up from the damage he'd created and saw Madhuri's mouth fall open.

"Hear me out before your voice gets all high-pitched and squeaky," Arjun said with a good-natured smile on his face. "Remember how I returned your mother's key back to her?"

"Yes…" Madhuri cocked her head to the side. "What does that have to do with us, though?"

"The same logic applies here. I don't need a piece of paper to hold me to my feelings. I trust you and I trust us, whether it's written into our prophecies or not. Besides, didn't we learn our lesson the first time around? Experimental relationships make everything more complicated."

Madhuri's cheeks hinted at a faint shade of pink. "You're right."

"Are we not doing the experiment?" Josie interjected, her eyes flicking to the clock behind their table. "What was the point in me coming here, then? The only thing I've been a witness to is your disgusting flirting."

Madhuri threw Arjun's slobbery pen at Josie, who screamed when it landed in her hair.

Auntie Iyer, obviously concerned by the ghoulish shriek to leave her sacred study, called their names from downstairs with a slight edge to her voice. "Don't make me regret open-ing the room for you three!"

Madhuri and Josie exchanged a look, trying their very best not to burst into a fit of giggles. Arjun wanted to join them, but one of them had to be the mature and responsible friend of their group. "We're so sorry, Auntie Iyer. We'll be out of here in a second."

"I'll be counting that second down," she responded, the edge in her voice slowly disappearing. Arjun could imagine the smile on Auntie Iyer's face, the subtle shake of her head as she questioned how a group of teenagers could possibly be so ridiculous.

Arjun grabbed Madhuri's hand as they left the table, his pen forgotten underneath. He cast a wayward glance toward the initials carved into their prophecies, a fading *AM* and *MI* once powered by a silent stroke of luck.

Madhuri pulled him down the staircase and out of the house with a bounce to her step, reminding Josie of the restaurant address she'd meet the rest of the Iyer family at. Raina and Uncle Iyer cracked horrible puns at each other, while Auntie Iyer doubled over in exaggerated laughter, her hand resting on the hood of the family SUV for support. The sky had turned to a shiny black since they first locked themselves in Auntie Iyer's study no more than an hour ago. Arjun tore his gaze from Madhuri's face, masked by the darkness of the night, and focused it on the brightest star above them. In its twinkle was a friendly wink, a promise whispered in his ear.

In that moment, Arjun knew that the Universe had been on his side all along.

★ ★ ★ ★ ★

ACKNOWLEDGMENTS

When I was seventeen years old, I wrote a sticky note with the names of every person who took a chance on me, and I stuck it up on the wall of my bedroom. I had recently made the transition from Wattpad to traditional publishing, and while I didn't know it at the time, this sticky note would serve as the foundation for the acknowledgments of my debut novel four years later.

Thank you to my literary agent, Ann Leslie Tuttle at Dystel, Goderich & Bourret, for being the first to notice the potential in my words, and for being my strongest advocate ever since. To Claire Stetzer for her work as my incredible editor—you are the reason why Kismat Connection exists in its truest form today. To Bess Braswell, Brittany Mitchell, Justine Sha, Kamille Carreras Pereira, Kathleen Oudit, Dana Francoeur, and the team at Inkyard Press for their unwavering support; to Tamanna for their insightful sensitivity reading; and to Jani Balakumar for illustrating the prettiest cover I've ever seen.

Kismat Connection is the story that officially made me an author, but I doubt I'd have completed it without the wonderful circle of writers in my life. To Swati Hegde, Morgan Watchorn, Safa Ahmed, Kalie Holford, Aarti Gupta, and Camille Simkin for the years of priceless feedback, in-line fangirling, and loyal friendship; to Jennifer Camiccia and Jessica Love for their mentorship at the earliest stages of my career; to Ali Hazelwood, Christina Lauren, Nisha Sharma, Michelle Quach, and Tracy Deonn for lending their time to my stories; and to Rebecca Mix, Chloe Gong, Ann Liang, Priyanka Taslim, Sarah Underwood, Miranda Sun, Alina Khawaja, Aamna Qureshi, Ann Zhao, Victoria Wlosok, Layla Noor, Birukti Tsige, Famke Halma, Birdie Schae, and Nithyaa Kodarapu for holding a seat at the table for me—at every festival and every conference, I am glad to have you.

Many of you may know that I wrote *Kismat Connection* as a teenager, which means that a majority of my acknowledgments must be dedicated to the people who have anchored me through my own coming-of-age journey. To Aly Gregorec, Alex Fraboulet, Manasi Patel, Sahil Jagad, Mehreen Mahida, Ansley Keane, Cynthia Nguyen, Riya Chandran, Ryan Lee, and Ayse Oztekin for being the greatest friends; to Ms. Miller for seeing a spark in me when I was a senior in your AP Literature class and urging me to follow it no matter what; to Dr. Kadandale, Dr. Radhakrishnan, and the countless professors at the University of California, Irvine, who have inspired me to pursue my deepest ambitions; to Evin Groundwater and the folks at the Writing Center for grounding me when my dreams threatened to swallow me whole; to Ramu Tata, Ganga Patti, and Venky Tata, who I know are smiling down at me as I write this; to Viji Patti for her endless love; and to

Amma, Appa, Anushka, and Ivan, who require no further explanation.

Finally, I would like to thank the community I write for. To the Indian American teenagers who resonate with Madhuri's desire for control in a Universe that never seems to listen and with Arjun's desire for belonging in a Universe that never seems to care; to the members of the South Asian diaspora who aren't quite sure how they identify but are willing to put in the work to figure it out; to the Desi parents who might've stolen this book off their child's shelf and found a familiar romance to root for in its pages; and most importantly, to you, dear reader, for choosing *Kismat Connection* and for making room in this industry for a plucky young author. I couldn't have done it without you.